Blood on
the Bayou

Blood on the Bayou

D. J. DONALDSON

St. Martin's Press
New York

Production Editor: David Stanford Burr

Library of Congress Cataloging-in-Publication Data

Donaldson, D. J.
  Blood on the bayou / D. J. Donaldson.
    p. cm.
  ISBN 0-312-05387-8
  I. Title.
PS3554.04679B55 1991
813′.54—dc20   90-19683
              CIP

10 9 8 7 6 5 4 3 2

Acknowledgments

The author expresses his gratitude to the following people for their kind assistance: Dr. O. C. Smith, Assistant Medical Examiner for Shelby County, Tennessee; Betty, Skeet, and Terry Rogers of the Bayou Pierre Alligator Farm; Dr. Allen O. Battle; Tim Jones; and Paulette Sutton.

Blood on
the Bayou

Chapter 1

Dawn was more than three hours away. Under cover of darkness, a sheet of thin gray clouds had crept over the city, bringing with it a steady drizzling rain. A rat with water drops glistening on its fur like crystal pearls stood on the curb at the deserted corner of Canal and Rampart as though waiting for the light to change. Behind it, water gurgled down a copper drainpipe on the side of the Maison Blanche building and spread over the sidewalk. Overhead, in a gray metal box, traffic-light relays clicked and tripped as busily as they had at rush hour. In numbers surrounded by a hazy wet halo, the illuminated marquee on the First American Bank alternately gave the time and temperature to no one. Abruptly, the rat turned and scuttled into the shadows. Seconds later, a silent ambulance sped by, its lights turning.

Across the Mississippi, in an antique bed equipped with extra slats to support his great bulk, Andy Broussard, chief medical examiner for Orleans Parish, sucked in air and blew it out in rhythmic contentment. Broussard was traveling. He was between his own sheets, but he was also in Brussels, seated at a long table covered with an immaculate white tablecloth. Spread before him were all his favorites: tiny whole lamb's tongues in a gossamer herb sauce; a mousse of Ardennes ham served in china thimbles with little spoons; sea urchins stuffed with mussels, scallops, and roe; slim trout fillets steamed in cream and arranged around a delicate spinach custard. He reached out with his fork for a small piece of calves' brains dusted with flour, and everything disappeared in the jangle of his telephone.

His small hand emerged from the bedclothes and groped over the nightstand. "Broussard," he muttered into the receiver. He listened quietly as the voice on the other end dispassionately recited the address where he was needed. "On my way," he said, hanging up.

He threw his legs over the edge of the bed and stood up in one continuous motion. Noticing the rain on his bedroom window, he grunted unhappily and padded into the bathroom, where he combed his unruly gray hair with his fingers and sent his toothbrush on a quick trip over his small, even teeth. Back in the bedroom, he cycled by the glass bowl of lemon drops on his dresser and popped one into each cheek.

The closets of most fat men contain two sets of clothes, one for the size the owners are, the other for the size they used to be or wish they were. The clothes in Broussard's closet all fit him perfectly. Not wanting the lifeless victim that awaited him to lie in the rain a second more than was necessary, he omitted his usual bow tie while dressing.

After putting on his yellow rain slicker and grabbing his bag, he went out through the kitchen to his gymnasiumlike garage and turned on the lights, setting the timer for five minutes. Stretching before him was a row of mint-condition 1957 T-birds, each of the six a different color, all with the original paint. From the moment he saw that it was raining, he knew he would be taking the red one, for it was the only one that was already dirty.

Princess, his Abyssinian cat, was asleep in her basket by the door. She had a little food left in her bowl, but not enough to last the day if he should get tied up and not make it back until evening. As he added to her food from the bag nearby, her whiskers twitched but she did not open her eyes.

Never a simple matter to get behind the wheel of such a small car, the extra fabric of even a rain slicker made the chore more difficult than usual. Nevertheless, he was out of the garage a full two minutes before the lights went out.

There were practically no cars on the road and he had the eight-lane Mississippi River bridge nearly all to himself, an exhilarating feeling considering how often he had sat on it mired in traffic. The dispatcher had given him an address on Royal. Since Royal was a one-way street running in the wrong direction, he went down Decatur and cut over to Royal on St. Philip. With the twisting blue lights of a police car and the orange lights of an ambulance raking the buildings on each side of the narrow street, it wasn't hard to tell he'd come to the right place.

He parked at the end of the block and struggled out of the car. Seeing that the drizzle had let up, he shucked off his slicker, put it on top of the car, and went around to the passenger side to get his bag, the humidity already pressing in on him.

The police cruiser was sitting angled in the street, so that the small entourage on the sidewalk was illuminated by its lights. Through its open windows, the two-way radio under the dash spit a guttural message into the night air.

"Shots fired at Sixteen-twenty Poydras . . . units eighteen and twenty-four . . . please respond."

Broussard took a deep breath. The lights and the radio, the apprehension before he saw the victim—it was all terrible and wonderful, and the old medical examiner's blood began to hum.

His eyes darted over the scene. Down to his left, wearing one of those flimsy raincoats that fold up into a package you can put in your shirt pocket, Lt. Phil Gatlin, ranking detective in the NOPD, was measuring the distance from an open umbrella in the gutter to a gold lamé purse lying on a sidewalk grate. Over him, holding a flashlight on the tape, was a uniform, a thin guy with a round little paunch that pulled at the buttons on his crisp blue shirt. Broussard thought his name was Cavenaugh. The uniform's partner, a young blond fellow whom Broussard had never seen before, was on the other end of Gatlin's tape.

Shifting his eyes to the right, Broussard saw Ray Jamison,

the homicide photographer, squatting at the head of a body
lying in a dark ocean of blood. Thankful for the awning, which
not only prevented loss of some of the evidence that would
allow him to fix the time of death but also protected the
unfortunate victim from further indignities by the weather,
Broussard stepped onto the sidewalk and lost sight of everything in the flash of Jamison's Polaroid.

As the blinding ripples of light behind Broussard's eyes died
away, Jamison stood up and let his camera dangle against his
chest. "I'm gettin' too old to squat like that," he said, swinging
his left leg back and forth at the knee. "How you doing?"

"I been better," Broussard said, staring at the body. "You?"

"Nose to the wheel. 'Asses and elbows,' as they say."

Broussard put his bag down at the edge of the pooled blood,
opened it, and took out a padded kneeling block. "Scuse me,
Ray. I need your spot." Taking the photographer's place,
Broussard looked down into the cold, unseeing eyes of what
used to be a young woman. She was wearing pink shorts and
a pink tube top that had been pulled down nearly to her waist.
Both had dark blotches of blood spreading into the fabric like
some sort of grisly camouflage. Her arms were lying palms up,
each at a forty-five-degree angle to the body. The blood on the
parts of them he could see was smeared. Her right leg was
cocked at the knee, so her ankle lay under her left calf. Except
for several red spirals around each thigh, her legs were
unbloodied.

In the raking beam from the police cruiser's headlights, he
could see bits of everted flesh poking out of her blood-covered
torso in dozens of places. His eyes traveled over the body,
measuring . . . sorting . . . moving quickly until they settled on the gaping crater in her neck.

Death has many forms, but its repertoire is not limitless.
Thus, it had been years since Broussard had run across a case
that did not already have a mental pigeonhole waiting. But
now, despite the poor lighting and long before he would say so
aloud, he believed this one was different; this was something
new. Yet if he had been listening, he might have heard the
small voice within, whispering that this was *not* something

new. It was old . . . very old. And softer even than the whisper was an old warning: *Never go* . . .

"So you finally got here," Gatlin growled.

"Main course always comes after the hors d'oeuvres," Broussard said, slipping easily into repartee he really didn't feel.

Gatlin's heavily lined face showed every month of his long career. In the unflattering light, his cauliflowered nose seemed enormous. "I swear this one gets me where I live."

"No argument there. I don't suppose you've got a suspect?"

"Not one I could show you, but he might've left his card over here." Gatlin pointed to the sidewalk a few feet from the body, and they moved over for a look.

Near the gray edge of the beam from the cruiser's lights was a single perfect footprint outlined in blood. "Probably an athletic shoe," Gatlin said.

"And fairly new, judging from the sharpness of the pattern," Broussard added.

"Triangles and squares," Gatlin said. "Should be easy enough to figure out the brand."

"Let's hope not."

"Why? . . . Oh, yeah. Easy to figure out means a popular brand and a million suspects."

"How do you know it wasn't made by somebody just passing by?" Jamison said.

"Unlikely," Gatlin replied. "Most people wouldn't come close enough to get blood on their shoes."

"A bum then, three sheets to the wind."

"No, Phillip's right," Broussard said. "It was the killer that left it. See those drops of blood beside the footprint?"

Jamison bent down for a closer look.

"The body's full of puncture wounds, which means whatever the weapon was, it came away covered in blood. Those drops are from the weapon. And since that's a right shoe and the drops are on the right side—"

"He's right-handed," Gatlin said. "Great. A million right-handed suspects. Now we're getting somewhere."

Broussard looked back at the victim. "Speakin' of gettin' somewhere, you through with her?"

"Yeah, go ahead," Gatlin said. He looked at Jamison. "Ray, get some shots of the umbrella and the purse. And one of her heels is stuck in that grate. Get that, too."

Broussard put his padded block on the sidewalk and knelt on it. He took a penlight from his shirt pocket and played it in the victim's eyes. "What time you got?" he asked, looking up.

Gatlin pushed up the sleeve of his raincoat and tilted his wrist into the cruiser's headlights. "Three-forty."

"Consider her pronounced," Broussard said, getting to his feet.

Gatlin wrote the time in the small spiral pad where he had already sketched the scene and entered the measurements he had taken.

The sidewalk was slightly slanted toward the street and most of the blood had run in that direction. Staying on the side of the body nearest the building, Broussard moved down and knelt beside the legs.

Seeing that Broussard would now be looking into the cruiser's lights, Gatlin stepped into the street and stood in front of them. As he whistled at one of the uniforms, a large drop of water from the awning hit the back of his head and ran down his neck. "Cavenaugh, bring your light over here."

Broussard raised the victim's leg that had been kept off the gore-soaked sidewalk by the opposite ankle, and bent it at the knee. He took the flashlight from Cavenaugh and examined the skin on the thigh and calf, making a sound that resembled a cat purring. After gently lowering her leg, he took a wooden applicator stick from the pocket protector in his shirt and drew it through the blood in which the body lay. He got to his feet and sent the beam of his flashlight up the brick and glass storefront. Then he handed the flashlight back to Cavenaugh and took out a little black book and a pen.

While Broussard made notes, Gatlin went back to the sidewalk grate. "Ray, you through with this?" he asked, pointing at the purse.

"Wait, lemme get one more, close-up."

Gatlin looked away from the camera flash, then pulled a pair of white gloves from the pocket of his raincoat and slipped them on. He picked up the purse and carried it to the cruiser, motioning for Cavenaugh's partner to follow. In the light from the uniform's flashlight, he turned the bag upside down on the hood. An assortment of objects clattered onto the car and stayed put, but a lipstick bounced once and hit the hood rolling. Evading Gatlin's gloved palm, which banged down a fraction of a second behind it, the lipstick rolled to the front of the car and tumbled down the grill, the delicate sound making the circumstances seem even more grievous.

As the uniform bent to pick up the lipstick, Gatlin grabbed his arm. By way of explanation, he wiggled his gloved fingers in front of the cop's eyes, then retrieved it himself. In addition to the runaway lipstick, the bag contained a compact, a pink comb, an accordion file of credit cards, a tin of Tic Tac, two Trojans with reservoir tip, and a change purse with a fat roll of bills inside.

"Wasn't robbery," Gatlin said, stating aloud what he already had known when he first saw the unopened purse lying on the grate.

"How much longer 'fore we can get movin'?"

Gatlin looked across the hood of the cruiser into the questioning face of the ambulance driver.

"You'll get outta here when we're through," Gatlin explained with exaggerated patience.

The driver raised both palms in a warding-off gesture and backed away. "Maybe next time you could, like, call us a little later."

Gatlin took a deep breath.

"Just a thought," the driver said, retreating a little more quickly.

Gatlin picked up the accordion file and let it unravel. In it was a Minnesota driver's license. "Paula Lyons," he said reverently. "Better she stayed in Minnesota." Tucked in one of the plastic sleeves was a check stub from a titty bar a few blocks away. He gathered everything up, put it back in the purse, and set the purse on the hood. "Bag that, will you?" he said to the uniform. "Then put it on the seat of my car. Bags are in the glove compartment. And use these." He stripped off the gloves and handed them over.

Then he walked back to Broussard. "How long you figure she's been dead?"

"Corneas are clear, no rigor yet, blood on the sidewalk thickening but not crusted . . . couple hours, tops."

"All the action take place here?"

"No doubt about that. Livor is consistent with the position of the body and that blood up there is right."

They both looked at the blood speckling the white *A* and *N* on the word ANTIQUES painted across the storefront's plateglass window. "Too high for spatter," Broussard said. "More likely cast off. Which means it wasn't a knife."

"You don't think a knife could have done that on the upswing?"

"Doubt it."

Broussard took a small evidence envelope and a scalpel out of his bag and scraped some of the dried blood from the window into it. "Gonna have it typed to be sure?" Gatlin asked.

"You wouldn't be after my job, would you?"

"Nah. Couldn't afford the cut in pay."

"She have an ID?"

"Driver's license said she was Paula Lyons. Also found a check stub from Tasha's, probably a dancer from the look of her."

"Any money?"

"Couple hundred."

"Guess you can forget robbery."

Gatlin nodded. "Somebody with a grudge, jilted lover, maybe."

Though neither said anything about it, both men felt a deep sense of foreboding about the brutality of the attack and what that could mean.

Gatlin looked back down the sidewalk toward the umbrella. "Whoever it was, she saw him coming and knew it was trouble. Dropped everything and tried to get away." He turned back to Broussard. "Did he do her?"

"When'd you ever know me to be able to answer a question like that on the scene?"

Gatlin shrugged. "Thought you might've learned a new trick or two since I last saw you."

"Do I sense that our time has come?" the ambulance driver said sarcastically from over Gatlin's shoulder.

Gatlin deferred to Broussard. "Andy?"

"In a minute."

Broussard got two large brown evidence bags and a couple of rubber bands from his forensic kit. Carefully, he slipped a bag on each of the victim's hands and secured them with the rubber bands.

"Now you can have her."

The two men in white tried not to walk in the blood while they lifted the dead girl and deposited her in a body bag on a folding gurney.

Overhead, the sky rumbled.

"How long before you can tell me the weapon?" Gatlin asked.

If it had been a garden-variety murder, like those that occurred at the rate of about two a day with relentless regularity, Broussard would have caught a few more hours sleep and picked up the case around nine o'clock. But with this one, that was impossible. "Call me in an hour."

On his way back to his car, the sky rumbled again and Broussard's stomach answered. He took a lemon ball from his pants pocket, separated it from some lint, and slipped it into his cheek. From all indications, it was going to be one lousy day.

Chapter 2

Aproned and gloved, Broussard stared into the murdered girl's face, now brightly lit by the bank of fluorescent lights over the stainless-steel autopsy table. How young she looked, how terribly young. Ordinarily, there would have been a morgue assistant in the room to help turn the body, but it was too early for them to be in.

He removed the bags he had put on the girl's hands at the scene. Then he took an applicator stick from a box on the shelves over the sink to his left and inserted it in the electric pencil sharpener beside the box. Carefully, he ran the sharp end of the stick along the underside of the girl's fingernails, collecting the scrapings from each finger into a separate piece of white paper, which he folded into a triangle and sealed with a paper clip. He wrote the case number and finger designation on the outside of each packet and put them on the creaky old desk across the room.

Picking up his Polaroid and several packs of film, he went back to the body and rapidly clicked off a dozen pictures, including four of the terrible wound on her neck, as well as two of each arm lying palm up, as she had been found, and two with them folded over her chest to show the surfaces not visible from the other view. As the camera delivered each picture, he flicked it with practiced ease onto the work area next to the sink, where the loathsome latent images grew bright and clear. Satisfied with the frontal pictorial record, he gently turned her over and took six shots of her back, then returned the camera to his desk.

Next, he filled a small test tube with distilled water from a carboy on a shelf to the right of the autopsy table and put the tube in a rubber rack. The remaining slots in the rack he filled with plastic screw-top tubes that each contained a long-handled cotton swab.

When Broussard had received his forensic training thirty years earlier, he had noticed that his teachers often set test-tube racks, saws, and other paraphernalia on the bodies they were autopsying, as though in death, the victim had no more rights than a doorstop. It was a practice he carefully avoided even though it frequently added extra steps or a measurable inefficiency to his movements. Since the girl on the table was slightly built and there was room beside her for the rack he held, today this cost him nothing.

After adding a stainless-steel bowl of warm tap water and a small sponge to the other objects he had assembled, he moistened one of the swabs in distilled water and applied it in a circular motion to an area of dried blood on the girl's left shoulder. When the swab contained as much blood as it would hold, he slipped it back into its tube and screwed on the cap. He repeated this on three different areas of the body, writing with an indelible marker the case number and a sample number on each tube. Corresponding numbers along with a brief description of the sample went onto a form attached to a clipboard hanging on the wall. Now she could be cleaned up.

Even though there was no one else to see her, he drew the curtain across the autopsy alcove before cutting off her clothing. Then he took several more photographs, documenting each step of his analysis.

He dipped the sponge in the bowl of warm water, then stood for a moment as though uncertain about where to begin. It was the throat wound that had brought him directly to the morgue, for he thought he knew what had caused it. And if he was right, it was bad, very bad—so bad that he was willing now to delay examining that wound until he had cleaned all the others.

He began at her collarbone and worked his way down. As the blood came away, a series of ugly puncture marks with everted margins appeared. The wounds seemed to occur in sets of four, with an equidistant spacing between members of a set. As he worked, he noticed a second pattern, in which the distance between the two members on the right was distinctly less than between the others. The discovery of some arc-shaped abrasions under her rib cage confirmed his suspicions about the relationship between the two types of patterns. And what he had learned gave him no comfort.

As he had suspected even before beginning the cleaning, the only wounds on her arms were defensive wounds on the outside surfaces, exposed when she threw up her hands for protection. The bloody smears on the inside surfaces were due to contact with her torso wounds. The blood on her legs was all from wounds higher up.

Now her throat.

He moved along the table, bent down, and tilted his nose slightly to the horizontal to bring the bifocal part of his glasses into position. The margin of the divot in her neck was surrounded by a thin film of blood that had dried in a smear. The wound itself went entirely through the sternocleidomastoid, the heavy muscle that runs from the collarbone to a ridge behind the ear. For such a wound, there was a minimal amount of blood in the resulting cavity. With a swab, he cleaned a small area in the bottom of the wound and verified his belief that the internal jugular vein was intact.

Switching to the sponge, he began to carefully clean the margin of the wound a little at a time, working his way slowly around the circumference. In a very few seconds, he found what he had feared. The sight stirred the old warning anew, louder this time. . . .

Never go . . .

If he had heard it, he might have been able to push the thought to completion. Ignored, it withered and died.

Hoping that it was not a futile effort, he returned to the

long-handled swabs and took several samples from the depths of the wound and from uncleaned areas of the wound margin. With all the wounds cleaned, he went to the desk and got his ABFO #2 ruler. Placing the ruler so that it would be included in each picture, thereby providing a record of the dimensions of the object photographed, he took several close-up shots of the various wounds he had found. As a last step before beginning work with a scalpel, he took swab samples of the contents of her mouth, vagina, and anus, even though he was sure that the serology lab would find no evidence of sperm or acid phosphatase, the cardinal signs of sexual assault.

The stillness of the morgue was shattered by the ring of the telephone.

"What can you tell me?" Gatlin said without identifying himself.

"We should talk," Broussard replied.

"What're we doing now?"

"I've got some things to show you."

"Not in the morgue, I hope."

"From pictures, if you'd rather."

"I'd rather. Your office in ten minutes?"

"Right."

"And make sure the door to Forensics is open this time, will you? I don't want to have to find a janitor to let me in like last time."

When Gatlin arrived, he found Broussard rocked back in his desk chair, fingers folded over his belly. He was watching the best coffee Gatlin had ever tasted issue in a hot stream from an old Mr. Coffee Broussard had bought because Joe DiMaggio said he should.

Gatlin took off his thin raincoat and hung it on a hall tree that already contained three large white lab smocks. He was dressed in a lightweight blue suit, white shirt, and a wide blue tie with a Masonic emblem on it. The knot in his tie was too small to hide the button extender at his throat. Over at the coffee maker, the stream had become a dribble.

Preferring a soft seat to a hard one, he avoided the wooden chairs in front of the desk and plopped onto Broussard's pea green vinyl sofa, where the stack of medical journals on the cushion beside him toppled into his lap. By the time he got them straightened up, Broussard was standing over him with some coffee.

"You read all this stuff or do you just keep it around to harass me?" he said, reaching for the cup.

"Thought for a minute you weren't gonna fall for it," Broussard said, returning to the coffee maker. He filled his own cup—a huge container decorated with a raised ring of dancing crayfish—and went back behind his desk. He sat down and tapped his finger on the glass bowl of lemon balls next to the telephone. Gatlin waved him off.

"Well, what have *you* learned since I last saw you?" Broussard asked, reaching into the glass bowl.

Gatlin watched Broussard put a lemon ball in his mouth, raise his cup to his lips, and take a healthy sip. "Someday you're gonna get one of those damn things stuck in your throat doing that," Gatlin said. "What have I learned? I learned that nine out of ten people who answer the door at three in the morning have bad breath. And nobody is interested in conversation."

"No one saw anything?"

"Do they ever? What about you?"

"I know the murder weapon."

Broussard liked the way Gatlin jumped up so quickly, he spilled some of his coffee.

"So give," Gatlin said.

Broussard spread some pictures across the front of his desk and gave Gatlin a few seconds to look at them. Then he leaned forward and pointed at the first photograph with a blunt dissecting probe he'd taken from a glass beaker full of pens and pencils. "The initial blows produced these wounds—sets of four with the members of a set equally spaced. Then as the weapon became slippery with blood, it twisted in his hand." He moved the probe to the second picture. "And she was struck several times with the side of it, causing these curve-shaped bruises." He moved the probe again. "When he finally got the weapon turned right again, it produced these wounds, still in sets of four, but with decreased spacing between the two on the right."

Gatlin looked up, the muscles behind his jaw pulsing. "That sounds like a—"

"Gardening claw," Broussard said, not wanting Gatlin to say it first, "a cheap one."

"Because the tines collapsed when he hit her with the side of it," Gatlin said.

Though he probably didn't even realize it himself, Broussard had mixed emotions about working with his old friend. Mostly he liked Gatlin's quick mind, but a part of him enjoyed explaining things to a more dependent audience. Gatlin's gaze had returned to the pictures. "The collapse of the tines could be useful," Broussard said, scratching his short gray beard.

Gatlin looked up. "Yeah, if we ever get our hands on it, that could help prove it was the actual weapon used." Gatlin saw something else in Broussard's eyes. "That *is* what you meant?"

"Sort of." Broussard hesitated, reluctant to say aloud what he had been thinking.

Then Gatlin got it. "Ohhh shit. I hope you're wrong about that. I really hope you're wrong. I do not need another one like this in my life. What makes you think it might happen again?"

Broussard added a picture to those already on the desk. "This is a close-up of the wound on her throat after I cleaned it."

Gatlin picked up the picture and studied it. "What *are* those . . . teeth marks?"

"Looks like he bit down hard, let loose for some reason, then got a grip he liked better, and—"

"Lord. Where's the piece he bit out?"

"Took it with him."

"What . . . in his hand . . . a damn souvenir?"

"Possibly. But maybe he *had* to take it with him."

"*Had* to? Why would he *have* to?"

"'Cause he swallowed it."

Gatlin's arms fell limply to his side. "Jesus. You stay awake nights trying to think of ways to gross me out?"

"From the relative lack of blood in the wound, and the

yellow color of the skin around it, it's clear that he didn't go for her throat until she was dead."

"Didn't want to move in before it was safe, I guess. She get to him at all?"

"Don't think so. No skin under her nails."

"Too bad. It'd help if he had some nice deep facial scratches. Something for his friends or the people he works with to notice. Anything distinctive about the teeth?"

"Not really. I'll make up a transparency that we can use as an overlay for when you get a suspect or . . ."

"Or we get another victim?"

"Let's try to keep a good thought about that."

"Didn't you once tell me you can sometimes get the blood type of a biter by typing his saliva?"

"That was a long time ago and I didn't think you were listenin'."

Gatlin feigned a look of hurt innocence. "Andy, you know I hang on your every word."

"Which I guess is why we nearly got struck by lightnin' the last time we went fishin' and I said there was a storm comin' and you said there wasn't."

"Jesus, so I was wrong once. Dwell on it, why don't you. So, can we get his blood type?"

Broussard shrugged. "Maybe . . . maybe not. 'Bout eighty percent of the population secretes blood-group antigens into their body fluids, includin' their saliva. . . ."

"That's good."

"It *can* be . . . *if* the killer was a secretor and the girl wasn't, which statistically isn't likely, and *if* the killer's salivary amylase hasn't digested the antigens were hopin' to find in his saliva."

Gatlin's face clouded up. "Suppose they're both secretors but have different blood types?"

Broussard stuck out his lower lip and nodded. "Yeah, *that* could be helpful. Been my experience, though, that when you really *need* for two folks to have different blood types, they usually don't."

"Jesus, I don't think I can stand all this optimism."

"Guess maybe I am takin' the short view. Probably because I want him caught so much."

"Didn't I read somewhere that you can get DNA finger-prints from semen?"

Broussard shifted his lemon ball to the other cheek. "For an old stone, you've still got some keen edges. What you say is true enough, but I wouldn't get my hopes up there, either. Her underwear was in place and undamaged. . . ."

Gatlin raised his eyebrows and rocked his head up and down with understanding. "Yeah, diddlers usually don't put things back when they're through with them. When'll we get the lab report? I don't want to start working my deev list if she wasn't done."

"Sometime this afternoon."

"Too long, but I guess that'll give me time to write up what we got so far, check out our shoe print with some athletic stores, and maybe talk to some of the people who knew her." He sucked his teeth in thought. "Could be this was a contract job made to look like a nut did it just to fool us."

"Pretty convincin' act."

Gatlin took a last sip of his coffee. Outside, thunder rumbled overhead. The sound called a similar noise from Broussard's stomach.

"You interested in some breakfast?" Broussard asked.

"Where?"

"Gramma O's."

Gatlin looked at his watch. "She open this early?"

"No. But we'll go around back and knock. I expect we can get her to rustle us up something."

"She still make her customers eat everything on their plates?"

"Ever know a grandmother who didn't?"

As they walked to Gatlin's Pontiac, the gray sky that stretched overhead like a shroud made it seem that the city had turned in on itself, as though ashamed for spawning Paula Lyons's killer.

Chapter 3

Kit left Shreveport at one o'clock with nothing settled. Was she going to follow David or not? She still didn't know.

David Andropoulas, assistant DA for the city of New Orleans, the man with whom she had been living for the last six months, had suddenly announced he was taking a similar post in Shreveport and wanted her to come along.

No discussion about it before he had accepted, just a pronouncement—a done deal. At first, she had been so infuriated at his selfishness, she had let him leave and hadn't answered his letters or calls for several weeks. But gradually, as she grew tired of eating alone and having no one to turn to in the night, she had relented and agreed to go up there and take a look. David had been overjoyed, even lined up a job interview for her as editor of a clinical psychology journal, a job that, from the comments of the interviewer, she could have if she wanted.

And it wasn't as though she couldn't do some good there. The journal operation was a mess, the other employees playing to their weaknesses instead of their strengths. That girl with the sharp eyes, Laura something, was a natural proofreader but had no feel whatever for layout. The slim brunette with the classy wardrobe was a born second in command. And they were letting their contributors get away with murder—no uniformity in submission format, no . . .

But how dull that job would be compared to what she did now. Was it murder? Suicide? An accident? Big questions. Important questions. And she was a part of it. Then, too, there was Broussard. In the year since he'd hired her, she'd grown quite fond of the old pathologist, not to mention the fact that he'd saved her life that time in the swamp. If that didn't earn someone's loyalty, what would? And there was her book on suicide, nowhere near finished. But as compelling as the reasons were for staying in New Orleans, Kit still felt drawn to Shreveport. *Glands* she concluded, bearing down on the gas.

It had been raining off and on, mostly on, in the whole state for nearly a week and the water stood a foot deep in what were once fields of cotton and sugarcane. At the moment, it was not raining, but the sky looked very gray and full of more water. Off to her left, she saw a train unable to proceed because the tracks ahead were completely submerged. Everywhere, the floodwaters were being plied by white egrets apparently enjoying the extension of their feeding grounds.

At 5:10, Kit left the interstate at the Bayou Coteau exit. In the passenger seat was a bottle of champagne with a pink bow on it, an anniversary gift for Claude and Olivia Duhon, old friends of Broussard who lived in Bayou Coteau. Before Kit had left for Shreveport, Broussard had called the Duhons and alerted them to her arrival. It had been arranged that she would spend the night, something she had been reluctant to do until Broussard told her what a grand old home the Duhons had.

From the largely treeless, marshy landscape on both sides of the road, the occasional shack on stilts, and the seedy little groceries advertising HOT BOUDIN AND CRACKLIN—whatever that was—on hand-lettered signs, it was hard to believe the area could boast of anything grand. But a few miles farther, the marsh on her left gave way to dry land that soon became populated with huge twisted live oaks heavily draped in Spanish moss.

Up ahead, the road turned gently to the left. As she came out of the turn, she saw something that brought her foot onto the brake. On the marshy side of the road, a guy in a straw hat was working the bayou with a long pole. On the other end of the pole, something was throwing water and mud everywhere. Beside the man with the pole, a thick-bodied fellow with a beer belly that made his shirttail dangle in front of him like a tablecloth watched the action, his hands in his back pockets.

Kit parked on the opposite shoulder, nose-to-nose with a red pickup, and reached for the lip gloss in her purse. Watching herself in the rearview mirror, she freshened her lips and reset the combs that held her long auburn hair away from her face. Though she personally did not like the sprinkle of freckles across the bridge of her nose, men seemed to find them appealing. They had certainly told her so often enough. Satisfied that she was presentable, she opened the door and stepped out into humidity so oppressive it was like a hand in her face.

Giving the two men a wide berth, she crossed the road and edged into the weeds that bordered the bayou, so intent on seeing what was going on that she failed to notice the mosquitoes that rose from the weeds and settled on her white slacks.

The end of the pole was held fast in the saw-toothed jaws of an armored horror that should have been a fossil in some shale bank rather than a living nightmare that you could find not six feet from a paved road. A thick tail whipped into the air and lashed the water, sending up an explosion of mud and duck-weed. Its ugly head and huge brown body began to roll, thrashing the water into a frothy soup.

Wondering why the savage twisting hadn't ripped the pole from the hands holding it, Kit forced her eyes from the great alligator and sent them along the pole until they found the answer. The pole was in two sections, one telescoped inside the other so that the end in the alligator's mouth could spin harmlessly.

Her eyes moved farther up the pole, to the primary reason she had stopped. He was wearing a stylishly shaped straw hat with a black band, a pale blue short-sleeved shirt of brushed oxford cloth, and khaki pants, all of which were well decorated with mud and duckweed. Below the brim of his hat, she saw a head of short black hair sharply defined by a fresh barber line. His features were delicate and refined and he had an elegance about him that transcended the mess the alligator had made of his clothes.

While sweat trickled into Kit's bra and crept down her back, the alligator continued to roll. After several minutes of this, it suddenly went limp and released the pole. The two men pulled the animal partway onto the bank and then the one in the straw hat came toward her.

"She'll stay quiet like that for at least an hour," he said, rubbing some duckweed from one forearm.

Kit's eyes went to his fingers. *No ring.* "Why will she stay quiet? What did you do to her?"

"Just wore her out is all." He offered his hand. "I'm Teddy LaBiche."

"Kit Franklyn," she said, taking it. He had cool gray eyes and was wearing a wonderful cologne. Kit was dimly aware that the man behind him was giving them a disgusted look. "What are you going to do with it?" she asked.

Teddy pointed at the pickup, which bore a picture of a baby alligator emerging from an egg. Under the egg, it read BAYOU COTEAU ALLIGATOR FARM.

"We'll use her as a breeder. Mostly, we collect our eggs from the wild, but that gets to be pretty expensive and it's not reliable. Are you interested in gators?"

"Very much," Kit said quickly, interested more in Teddy LaBiche than in dirty brown reptiles.

"Maybe we could get together and trade notes. Are you staying nearby?"

"With the Duhons."

Teddy's lips parted in a grin that showed strong white teeth. "Around here that doesn't say much. There are at least six Duhons within a mile of where we're standing."

"Claude and Olivia."

"Now *that* helps."

"Do they live nearby?"

"We don't tend to business, we're gonna lose this gator," the fellow with the big gut shouted from where he was leaning on the truck.

Teddy ignored him. "Straight ahead two miles. When you hit the town square, keep to your right and look for Rue Patoit. The Duhon place is at the end of the street, about a quarter of a mile from the square. You can't miss it; theirs is the only house on Rue Patoit."

These were facts already in Kit's possession, but she allowed him to relate them anyway, liking the sound of his voice, especially the way he said Rue Patoit with a slight French accent.

"There's a dance tonight in Boudreaux," Teddy said abruptly. "Would you like to go?"

As much as she was attracted to him, Kit's internal warning system would not permit her to accept a date with a man about whom she knew nothing. Still, no sense in *slamming* the door.

"I don't think that would be polite. I should stay in and visit with the Duhons."

Teddy grinned. "I'm not doubting your conversational ability, but I'd have to guess that about nine-thirty tonight, Olivia, bless her heart, will start to nod in her chair. And if you look closely, you'll catch old Claude yawning in his throat. By ten, you'll be talking to the walls. They're just not night people. So I'll be by at ten."

"How do you know so much about them?"

"Been friends for years. And I know they'll be happy that you found something to do that will let them go to bed without feeling guilty. As for that other problem—"

"What other problem?"

"The one that I saw in your eyes a minute ago. You ask Olivia if I'm okay, and if she doesn't put your mind at ease, call me and cancel. She has my number. Deal?"

Kit's warning light grew dim and began to flicker. It was good to be careful. But it was also important to know when you were overdoing it. As her resolve began to crumble, she reminded herself that a woman should never appear too eager. Holding a man off awhile was the best way to encourage him.

So she was surprised to hear herself say, "How should I dress? I'm traveling light and don't have much choice."

Teddy grinned. "Believe me. It doesn't matter what you wear."

It was only after returning to the car that Kit felt the itching. Lifting her slacks off her shoes, she saw that her ankles were peppered with mosquito bites.

Bayou Coteau was as lovely a little village as Kit had ever seen. In the center of the square was a large two-spired church whose gray stucco bore a faint green patina of moss. Scattered over the grounds were more bearded oaks. The two-story shops lining the square were also stuccoed and had lots of wrought iron and balconies. Between the shops, oak-lined streets identified by black wrought-iron signs bearing white gothic lettering radiated for short distances away from the square. The homes she could see dotting the streets were large wood structures with big porches. Most of the houses were painted in the traditional southern scheme: white with green shutters. And the houses looked as tidy as the shops.

Seeing a drugstore, she pulled into one of the vertical parking places in front and went inside to get something to treat her bites. With that taken care of, she set out once again to find the Duhons.

The oaks on Rue Patoit were even larger than those she had seen along the road coming in, their thick, twisted branches touching overhead like noble couples performing an ancient court dance. Kit let the car creep along the street, appreciating the quiet splendor. Could the Duhon home possibly measure up to its surroundings?

Then she saw it; a huge colonnaded mansion sitting far back from the road. At the entrance to the grounds, she stopped the car and admired the oak alley that exactly framed the front of the house. Here, in addition to mossy beards, the branches of the trees were fuzzy with tiny ferns growing from the bark. It all looked organic and primeval, as though the house had not been built at all but had simply grown from seed. It seemed right that the approach to the house should be packed sand strewn with Spanish moss rather than asphalt.

The house had nine columns on each of its three visible faces and was wrapped with wide upper and lower porches. As she neared it, Kit saw two figures off to her right, standing near a black-water bayou that ran parallel to the lawn. One of the figures had something white in one hand.

In front of the house, the drive curved into a large flattened oval that took her to the front steps. The windows of the house were the kind that could be converted to doors by simply raising the lower sash. Up close, the house was not as pristine as it had appeared from the street. A few of the shutters were coming apart and a large patch of stucco had fallen off one column, revealing to Kit's surprise that they were brick not wood.

As she got out of the car, one side of the double front door opened and a small woman with her gray hair pulled back in a bun came onto the porch. She was wearing a black dress that looked as though it had come from one of those shops that show them to you one at a time. At her throat was a string of freshwater pearls.

Beautiful when she was young and beautiful still, Kit thought.

"Welcome to Oakliegh," the woman said, spreading her arms in a welcoming gesture. "You must be Dr. Franklyn."

"Please, it's Kit," Kit said, going up the steps.

The woman took Kit's hands warmly in her own. "I'm Olivia Duhon. Did you have any trouble with the roads being underwater?"

"The ones I traveled were clear. But I could see some that weren't."

"Yes, I know, its been a terrible summer. Do you have luggage?"

"Just a suitcase, a small one . . . in the trunk. I can manage it."

"Nonsense. Martin will bring it in." She glanced toward the bayou where Kit had seen the two men. "Ah, here's Claude."

Like Olivia, Claude was dressed for company; pale yellow shirt, brown tie with a cream paisley print, and tan pants. Were it not for the crutches holding him up and the slit in his pants that allowed them to slide over the cast on his foot, Claude would have been fashion-catalogue material. A dozen yards behind Claude, Kit saw a man heading for the back of the house. This, she concluded, was Martin. He was carrying a dead chicken.

"He won't take it," Claude complained to Olivia. "It's almost like he knows it's poisoned."

"Claude, this is Dr. Franklyn . . . Kit Franklyn, Andy's friend."

Claude Duhon struggled up the steps and offered Kit his hand. His face reminded her of a mountain that had been worn away by wind and rain. There was strength there, and Kit felt that Olivia had chosen well.

"Happy to see you. Sorry about blowing off like that. But there's a gator down there somewhere that got my dog last week, and me not fifty yards away. It missed him the first time and while I was running to help, I caught my toe in a root and fell on my leg. Fool thing, really. Makes me sound positively doddering. We've been putting out poisoned chickens hoping he'll take one, but he seems to know what we're up to."

"Teddy warned you it probably wouldn't work," Olivia said.

"Teddy LaBiche?" Kit said.

"Yes, do you know him?"

"I met him coming in."

"He's a nice boy, isn't he?"

Already fond of Olivia, Kit was heartened by her good opinion of Teddy and the fact that no probing had been required to discover it.

"But such a peculiar occupation," Olivia said. "Still, if it wasn't for people like him, we wouldn't have all those nice shoes and bags, would we? Well, let's go inside where it's comfortable."

"Oh, I brought you something." Kit returned to the car and got the champagne.

"Happy anniversary, with Dr. Broussard's compliments," she said, handing the bottle to Olivia. "When exactly is the big day?"

"Tomorrow," Olivia said, going inside as Claude held the door.

Kit was relieved at her answer. From the way they both were dressed, she had feared that it might be today, a circumstance that would have made it very awkward to leave them for Teddy. "How will you be celebrating?"

"Quietly," Claude said.

"We don't go out much," Olivia added.

The entry hall took Kit's breath away, especially the stairs, which swept down from two sides to unite in one wide expanse of turned balusters and plush carpet. For a moment, Kit almost could see Scarlett pausing halfway down, her hand on the rail, her eyes searching the throng of partygoers below for Ashley. Olivia led them into a parlor, where she tugged on a braided cord beside a mantel whose glistening finish reflected off intricately carved garlands of flowers and berries.

So quickly that he must have anticipated her, Martin appeared in the doorway. About the same age as the Duhons, he was a large man with prominent ears and a simple, open face. His dark suit had been with him a long time and needed pressing.

"Yes Mrs.?"

Olivia gave him the champagne. "Please see that this is served with dinner. Right now, we'd like some iced tea."

Olivia looked at Kit. "With or without sugar?"

"Without please."

"And when you have a moment, would you get Dr. Franklyn's suitcase and put it in the blue room?"

Kit reached in her pocket for her keys. "You'll need these."

Martin left the room and Kit turned to Olivia. "Your home is magnificent."

"It was built by my great-grandfather," Olivia said. "He made his fortune in lumber. The house has never been out of the family."

Aside from the natural aging process, Kit thought she saw the effects of strain and worry on Olivia's face. As she was given a tour of the house, Kit believed she detected the cause of this concern. The furniture was all elegant, but the flow of its placement was wrong, like a suicide case that didn't quite hang together. When she saw a rectangle of wallpaper that was faintly brighter than the rest, she understood. The Duhons were in financial trouble. The furniture flow was wrong because they had been selling it off piece by piece. The lighter wallpaper used to be under a painting that might this very minute be hanging in a gallery on Royal Street. Feeling like a participant in ill-intended gossip, she averted her eyes from the wallpaper and complimented Olivia on the drapes.

The last stop on the tour was Kit's bedroom, a palatial space with plush blue carpet, a marble fireplace, and a Prudent Mallard canopy bed, typical right down to the carved egg on the headboard. After a long, cool shower, she joined the Duhons in the dining room for a meal of Cornish game hens, wild rice, and a sparse amount of conversation—most of that from Claude, who didn't seem interested in anything but oil: what the price used to be, what it was now, and what it was likely to be by the first of the year. Kit thought she did a good job of appearing interested, but she was actually considering the various ways she might tell them she had a date.

After dinner, when they went into the parlor for coffee, she still had not broached the subject.

"Refill?" Olivia asked, the china coffeepot poised for pouring.

Wanting to appear appreciative of Olivia's attention, Kit held out her cup even though she didn't particularly want any more. When it was half full, there was a long roll of thunder directly over the house. Olivia jumped at the sound and the coffeepot slipped from her hand. It crashed into Kit's cup and both cup and pot fell to the floor, shattering when they hit. Olivia's hands flew to her face and she began to cry.

Claude jumped to his feet and tugged on the braided cord by the fireplace. He went to Olivia and put his arm around her shoulder. "It's all right, dear. There's been no harm done. Dr. Franklyn didn't even get her clothing soiled. And here's Martin to set things right."

While Martin picked up the broken china, Claude patted Olivia's hand and cooed into her ear—but to no avail, for she just couldn't seem to get control of herself. Finally, Claude led her from the room, reappearing a few minutes later alone.

"It was the thunder," he explained. "It reminds her of . . ." He pointed to a picture mounted in a shadow box on the wall beside the fireplace. Also in the box was a medal and a little explanatory note. "Our son. Killed in a helicopter crash in Vietnam. That's the medal they gave him for bravery in the face of fire. He carried his wounded platoon leader through a mile of VC-infested jungle to get to an air rescue site, but the pilot was hit on takeoff and they crashed, killing everyone on board. I always assumed Olivia would eventually get over it, but now I don't know. It's been so long. Sometimes thunder doesn't bother her, other times . . . well you saw for yourself. The sound makes her see the crash . . . the explosion. She'll be fine in the morning. But I'm afraid we'll have to do without her the rest of the evening. It's a sorry way to treat a guest I know, but . . ."

"Actually, Teddy LaBiche asked me to go to a dance with him but I . . ."

Claude's grave expression brightened. "By all means, you must go. Then perhaps you'll have pleasant memories of your visit rather than unpleasant ones."

"I don't want to be . . ."

"Go. Go. It'll make me happy."

Kit looked at her watch—8:30. "We thought we might leave around ten—"

"No need to wait that long on my account."

"You're sure?"

"Absolutely."

"Maybe if I called him . . ."

Teddy arrived in his red pickup shortly after Kit made the call. He was dressed about the same as earlier in the day, but without the mud and duckweed. It was the first time since she was a kid that Kit had gone on a date in a truck. But he *did* open the door for her.

"Why the change in plans?" Teddy asked, climbing into the driver's seat. The cologne Kit had smelled when they first met filled the cab with a light spicy aroma.

"Olivia wasn't feeling well and Claude thought I'd enjoy myself more if I went out."

"And so you shall."

"What does Claude do . . . for a living I mean."

"Oil."

"That explains his conversation at dinner."

"One-dimensional was he?"

"Sort of."

"If he'd given you a chance to talk about what you do, what would you have said?"

"As little as possible, I suppose. It doesn't make very good dinner conversation."

"Intriguing. Go on."

"I'm primarily a suicide investigator for the medical examiner in New Orleans. I do psychological profiles of all decedents when there's some question as to whether the death was accidental, a suicide, or murder. Sometimes I get loaned to the police as a psychology consultant on murder cases and I help develop a profile of the perpetrator."

"Do you know how many conversations you can have in this part of the country and never hear someone say *perpetrator*?"

"Which reminds me. When I walk into this dance, is the music and all conversation going to stop while everyone turns slowly toward the doorway?"

"You feeling out of place?"

"Like I'm in another country. By the way, what the devil is boudin?"

"It's pronounced boodanh. It's a sausage mixed with rice. There's an old saying around here that a seven-course meal to a Cajun is a six-pack of beer and a pound of boudin."

"They say that about themselves?"

"*We* say it. LaBiche, remember? Sure, Cajuns are open, fun-loving folks with no hang-ups. You'll see."

"Who was that with you today on the road?"

"Carl Fitch. Been with me since I started in gators five years ago."

"Partner or employee?"

"Employee; why?"

"As unhappy as he was about you talking to me, I thought *he* might be the boss."

Teddy laughed, a gentle sound that wrapped around Kit like a soft blanket. "I honestly think he *does* believe he's in charge." Teddy's grin faded. "But I've got to get rid of him. He's started drinking on the job again and the other day he fell down in one of the pits. You just can't be doing that. With some exceptions, a wild gator won't attack people. But you take a farm-raised gator or one that's been in captivity awhile, anything falls in the pit, they think it's food. Carl won't carry a gun even though I've warned him dozens of times to do it. And when he cleans the pits, he lets them get behind him."

Lets them get behind him. Until that moment, Kit had been carrying a sanitized version of alligator farming in her head, imagining that it was all mechanized, with no real danger. Apparently, she was wrong.

"One day, I'm going to walk in and find nothing left of Carl but his boots."

"I had no idea of the risks involved," Kit said.

Teddy stiffened against the floorboard and pulled a tiny pistol from his pocket. "I never go anywhere without this," he said. "Fires twenty-two longs that'll make short work of a gator. I make it a habit to put it in whatever pants I'm wearing, even if I'm not planning to go in the pits. That way when I do, I won't be caught without it. Sometimes, though, even that won't help."

"For instance."

"Friend of mine who's got a lot of breeders lost an arm collecting eggs. The way it's done, you approach the nest and when the female comes at you, you work her with the pole the way you saw us do with that gator beside the road. Then when she wears herself out, you get the nest. Well, he went after this one nest and the female charged him just like he expected. Except the nest he was after wasn't hers. Hers was behind him and he hadn't seen that one. Well, he works her with the pole until she can't move, then he reaches for the nest he thinks is hers. The female for that nest was just under the water a few feet away. She's got her tail all curled up under her like a coiled spring. When they get their tail coiled like that, they can launch themselves almost their full length, which she did and got him across the elbow. One good twist and she tore off his arm."

Kit shuddered. "So did he give up alligator farming?"

Teddy looked at her perplexed. "Why would he want to do that?"

A few miles farther on, Teddy turned into a grassy field full of cars and trucks beside a gray clapboard building that didn't look like anything special. He parked next to a van with a beach scene painted on the side and hung his hat on the pickup's rearview mirror.

Leaving the parking area on foot, they picked their way between rutted tire tracks of matted grass and mud until they came to a large puddle that stretched from the bumpers on one side to those on the other. While Kit was looking for a way across, Teddy swept her up in his arms.

Before she could stop herself, she slapped him.

Horrified at what she had done, her hand went to her own cheek, which felt as hot as though *she* had been the one slapped. "Oh Teddy . . . I'm so sorry. . . . It was a reflex. I really didn't mean to do that."

"Then you don't want to be put down?"

She did and she didn't. The part of her that had slapped him felt violated. To snatch someone off their feet like that, make them helpless and dependent without warning, it was unforgivable. Not an act of chivalry at all but a chauvinist reminder of which sex ran things. But it was the part of her that had memorized all the dialogue in the last five minutes of *Casablanca* that said, "The other side of the puddle will do."

After Teddy paid the two-dollar cover charge, which was collected at the door by an old lady in an old-lady dress, Kit found herself in a dark, low-ceilinged room packed with people. Around her couples were doing strange steps with so much fervor, she could feel the floor vibrating. Considering all the straw hats in the room, Teddy needn't have left his behind. Of course, with all their feathers, these were probably *dancing* hats.

To her right, on a low plywood riser, the lead singer in a small band was wailing an upbeat Cajun song with no discernible melody into a sound system that couldn't possibly have been set any louder. Near the far wall, people stood three deep at a long wooden bar. On her left, those not dancing were seated at rows of picnic tables covered with checkered tablecloths. Scattered around the room, on little platforms hanging from the low beams, electric fans made sure everyone got their fair share of cigarette smoke and beer fumes.

Teddy guided her through the dancers to a pair of empty seats. Judging from the reception they got from the other couples at the table, Teddy was a regular. Despite music so loud that conversation was nearly impossible, everyone wanted to introduce themselves. She met the Thibodeauxes, the Fontenots, the Theriots, and the Delahoussayes.

Now Kit saw what Teddy had meant when he said it wouldn't matter what she wore. It was a most unusual mixture of people: octogenarians, twenty-year-olds, men in ties, men in polyester jumpsuits, women dressed to go out, and women dressed to stay home. There seemed to be no age or class distinction at all observed by those present. In the space of three dances, a wiry little lothario in denim coveralls and knee-high rubber boots worked his way through an attractive young brunette in a pink sunsuit, a fat woman in a tight red dress with a big sash at the waist, and a thin woman old enough to be his grandmother.

We shouldn't let them have all the fun," Teddy said, standing up. "Come on." He took Kit's hand and pulled her toward the dance floor.

"I don't know how to . . ."

"I'll teach you."

Teddy was a good instructor and Kit was soon giving a fair approximation of what he was showing her. After a couple of dances, the band took a break and Kit and Teddy went back to their table.

Scanning the crowd, Kit saw a striking blonde coming their way. Tanned and smooth as a mink, she was wearing a tight black miniskirt that showed off her long legs, and a sleeveless white pullover that fit tightly enough for Kit to see with some satisfaction that she was small-breasted. Teddy was watching her, too.

"Bonjour, Teddy," the girl said, letting her hand rest on Teddy's shoulder.

"Hello, Maria. Enjoying the dance?"

The girl replied in rapid-fire French, in which Kit caught the phrase *L'Americaine* as the girl gave her one of those looks she had been expecting from everyone else there.

"Maria, this is Kit Franklyn, Kit . . . Maria St. Julien."

As Teddy introduced them, he gestured at Kit with his left hand. Ignoring Kit, Maria's eyes went to Teddy's hand and her expression progressed from mild annoyance to anger. Without taking a breath, she began to give him a verbal shellacking.

Teddy put his hand over hers where it rested on his shoulder. "Maria, as terrible as it sounds, the truth is, I lost it."

Maria pulled away as though burned by his touch, and uttered two sharp words. Both hands went to her hips and she lit into him again. Finishing with a stamp of her foot, she flipped her hair and stormed away.

"Sounds like you're in trouble," Kit said.

"She's upset because I lost the bracelet she gave me for my birthday. Understandable reaction. Not like me to be so careless. She's not a girlfriend or anything. We're just regular friends."

"Doesn't she speak English?"

"As well as I do. She just wanted you to feel left out."

"I guess 'L'Americaine' was me."

"That's what Cajuns call anybody that doesn't speak French, even if they were born here."

Kit couldn't remember *when* a tiff between two people had made her feel so good.

The evening ended before Kit was ready. All too soon, she found herself at Oakliegh's front door, which Teddy opened with the key Claude had given her.

"This was fun," Kit said.

"I'm glad," Teddy replied, taking her hand and pressing the key into her palm. "I'd like to see you again."

"Me, too, but how?"

"No problem. New Orleans is only two hours away and I'm there all the time. In fact, I just got back this morning from taking a load of skins to the auction house on Dryads. Is your name in the book?"

"Yes."

"I'll call you next time I'm in town."

"Do that."

As Teddy was getting in the truck, Kit said, "Don't let 'em get behind you."

Teddy waved and Kit watched the truck until it turned onto the road out front.

Chapter 4

While Kit slept soundly in the Duhons' canopy bed, Deke Barnes was standing under a balcony on Bourbon Street, his fingers plucking out the first bars of "Dueling Banjos" on a guitar he'd bought from a guy that said it once belonged to Les Paul.

Deke finished his part and the old man responded on his harmonica. The old man didn't have a name, or at least Deke didn't know what it was. Nobody on the street did, either. He was just the "old man." If you wanted to find him, you could just ask a regular where the old man was, and they'd know who you were talking about. The old man finished his part and waited for Deke to come in.

"Dueling Banjos"—with a guitar and a harmonica. The old man was always comin' up with weird shit like that, Deke thought.

"C'mon son, you're missin' your cue," the old man said.

Deke took his fingers off the strings. "Who the hell we doin' this for?" He gestured to the nearly empty street. "Ain't hardly nobody out. And with this drizzle, ain't gonna be, neither." He picked up the old man's greasy hat and looked inside. "Whoa, can you stand the prosperity. There's all a two dollars and thirty cents in here."

"Once you start a piece son, you gotta finish it," the old man said. "It don't matter if anybody's around or not. You gotta finish it." He moved around in front of Deke and took him by the arm. "You finish it because you started it. When music is all you got, you gotta respect it. A man that don't respect his work is a bum." He looked up and swept his harmonica through the air. "And an unfinished piece of music hangs in the air forever like a lost soul that can't find rest." He looked back at Deke, his eyes pleading. "Do you see what I mean, son? Do you?"

When the old man started in on this kind of shit, he could go on for hours, and you only had two choices: give in or walk away. If you walked, he'd make you beg before he'd work with you again, and it was nice havin' someone to work with. Pay me now or pay me later, Deke thought. He decided to pay now and get it over with. "Okay, old man, let's finish it."

Deke raised his guitar and gave the best performance he could considering his heart wasn't in it. But the old man had just said finish it; he didn't say it had to be good. As the drizzle sucked away the last chords, Deke reached again for the hat and took his half of the take. "Now, old man, I'm gone."

While the old man fished the remaining coins from the hat, Deke slipped his guitar into a plastic bag he'd found in the trash from the cleaners on St. Peter Street. He tore a hole in the bag and pulled the strap out so he could still wear the guitar around his neck. Slinging his duffel bag over his shoulder, he stepped into a light rain.

A dollar and fifteen cents—either a flop or somethin' to eat. It was late and the trash had already been picked up at McDonald's, so there'd be no pickin's there. It seemed like it had been rainin' forever and he wanted a dry bed, even though he might have to share it with a few bugs. What the hell, they couldn't get to you much if you kept your clothes on, and who in their right mind would take 'em off . . . might be the last time you saw 'em.

What he disliked most about wet weather was the way it made his guitar sound all mushy. He began to think about what the old man had said about respecting the music and Deke saw what he'd been getting at. The music was what set them apart from the ones who didn't have it. He was glad the old man had made him finish the song.

He had about decided on a bed instead of food when he saw a Lucky Dog wagon being pushed back to the warehouse on Gravier by a fat vendor in a red and white striped shirt.

"Hey man," Deke said. "How about a dog and half a Coke."

"I'm closed," the vendor said. "And the dogs are probably cold, anyway."

"Hot as it is, they ain't likely to be all *that* cold," Deke said. "C'mon, whadda you say, gimme a break. I ain't had anything to eat all day and where'm I gonna find anyplace open this late?"

Reluctantly, the vendor lifted the cover on his wagon and put a dog on a bun, using his fingers instead of metal tongs.

"Whadda you want on it?"

"Everything you got, only don't put it on with your fingers. And half a Coke."

"What are you big spender, food critic for the *Times*?"

Deke wolfed down the dog on the spot, stretching his half a Coke so that he had one swallow left to wash down the last bite. No longer hungry, he wished he had chosen a bed instead. It didn't really matter though; he'd slept on the street before and could again.

With his duffel bag over his shoulder and his plastic-bagged guitar hanging in front of him, he walked a few blocks farther and turned left on St. Ann, heading for a nice deep doorway he knew. If you were in a deep doorway, there was less chance of some dog peein' on you while you slept.

A few minutes later, a drunk who had beaten Deke to the prize doorway was aroused from beery slumber by the sound of mindless strumming and splintering wood as pieces of guitar and shreds of plastic were driven into Deke's chest.

Kit arrived in New Orleans the next morning a little after ten. from the way her dog, Lucky, acted when she picked him up at the vet where he had been boarded, you would have thought she had been gone a month instead of just three days. It was such a short time that she hadn't bothered to cancel the newspapers, and they lay scattered over the lawn, still dry in their plastic sleeves even though it had rained every day according to her car radio.

As she passed the FOR SALE sign stuck in the lawn, she considered once again buying the place herself, but not at the price David was asking. She knew he was getting anxious, what with two mortgage payments and all. And that was really the problem. How do you sleep with someone and then take advantage of them in a business deal? If he had let her pay rent, then he wouldn't be so vulnerable to a low offer, which, if she decided to join him in Shreveport, was all irrelevant. "Aggggh." Kit groaned aloud at the complexity of it all as she unlocked the front door.

She went directly to the bedroom and tossed her suitcase on the bed. Always on the lookout for a way he could get closer to her petting hand, Lucky jumped onto the suitcase and yipped for some affection. She responded by giving him one of his favorite treats; her knuckles rubbed across his skull until the friction almost set his fur on fire.

"Now that's *enough*," she said finally, putting him on the floor.

Eager to see what had been happening in the examiner's office during her absence, she phoned in to tell Broussard she was back, learning from his secretary that he had left not ten minutes ago on a call to an address on South Hector, a street only a few minutes away.

Officially, her job as suicide investigator did not require her to accompany the medical examiner when he was called out. It was something Kit herself had begun to do after deciding that her forthcoming book on suicide should include a section on forensic details of the suicide scene. It was a decision that could have required far less of her time if Broussard had been willing to let the cops at the scene give him a preliminary report over the phone as to what had happened. His refusal to allow anyone to interpret a scene for him before he had seen it himself meant that *she* ended up at a lot of scenes that merely made her ill without contributing anything to her book.

* * *

Through the wipers and the fine drizzle that speckled the windshield, Kit saw that South Hector was lined with small one-story houses, most of them with full garages instead of the carports you'd expect to see in such modest homes. The Bermuda lawns were all closely cut and edged; a street where the dinner conversation might include speculations on the cause of that brown patch of dead grass in the neighbor's yard.

Kit didn't need to check house numbers to locate the scene. The NOPD cruiser, a couple of unmarked civilian cars, and one of Broussard's '57 T-birds stretched in a line along the curb did that for her. On the sidewalk across the street, two women sharing an umbrella watched her drive up.

Both the front door and the garage door on the house were open, as were all the windows. She didn't recognize the cop posted outside, but he seemed to know her and her presence wasn't challenged. Inside the house, camera flashes drew her into the den, where she found Broussard writing in his little black book.

The photography subjects were a man and a woman in their late forties sitting side by side on a sofa in front of the TV, their heads touching like young lovers. With their shoeless feet on the coffee table amid some partially filled wineglasses, they looked like a contented couple spending the evening at home. Most of all, they didn't look dead. In fact, with their rosy complexions, they appeared healthier than anyone else in the room.

Looking up from his black book, Broussard saw her and raised his bushy eyebrows in greeting. His eyes took on a distant glaze and he stroked the bristly hairs on the tip of his nose in thought. She would have bet everything she owned and all she could borrow that the bulge in his cheek was a lemon ball.

The detective on the case was Woodsy Newsome, a tall, athletic bachelor who spent all of his vacations camping in Michigan. While Broussard and most of Newsome's colleagues routinely dropped the "ing" ending on words, Newsome never did, sometimes even adding it to words where it didn't belong, producing creations like chicking and cotting. Newsome was tipping a wallet on top of the TV into a Baggie with the back of his index finger.

Ray Jamison, the photographer, circled by and shared a thought. "I bet they didn't look that good when they were alive."

Newsome winked at her and handed the Baggie to a uniformed cop. "Put this in my car, will you?" He put a hand on Broussard's shoulder. "Andy, me and Ray are going out to the garage."

"So are we," Broussard replied, motioning Kit over. "How was your trip."

"Interesting," she said.

"Can't ask for more than that. Seen the papers?"

"Haven't had a chance."

"Well, we had some trouble in the Quarter while you were gone. Somethin' we need to discuss. After we're through here, we'll get together with Phillip and talk about it."

The garage door was open now, but it was obvious from all the soot on it that the car had been running for a long time with the door closed.

"Anybody touch the car?" Broussard asked.

Newsome shook his head. "All the uniforms did was open the garage door to clear out the exhaust fumes. It wasn't running when they got here, so it's probably out of gas."

Broussard looked at Kit. "Cable TV installer found 'em," he said, shifting the lemon ball in his mouth to the other cheek. "When they didn't answer the bell, he went around back and saw 'em through the patio doors."

"No keys in the ignishing," Newsome called out.

Broussard continued with his story. "Air conditioner had cleared the carbon monoxide out of the house by the time help arrived, but apparently it was still pretty thick in here. Hemoglobin has a choice it'll take carbon monoxide over oxygen. When it's saturated with carbon monoxide, it can't carry anything else.

"Carboxyhemoglobin is what makes 'em look so pink. Now we got to figure out why it happened."

"What do you make of this?" Newsome said from the front of the car.

Kit followed Broussard to where the detective and the photographer were standing and saw what looked like an electrical plug coming out of the grill.

"I make that to be the last piece of the puzzle," Broussard said.

Jamison snapped a quick picture and they all followed Broussard back into the den, where he bent over the bodies and slipped his hand into the space where the thighs of the two corpses touched. "Woodsy, gimme a hand here."

"What do you want me to do?"

"Slide her a little to the right."

"You want the cushing moved, too?"

"No, just her . . . that's it."

Broussard opened his black bag and removed a large pair of chrome surgical scissors that he used to cut open the right pocket of the male corpse's pants. As he laid the fabric back, Kit saw a thin gray object in the pocket.

"Ray, get a shot of this in place, will you?"

Kit averted her eyes from the flash. When she looked back, Broussard was teasing the object into a handkerchief by using a tongue depressor.

"What is it?" Newsome asked.

"Indirectly, the cause of these deaths. When you check it out, I expect you'll find that this couple and the car recently came here from Alaska, Anchorage most likely."

"Based on what, that electrical cord on the car?" Newsome said.

"That's one way they keep the cars from freezin' up in arctic climates. In the big cities, most parkin' meters have outlets you can plug into."

"Why Anchorage?" Newsome asked.

"There was a membership card to the Anchorage Zoo in that wallet on the TV."

Newsome pointed his finger at Broussard. "Which not only tells us where the car came from but shows that they lived there, too."

"Excellent point, Woodsy."

Crafty old devil, Kit thought, catching Broussard at one of his favorite tricks: giving others the credit for something *he* had figured out. She had come to know him so well that it no longer worked on her.

"This little gizmo"—Broussard held the gray object up so they could get a good look at it—"explains why there was no key in the ignition even though the car had been runnin'. Here, I'll show you."

They followed him back to the garage, where he made the car's engine turn over by pressing the button on the object with his tongue depressor.

"Sometimes in the Arctic, you find yourself havin' to park for several hours in an area where there's nothin' to plug into. That's where a gizmo like this is useful. You can start the car every hour and keep it from freezin' up without goin' outside. Question is, was the wine to toast a suicide pact or did the gizmo get set off accidently while they were snugglin'? The absence of a note and the fact that the gizmo was in his pocket and not on the coffee table suggests an accident." He looked at Kit. "When you work this one up, see if you can find out why he'd been carryin' this thing around in a climate like ours."

As usual, on the way downtown, Kit was caught by the first traffic light she encountered, while Broussard slipped through. Invariably, if she was following him, the lights would be green for him and red for her, as if they were cooperating with him because he was a native. Consequently, by the time she reached Broussard's office, he had been there long enough to be on the phone already.

"How much hair?" he said into the mouthpiece.

While the person on the other end figured out how to answer such a question, Broussard put his hand over the phone and said, "Phillip's on his way." Then to the phone: "You think it's a contact wound?" He picked up a folded newspaper, tossed it to the front of his desk, and jabbed his finger at the headlines: MUTILATION MURDER IN THE FRENCH QUARTER.

"Do you know the kind of ammo? 'Cause federal ammo burns

real clean. . . . Go by your naked eye. . . . Sections are only supportive. . . ."

While Broussard talked, Kit scanned the article: Young girl . . . mutilated with a gardening claw . . . sources close to the investigation said that the victim's throat had been torn out by human teeth.

Kit looked up at the sound of the door: Phil Gatlin, his wet hair lying on his head like somebody had dumped a plate of black spaghetti on him. "Anybody remember what the sun looks like?" he growled, shucking off his raincoat. He looked over Kit's shoulder at the newspaper. "'Sources close to the investigation.' I'd like to get my hands on those sources." He went to the coffeepot, poured himself a cup, and then, remembering his manners, offered it to Kit.

Knowing how strong Broussard liked his coffee, Kit shook her head.

"What we need . . ." Realizing for the first time that Broussard might be finding it difficult to talk with other conversation in the room, Gatlin tapped the paper with a huge finger and whispered, "What we need in this country is to repeal the First Amendment . . . to where it doesn't apply to reporters."

"You found soot?" Broussard said into the phone. "And a flash burn? That's six inches. . . . Right. Let me know."

"How'd the paper find out about the throat wound?" Gatlin asked.

"Leaks," Broussard said. "Big leaks."

Gatlin looked at Kit. "We found another victim this morning . . . street musician. That one'll be in tonight's paper."

"Also with a throat wound?"

"This wound was located a bit more anterior than the first one but was significantly deeper," Broussard said. "All the way into the trachea."

Suddenly, Kit saw why they were relating all this. When she had told Teddy LaBiche that she occasionally helped develop profiles of murderers for the police, it was all true, except that she had not yet been given an assignment. This case was to be her first.

"The musician, male or female?" she asked.

"Male," Gatlin replied.

"Any chance it's a copycat of the first one?"

"None," Broussard said. "The puncture wounds in the first victim showed a distinct pattern that was also present in the second victim."

"Robbery?"

"The guy didn't have anything worth stealing," Gatlin said. "The girl still had money in her purse."

"I take it she wasn't sexually molested?"

Broussard rocked back in his chair, folded his small hands over his belly, and shook his head.

Kit felt the eyes of both men on her. It was like being back in school taking her Ph.D. orals again, only this was worse. If she screwed up here, a murderer might remain free long enough to kill again . . . and *there* was Broussard, keeping a scorecard on her. She had never wanted to please anyone as much as she wanted to prove herself to Broussard. "I guess you've had time to talk to some of the girl's friends," she said to Gatlin.

"All day yesterday. If you had a popularity contest between this girl and Mother Theresa, you'd have to have a runoff." Gatlin crossed himself to make sure his Mother Theresa remark wouldn't be used against him in the hereafter.

"One female, one male," Kit said. "Serial killers usually stick to the same sex. What did the girl do for a living?"

"Exotic dancer," Gatlin said.

"Any hooking on the side?"

Gatlin shrugged. "Haven't found anyone so far who'll say so. What do *you* think?"

"Neither victim was what you'd call an asset to the community," Kit observed.

"Depends on your point of view," Gatlin replied.

"Exactly. Could be we're dealing with someone out to clean up the Quarter . . . get rid of all the undesirables. But . . ."

"But what?" Gatlin asked.

"The brutality of the attacks is puzzling. That doesn't sound like someone carrying out a plan."

"So what are we looking for, Doc?"

"I'm not sure. Let me study the files on the two cases and see what I can come up with."

From the look on Gatlin's face, he had expected more. And why not; she had expected more from herself. But after all, they had sprung this on her without even giving her a chance to review the available written material. She glanced at Broussard and saw that *his* face was unreadable.

"Well, he won't be getting away with anything tonight," Gatlin said. "We've put everybody on double shifts and practically cleaned the Salvation Army thrift store out of undercover clothes."

Chapter 5

It took Kit thirty minutes to read the files on the two murders. There was actually not much to review. The girl's file included the autopsy findings, Gatlin's description of the scene and his conversations with the girl's friends, as well as a stack of photographs that brought the case out of the abstract into gruesome reality. While it was nothing that would help *her*, she was impressed with Broussard's thoroughness. At least he was doing *his* part. The file on the second case was even thinner. So little time had elapsed since the murder that Gatlin had nothing personal on the victim and Broussard had only completed a superficial examination of the body. While she was looking at the scene photographs of the second victim, Broussard came into her office waving a sheet of paper.

"Well, we know the murderer's blood type," he said, plunking the serology report down in front of her. "He's type B."

"How'd you get that?"

"From saliva traces around the bite on the second victim. Tried it on the first one but couldn't be absolutely sure of the results because she was an AB secretor. But the musician was type O, no B antigens to mask what the killer left."

Kit only partially understood what he was talking about, but she got the important point.

"How common is type B?"

"Ten to fifteen percent of the population."

"That's good. Wish I was doing as well."

"But then your job is harder," Broussard said. "When two objects come together, there's always a transfer of physical evidence. All I've got to do is find it. There isn't always a piece of the murderer's psyche left behind."

Kit shook her head. "I disagree. It's there, just like the physical evidence. Unfortunately, I may need to see more of his work before I understand him."

"Maybe they'll catch him tonight and that won't be necessary."

"I pray they do."

Unable to glean anything further from the scanty files, Kit decided to see what she could learn about the dead couple they had found that morning.

After filling out a requisition in triplicate at the police property room, she was allowed to see the contents of the wallet that had been on the couple's TV. Among those items was an ID card from the Frigi-King ice cream plant in Kenner.

When she got to the Frigi-King plant, the receptionist directed her through a wide metal door to the novelty production section. Always having imagined the manufacture of ice cream products to be a quiet process, she was surprised at all the hissing and clanking. Apparently, she didn't know much about alligators *or* ice cream.

Waiting for her next to a massive vat of brine filled with rows of metal forms containing embryonic orange Popsicles was a man in a white jumpsuit—the production foreman. He had long brown flyaway hair that made Kit wonder how much of it had been shipped out in the company's products over the years. In a glassed-in freezer behind him, a man in a white jumpsuit and a Russian hat was scraping the ice cream from crushed half-gallon cartons into a large galvanized milk can with his fingers.

"Where'd you say you were from?" the foreman asked over the noise.

"Orleans Parish Medical Examiner's Office," Kit said. The man in the glass freezer dropped a large chunk of ice cream on the floor, picked it up, and threw it in the milk can. "Do you have an employee named Dennis Chapman?"

A wary look crept over the foreman's face. "Chapman? Yeah, he's a manager trainee. And he's late. Real late."

The plant had obviously not been informed of what had happened. "I'm afraid Mr. Chapman won't be coming in at all. He and his wife were found dead this morning in their home."

"Oh well," the foreman said, shrugging his shoulders. "We'll just hire another trainee. Ain't as though they're hard to get." He looked expectantly over Kit's shoulder at the door through which she had come.

Thinking that perhaps he hadn't heard her correctly over the noise, Kit repeated herself. "I don't think you understand. Mr. Chapman is dead."

"Oh I understand," the foreman said, still looking at the door. "I hope he don't expect me to come to the funeral. 'Cause I wasn't *that* crazy about him when he was alive." An amused smirk appeared on his face. He pushed past her, leaned on the door, and stuck his head into the next room. "So where is he?" he asked, pulling his head back and letting the door swing shut.

"I certainly didn't bring him," Kit said. "He's probably in the morgue."

A gray pall spread over the foreman's face. "Then you're serious? This isn't another one of Dennis's pranks?"

"This is no prank. He and his wife died of carbon-monoxide poisoning."

"Jesus . . . the things I said. I didn't know. I thought . . . I mean he's always pulling crap like this on us."

"I'm trying to find out if it was an accident or—"

"Suicide? No way. He and his wife were taking scuba lessons. They were planning a Caribbean diving trip for their anniversary. Already had the reservations. He talked about it all the time. Like to drive us nuts with it."

"Did he carry a remote car starter around with him?"

"Oh that. Yeah, he used to tell people he could make his car start by whistling for it like it was a horse or something. Used to pull it every chance he got."

Before letting the foreman go, she asked him one last question. "By the way, what are you going to do with the ice cream that man is collecting?"

The foreman shrugged. "Make chocolate."

Kit verified with another employee what the foreman had told her and was then satisfied. Chapman's anticipation of the couple's forthcoming trip was a major factor in her conclusion that the couple had not taken their own lives. The only things suicidal mentalities look forward to is the day they plan to kill themselves. The men at the plant also had explained why Chapman had the remote control in his pocket. It was simply an accident. Ordinarily, she would have been pleased at being able to reach a decision so quickly. Today, she would have preferred a more complicated case, one she could use as an excuse for not coming up with any bright ideas on the French Quarter murders.

Late that afternoon, the sun broke through for a few hours and was then obscured again as yet another front pushed into the city, bringing more rain. This time, Gatlin was happy to see it, for he wanted things to be just as they had been the previous two nights when the killer struck.

Gatlin gave himself the best location, spending the night shuffling around the two-block area where the previous killings had occurred. In the left pocket of a hot old raincoat that smelled like a wet horse, he carried a Handie-Talkie that gave him direct access to the undercover command post in a Winnebago parked in Exchange Alley. Every few minutes, he would put a Gilbey's gin bottle filled with water to his lips and pretend to take a long drink. Whether he and the other undercover cops cruising the Quarter were dressed wrong or were too clean-shaven or were just lousy actors was not clear. Whatever the reason, nothing happened that night or the next. Citing the cost, the police commissioner suspended the operation.

The following day, it occurred to Kit that one reason she was having trouble getting a handle on the murderer's mental state was that she did not have a clear picture of the environment in which the murders had taken place. Sure, there were plenty of photographs, but they could not convey the *feel* of the place, the intangibles that might have influenced his choice of victims or his decision to act. She could learn that only by visiting the scene, not during the day but at night, around the time each murder had occurred.

The thought raised gooseflesh on her arms, but that didn't change her mind. It was something she had to do. But how? She couldn't go down there unprotected. And she definitely did not want to take Gatlin or any other member of the police with her. That would only cast further doubt on her abilities if she failed to learn anything. Better to keep a low profile. So whom could she take? Someone discreet . . . someone who owned a gun . . . someone like . . . Bubba Oustellette.

When Kit arrived at the NOPD vehicle-impoundment station on Poydras, she saw Bubba through the glass window in the small concrete-block building just inside the lot's chain-link gates. He was eating a sandwich and reading a comic book.

She pressed the button like the sign told her to do if she wanted help. The bell caught Bubba by surprise and he nearly fell off his stool. Seeing who it was, he grinned and motioned for her to come around back.

"Hey, Dr. Franklyn." He threw the door open and stood aside. "C'mon in here where it's cool."

Bubba was wearing what he usually wore: navy blue coveralls over a blue T-shirt, and a green baseball cap with the Tulane football logo on it—an ocean wave showing its teeth and carrying a football. With his long black hair and bushy black beard, he always reminded Kit of a chipmunk, a comparison called to mind by Bubba's kind nature and extremely small stature. He was the one that kept Broussard's fleet of '57 T-birds running smoothly.

Bubba pulled out another stool. "Maybe you wanna sid-down."

While Kit climbed onto the stool, Bubba dug in his lunch box and brought out half a sandwich.

Kit shook her head when he offered it to her.

"Fried baloney," he said, as if she ought to know what she

was missing. Still no sale. "Somethin' to drink den," he said, lightly kicking the short refrigerator under the counter. "Ah got Mellow Yellow and Mellow Yellow. Whadda you think?"

"I had lunch before I came over. I'd like to ask a favor."

Bubba slid off his stool and wiped his hands on his coveralls. "Your car actin' up?"

"It's not that. You do a lot of hunting, don't you?"

"Allatime."

"Then you have a gun?"

"Pretty hard to shoot ducks with a fishin' rod. Ah tried it once and didn' get nowhere near da limit." He touched her arm. "Sorry for dat. It's one a mah wors' habits. Gramma O says Ah'm goin' to hell if Ah don' quit it."

"Do you have any small guns? Like a pistol, something that you could carry easily?"

With each question Kit asked, another line appeared on Bubba's forehead. "Scuse me for sayin' dis, but when Ah dance with somebody, dere's usually music playin'." He wiped the air in front of his face. "Sorry."

"It's all right. I'm the one that should apologize for being so obtuse."

"Obtuse?" Bubba's mind struggled with the word and he said it again. "Obtuse. Nice word. Gotta kinda French sound to it."

"It means not getting to the point."

"Ahhh. Dat's why Ah was havin' trouble figurin' out what we were talkin' about. You were jus' bein' obtuse."

"I guess you've read about the two mutilation murders in the French Quarter. . . ."

"Yeah, sounds like dat guy's a real animal."

"Well, I'm trying to help the police by figuring out what's going on in the killer's mind, what kind of person he might be during the day. To help me do that, I want to go to where the murders were committed and get the feel of the place. And I want to go around three A.M., the time when they think both crimes occurred."

"An' you'd like for me to go with you?"

"If you would."

"An' bring a gun . . . a small one."

Kit nodded, convinced that he was going to refuse to help her.

"You mean go right down dere where we might meet dis fella face-to-face?"

"I suppose that's possible. I certainly hope we don't."

"What time you want me to pick you up?"

Kit drew Bubba a map of how to get to her place and they agreed to meet at 2:30 A.M. the next morning.

"Wear dark clothes," Kit said as she was leaving. "And bring a black umbrella."

Though she had not said so back in Bayou Coteau when Teddy LaBiche was telling her how the Duhons liked to turn in early, Kit was not a night person either. Ordinarily, if she didn't have a date, she would become drowsy around 10:30 and would barely be able to keep her eyes open during Johnny Carson's monologue. Rarely did she ever make it to his first guest.

Tonight, her adrenaline was flowing so freely that she was still wide awake when David Letterman signed off. Two hours to go before Bubba arrived. She passed that block of time by watching an old black and white musical, marveling at the truly ludicrous routines, which included one in which a chorus line performed on the wing of an airplane for an audience at a posh party on the ground. How those watching below were able to see the dancers through the wing of the plane was a real puzzle.

Bubba arrived a few minutes early in a battered pickup. He didn't have to ring the bell because Kit was watching for him through the window. He was dressed as she had requested, in dark clothes—the same ones he had been wearing when they spoke that afternoon. When she asked if he was armed, he patted a bulky pocket in his coveralls.

As they drove downtown in Kit's little Nissan, a light mist drifted onto the windshield. The well-publicized killings and the weather made the French Quarter quieter and more lifeless than Kit had ever seen it, as though the Quarter itself had been mortally stricken. She shivered and was glad that Bubba had agreed to come along.

The first murder had occurred on Royal, a few doors from its intersection with Dumain. She parked a block away on St. Philip and gave Bubba his instructions.

"I want to walk by myself. You follow about a block away. Try to look casual."

Kit got out of the car and raised her umbrella against the light rain that had seemed to become a permanent resident of the city. As she turned the corner onto Royal, she saw something peculiar: Someone was playing a flashlight over the sidewalk and the doorway where the first body had been found. Wanting to see what this person might do next, Kit stepped into a dark doorway, closed her umbrella, and stole another look.

Flashlight still in hand but now turned off, the man—and she was sure from the walk that it *was* a man—was heading down Dumain, toward the French Market. Still curious, Kit decided to follow.

She went quickly down Royal, past the famous cornstalk fence, and crossed over so she could get a look around the next corner. The man had stopped opposite a partially collapsed building that had dropped away from those on each side to which it had been attached. He sent the beam of his flashlight over the rubble for a minute or two, then closed his umbrella, telescoped the handle, and put it in the pocket of his raincoat. Then he slowly crossed the street, his movements wary and calculated, almost as though he was expecting something to burst from the debris.

Unexpectedly, he glanced toward the French Market. Kit drew back, fearing that he would look her way next. When she had summoned enough courage to look again, she saw the man leaning forward, his hand cupped to his mouth, saying something over and over into a dark recess between what was left of the first floor of the collapsed building and an old gate that had been nailed over a large hole in the brickwork. After a short time had passed, he raised his umbrella again and moved on toward the French Market. Kit let him get two blocks away before she went after him.

As soon as Bubba had gotten out of the car, he had become

absorbed in a display of knives in a shop window on St. Philip. Now when he looked up, he realized Kit was gone.

Kit moved slowly down Dumain, not wanting to get too close to the man she was following. He crossed Decatur and walked toward a fountain between the stuccoed market buildings on the other side of the street. After working his flashlight around the trash-collecting area behind the building on his left, he disappeared through the gate in the wall that separated the market from the riverfront.

Afraid she might lose him, Kit began to walk faster. Suddenly, her legs became tangled and she pitched to the sidewalk. Her umbrella rolled crazily into the gutter. Hands were scrabbling at her clothing. Grasping fingers closed on her flesh and she was dragged into a dark doorway.

Chapter 6

Before Kit thought to scream, a calloused hand was clapped to her mouth, catching her lip hard against her teeth. The smell of alcohol and urine catalyzed the nausea that fear had already set in motion. She was dimly afraid that she might throw up and, because of the hand at her mouth, aspirate vomitus into her lungs.

The man holding her had been sitting in the doorway like a spider waiting for something edible to pass. He had tripped Kit with his feet and had pulled her onto his lap.

"I'm not gonna hurt you lady," he said, his face so close, she couldn't focus on it. "All I want is money enough to get off the streets until whatever's down here is caught. That ain't bein' unreasonable, is it? Ain't I got the right to be as safe as you when I sleep?"

"Maybe you oughtta let da lady go," a voice said from above and behind the bum's head. Bubba put the barrel of a huge pistol on the man's nose.

The bum's hand slipped from Kit's mouth and he slithered out from under her, flattening himself against the iron bars covering the glass door behind him. As Bubba helped Kit up, he never let the pistol waver from the cowering man's face.

"You okay, Doc?"

Kit brushed herself off, plumped her hair, and carefully touched her tender lip. "I'm a little wet and dirty, but that's about all."

"So Ah guess Ah should shoot him," Bubba said, leaning into the doorway.

The bum threw his hands in front of his face and sucked in a breath, the rushing air rattling wetly in his nose.

"I'd be satisfied just to see him running as quickly as he could that way," Kit said, pointing away from the French Market. Ordinarily, she might have had Bubba hold him until he could be turned over to the police, but she still didn't want it known that she had come down here.

"You hear da lady?" Bubba asked.

"Yes, sir, I heard her."

"Den why you still here?"

The bum got to his feet, oozed out of the doorway, and slid along the wall, Bubba's pistol touching his nose. Then he ducked under the gun and began to run, stumbling for a few steps over his own feet.

Bubba put the gun back in his pocket and got Kit's umbrella from the gutter. Kit remembered the man she had been following. By now, he could be anywhere.

"Thanks, Bubba. That's one I owe you."

"Maybe we oughtta go home now."

"Not yet. There's something I still need to do. You follow from behind, like before."

Kit hurried to the gate where the man she was following had disappeared. She looked up and down the long parking lot that separated the wall from the riverfront levee. Far to the right, she saw a figure on the raised sidewalk leading to the river.

Crossing the parking lot and the riverfront trolley tracks, she scaled the wet grass of the levee and worked her way toward the man, using the trees on the crest of the levee for cover. From behind one of those trees, she saw the man play his flashlight along the edge of the timbered steps that led down the other side of the levee into the Mississippi, as though he was trying to see under them. Then he moved to the other side of the steps and did the same thing.

From there, he retraced his path and went up to the moon walk overlooking Jackson Square, using his flashlight to examine the beds of foliage flanking the stairs.

By the time Kit had gone up those same steps, he was already down the other side and halfway across the square. Hurrying after him, Kit used the statue of Andrew Jackson and his horse to shield herself from view, getting closer to him than she had ever been. From behind a crepe myrtle in full flower, she saw him pause at the scaffolding that had been erected in the passageway between St. Louis Cathedral and the Presbytere, the building that once served as home to the cathedral priests. He sent the beam from his flashlight up the scaffolding and stepped back so he could pick out the dormers that projected from the slate on the Presbytere's mansard roof. Then he entered the passageway and checked each of the cathedral's empty planterlike recesses, his face pressed against its wrought-iron fence.

Deciding that she *must* see this man's face, Kit gambled that he would turn left when he came out onto Royal Street. She rushed past the cathedral and hesitated at Pirate's Alley, another passageway that led to Royal. If she went down Pirate's Alley and missed, she'd still be behind him. Better to go on to St. Peter and cut over. He must have quickened his pace, though, after Kit had lost sight of him, because they collided at the corner of Royal and St. Peter.

"Sorry," she said, getting a good look at him. He had a long face with a prominent oval chin. His deep-set eyes were surmounted by sharply arched hoary eyebrows. Below, they sat on puffy pouches of skin that would have made a plastic surgeon cluck with disapproval. At each corner of his mouth, there were small fleshy bulges below his lower lip, suggesting that his glum expression had nothing to do with what had just happened but was something he carried around all the time.

Without looking at her, he mumbled a reply that included the word *clumsy* and continued on. When he was a block away, Kit set out after him. A few minutes later, she saw him ring the bell at Maison Toulouse—one of the Quarter's most exclusive small hotels—and go inside when the concierge answered.

Most curious, she thought as she looked behind her for Bubba. Spotting the tip of an umbrella sticking out from the edge of the building at the corner, she motioned with one finger and Bubba stepped into view. She could hear the legs of his coveralls rubbing together as he came briskly toward her.

"Doc, you sure cover a lotta ground when you take a walk. Ain't you gettin' jus' a little bit tired?"

When she was following the strange man, she had been too preoccupied to notice anything else. Now that he was off the street, she realized she was not only tired but her knee hurt. And her lip felt like a basketball. "Well, if you're ready to call it a night, I guess I am, too."

Before allowing Bubba to go home, Kit gave him some tea and a small plate of butter cookies, which he avidly consumed. As they said good night, she took off his cap and gave him a sisterly kiss on the forehead. Bubba responded by turning the color of a boiled crayfish.

Despite all that had happened, Kit fell asleep almost immediately after she got into bed. In the morning, while showering, she found a yellow bruise on her arm where the bum had grabbed her and one on the knee that had absorbed most of her fall. Her lip, though, felt almost normal.

Later, as she poised over Lucky's bowl with a Gainesburger, she asked his opinion of what she had seen. "He's out looking at the murder scene, walks all over the area where the murders occurred, looking in corners, looking in the shrubbery. And what about that collapsed building? I'm sure he was saying the same word over and over. What was *that* all about?"

While she questioned him, Lucky sat on his hind legs, his head cocked to one side, his big brown eyes giving the impression he understood everything she said. Kit put the burger in his bowl, and while he ate, she scratched his neck and gave the problem a little more thought herself. Maybe she was making too much out of what she had seen. The guy could have been an undercover cop. But would a cop be staying at a hotel in the Quarter? Not likely . . . unless, of course, he was a really *good* undercover cop.

The morning was clear and bright, the kind of day where nothing unpleasant could possibly take place and where problems could be solved. But as Kit pulled onto South Claiborne, the sun disappeared behind a cloud bank that plunged the city into a gloom that robbed Kit of her optimism. A few minutes later, the sun reappeared. Having already been fooled once, Kit lapsed into a neutral attitude.

Upon reaching her office, she called Phil Gatlin and asked whether there was an undercover officer with a long face and heavy, arching eyebrows working the Quarter late at night. Assured that there was not, she parried his curiosity as to why she thought there might be, and hung up.

She spent the next hour proofing and polishing a description of her activities for the last six months to be included in Broussard's semiannual report to the Orleans Parish hierarchy. Finally finishing the blasted thing, she wanted to personally place it in Broussard's hands. To do that, she went down the hall and knocked on his door, trying hard to tune out the old air-handling unit overhead that lately had begun to clank and clatter as if it was about to fly apart. Thinking she heard a faint "Come in," she pushed the door open and saw Broussard behind his desk, one hand digging in his bowl of lemon balls.

"Hello, Kit." He motioned her inside with the hand that wasn't in the bowl. "There's someone here I want you to meet."

One of the two wooden chairs in front of Broussard's littered desk was occupied. As the man in it turned toward her, she felt her jaw drop.

"Henry, this is Kit Franklyn, the psychology arm of our operation. Kit, meet Henry Guidry, an old friend from Bayou Coteau."

"My pleasure," Kit said, shaking hands with the man she had followed the previous night. From his expression, it was obvious he did not recognize her.

"Kit just got back from visiting Claude and Olivia," Broussard said.

"How do you know *them*?" Guidry asked.

"I don't really. I dropped off an anniversary gift from Dr. Broussard on my way back from Shreveport and they allowed me to stay the night. How long have you been in town?"

"About an hour. Came to see if I could pick up a good bull at the Laplace livestock auction later this afternoon."

"Henry's a vet turned cattle rancher," Broussard said. "What do you run Henry, about a thousand head?"

"More or less."

"Kit, Henry and I are gettin' together tonight for dinner. Why don't you come, too?"

Kit didn't have to think at all about her answer. There was absolutely no doubt that this *was* the man she had followed. By itself, his behavior the previous night was merely peculiar. But add to that the lie about just arriving in town . . . How could she pass up an opportunity to learn more? "I'd love to join you."

"You mind meetin' us at Gramma O's? Three just won't fit in a bird."

"When?"

Broussard looked at Guidry. "Say . . . seven?"

Guidry nodded.

Back in her office, Kit lugged out the Yellow Pages and looked up the number of the Laplace livestock auction. They picked up on the third ring.

"Yeeellllo."

"Could you tell me when the next auction will be held?"

"Not only *could* but *will*," the voice on the other end said. "You want some prime beef on the hoof, you be here nine o'clock sharp week from today and we'll see you get fixed up proper."

Kit thought she could smell cow manure through the phone. "Then there's no auction today?"

"Not to my knowin', and I run 'em."

"Thanks."

As Kit replaced the receiver, she wondered whether Guidry *ever* told the truth.

Chapter 7

Kit spent the afternoon in the LSU medical school library, becoming so engrossed in what she was doing that she had to go directly from the library to meet Broussard.

Grandma O's was Broussard's favorite restaurant. Located near the Quarter but on the opposite side of Canal, it had something French Quarter restaurants didn't: a parking lot. When Kit pulled into it, she saw Broussard and Guidry getting out of Broussard's red T-bird. Despite the misty rain that had begun to fall, neither of them had umbrellas or raincoats. Even so, they waited for her to join them before going inside.

They were met by Grandma O herself, a large woman whose hips made it look as though she wore an inflated inner tube as an undergarment. While others called her Grandma because she wanted them to, Bubba Oustellette did it because she had borne his father. As usual, she was wearing a black taffeta dress that flared so widely from the hips that she inadvertently rearranged the empty chairs and dusted the customers in the occupied ones as she walked through the narrow spaces between tables.

"Don' stand in da doorway," Grandma O said. "It'll make folks think de'll have to wait for a table." She pinched Broussard's arm. "City boy, you feel like you losin' weight. We better get some food into you quick." Then she let loose with a loud cackle that showed the gold star in her front tooth. "Doc Franklyn, you lookin' fine, and who is dis handsome fella?"

Broussard introduced her to Guidry, and she led them past a lot of small round tables with white marble tops to one much larger than the rest.

"Any man spends as much time in here as city boy does, gets da best Ah got," she explained to Guidry as she put in front of each of them a menu made up to look like a shack on stilts. "Ah know dat city boy wants a strawberry daiquiri to start," Grandma O said. "And Doc Franklyn, Ah bet you want a rum and Coke."

Kit nodded.

"A draft . . . whatever you have," Guidry said when Grandma O looked his way. She went off to fill their order and Guidry picked up the menu.

"Red beans and rice is what you want," Broussard said. "Nobody makes andouille sausage like Gramma O."

"Well," Kit said to Guidry, "did you find anything at the auction today?"

There was a fleeting trapped look in Guidry's eyes that made it appear as if he was sifting answers.

"I'm embarrassed to say that I got over there and discovered that the auction wasn't today; it's *next* Tuesday."

Kit did not know what to make of his answer. Had he somehow detected that she was testing him and had decided he'd better cover himself? Or was this the truth?

She decided to probe deeper. To make her interest seem innocuous, she directed the next question at Broussard. "How did you and Henry meet?"

"As I recall, it was when I fell on him."

Kit shook her head. "I don't—"

"Football . . . when we were kids," Broussard explained. "I was on one side and Henry was on the other."

"I wondered why no one else was trying to stop him," Guidry said. "Then when I hit him, I found out. How long was I unconscious?"

"I don't think you were ever really out," Broussard said. "Just a little confused."

"Like when I went after you in the first place. After that, I always made sure we were on the same team."

Grandma O brought their drinks and took their orders—red beans and rice all around. As she went off to the kitchen, Broussard said, "Henry, Claude, and I were best friends all through high school. Compared to Henry, Claude and I were choirboys. Henry spent more time in detention than anybody else in the history of the school."

"That's probably not far from the truth," Guidry said. His heavy brows crept together, partially hiding his eyes—a signal to Kit that he was about to change the tone of the conversation. "Andy, I've never told you this, but I always admired the way you handled yourself after the accident. Don't know if *I* could have done as well."

"The accident?" Kit said.

"Truckload of cypress logs on their way to the mill," Broussard said, stirring his daiquiri with his straw. "Chain came loose just as my parents were passin'."

"And they were . . ."

He nodded.

"How awful."

"I remember when the call came," Guidry said. "Andy, Claude, and I were helping Claude do some bodywork on the car his father had given him. I can see that moment in my mind as clearly as if it happened an hour ago."

"So can I," Broussard said. "It wasn't an easy time for a sixteen-year-old, that's for sure. Would've been worse, though, if I hadn't had a grandmother to look after me. Course it meant I had to leave my friends and move over here, which, as it turned out, wasn't such a bad thing. It's criminal, though, how rarely I get back. In the last ten years, I'll bet I haven't been in Bayou Coteau more than . . ." He thought it over and came up with ". . . twice. Only twice."

Further reminiscences were put on hold by the arrival of the food. Before she left them to enjoy it, Grandma O looked sharply at Guidry. "Ah don' know if city boy tol' you da rules, but you gotta eat everything on your plate or explain to me why you didn'. An Ah ain't likely to believe you if you say you jus' weren' hungry."

"That's why she's Gramma O," Broussard said as she swished back to the kitchen.

"Looks good," Guidry said. He cut himself a slice of the plump sausage that lay across his generous portion of Grandma O's renowned red beans and rice, skewered it with his fork, and carried it to his mouth. His eyes closed in reverence. "I don't think I'm going to have to explain anything," he said.

They ate in silence for a minute or two, then Guidry said, "I see from the papers that you've had a couple of unusual murders in the Quarter. Making any progress on solving them?"

The conversation about their days as kids had lulled Kit into complacency. Guidry's question stripped that away.

"If we knew ten times as much about them as we know now, we'd still be pretty much in the dark," Broussard said.

"What kind of person is able to commit murder?" Guidry asked Kit.

"Practically anyone," Kit answered. "Given the right circumstances . . . maybe even you." She was disappointed that Guidry took no notice of her attempt at a personal jab.

"The right conditions . . . like anger or jealousy?"

"Those are some of the more common ones. But there's also evidence to indicate that normal people can kill in a cold, dispassionate way."

"What sort of evidence?"

"You thinkin' of the Milgrim experiments?" Broussard said.

"Yes," Kit replied, once again surprised at the old pathologist's breadth of knowledge. She turned to Guidry. "A large number of volunteers agreed to participate in what they thought was a motivational learning study to determine the effects of punishment on learning. Each volunteer was given the designation *teacher*. The role of the teacher was to deliver an electric shock for every mistake to a learner who was required to learn a list of word pairs. With each mistake, the teacher was asked to increase the severity of the shock. In truth, the learner was actually an actor hired by the experimenter, and there was no electric shock at all. But the actor

made it appear as if there was, faking mild discomfort at supposedly low voltages, obvious distress at high ones, and even
screaming and pleading at the highest voltages to be released
from the straps that held him to his chair. To the experimenter's
astonishment, over ninety percent of the teachers were willing
to inflict pain on the learner if the experimenter agreed to take
the responsibility. Many of them were even willing to force the
learner's hand onto a metal plate to give him the shock."

From behind Kit came the voice of Grandma O. "Doc
Franklyn, Ah notice you don' seem to be eatin' much. You
know what dat means. Can Ah get anybody anything?"

They all shook their heads and Grandma O moved off to
warn other customers who were dawdling over their food.

"But would these same people have been willing to *kill* the
learner?" Guidry asked.

"We have to assume they would. After all, a severe shock
could cause a heart attack. It was at least theoretically
possible that they already had engaged in homicidal behavior.
Apparently when atrocities are part of a large program in
which an individual plays a subordinate role, however proxi-
mate to the actual infliction of the atrocity, he's able to
dissociate his moral sense from the act. That's one explanation
for the willingness of so many Germans to participate in the
operation of Nazi death camps."

"Fascinating stuff," Guidry said. "But if you'll forgive me for
saying so, not very applicable to these French Quarter murders. What do you think of the guy that did *that*?"

When she had first met him in Broussard's office, Guidry
had seemed morose and passive. Now there was an energy
about him that took ten years off his age. Before Kit could
reply, Broussard said, "Come on, Henry. You don't want to
dwell on such sordid things as that. Tell us about the time you
put a five-hundred-pound pig in the principal's office. I never
did know the details of that caper. How'd you get him up the
stairs?"

"Jesus, Andy. That was so long ago, I don't think I can
remember it all."

"Try."

Guidry rolled his eyes in thought. "It was the weekend before . . . no, *after* the Bristol game. . . ."

The net result of the evening was that Kit found Guidry to be a likable man. But he did have an uncommon interest in the subject of murder.

Ordinarily, she could hear Lucky's paws on the door even before she opened it. Tonight, though, all was quiet. When the lights came on, she saw Lucky on the sofa with his head under a pillow, which could mean only one thing. "All right. Show me," she said sternly.

Whimpering, head down, Lucky led her to the bedroom, where she found her new box of face powder upside down on the carpet. Crossing the room in two strides, she snatched the little dog up and cradled him in her arms so she could look into his face. "What am I going to do with you, you little *varmint?*"

He blinked and cowered so helplessly when she said "varmint," that she had to forgive him. After the mess was cleaned up, she went into the living room and flicked on her answering machine. To her surprise, it contained one of the last voices she expected to hear.

"Kit, this is Teddy . . . Teddy LaBiche. Was in town for a few hours and thought we might get together. Sorry I missed you. Now that I know your number, I'll call ahead next time."

"Nuts," Kit said aloud. She plopped down on the sofa and took Lucky into her lap. "An alligator farmer," she said, scratching the dog's neck. "I'm attracted to an alligator farmer who takes you dancing in a pickup truck. What am I doing?"

In the heart of the French Quarter, Melanie Conroy glanced around her at the empty tables. "Where do you suppose all the customers are?"

"Probably the rain," Del Ferris replied, running a toothpick up and down the crack between his lower front teeth.

"Let's just split it three ways," Roy Hanover, the other man that had made the trip, said, studying the bill.

Del wiped the toothpick on his napkin. "What difference

does it make. It all goes on company cards. Just take care of it."

While they waited for the waiter to pick up Roy's card, Del rubbed his hands together. "Well, what now? There's a lot of the evening left."

"I don't know about you two, but I'm going back to my room," Melanie said.

"And practice?" Roy said in a smirking tone.

"Maybe you two have forgotten," Melanie said. "The Filmore account is worth a million-two a year, and for that we need to be letter-perfect tomorrow."

Del turned his palms to the ceiling. "Hey, I'm ready."

"Me, too," Roy added.

"You better be. 'Cause if either of you leaves me hanging out there naked tomorrow—"

"Naked," Del said. "Sounds interesting. Why don't we pursue that thought for a few minutes."

"Cretins," Melanie said, thrusting back her chair and stalking away.

Word was that the CO at Filmore had been considering changing agencies. So everything had to go smoothly tomorrow, and even that might not be good enough. In her room, Melanie practiced her presentation twice, complete with easel and graphs, watched TV for awhile, then turned in early.

Several blocks away, it started as it always did—with an olfactory hallucination, at first faint and then full-blown, the smell of a grass fire. Then the headache, beginning as a dull pressure in the back of his head that slowly spread in all directions until the pain drove him to the floor in agony. Pain. There was nothing else in his world now but a white suffocating blanket of pain.

Reluctant seconds passed into plodding minutes as he lay on the floor with his knees pulled up to his chest, his hands and arms clasping his head, unable to form any kind of thought, a creature linked to the present only by unendurable pain.

Gradually, as the raging fire in his brain waned, his senses returned, sharpened now, making colors brighter, sounds louder, and smells . . . He lowered his knees and dropped his arms to his side, absorbing the sounds and smells around him. A fly buzzed against the window. Over the sound of its wings, he heard its legs drumming against the glass. From the corner came the roar of a cockroach nibbling the glue off the edge of a stamp on an old envelope. As his chest rose and fell, he could feel the ebb and flow of the air in the room as it nudged the hairs on his arms.

His nostrils began to flare in rhythm to his thudding heart, drawing in a thick soup of odors so vivid, he could taste them, could hear them, could see them mingling and swirling: the pungent smell of pasteboard from the collapsed boxes on which he lay, the soft caress of oak and the shrill voice of glass from the makeshift walls, the bitter taste of steel. It was all mixed-up; odor was color, color was sound. And cutting through it all, like church bells crashing into each other, were odors from the street, each tone a hammer blow to his head, which had begun to hurt again.

He staggered to the window, opened it, and looked out. In the street below were two umbrellas, and under them the bells . . . clanging. Across the square, more bells . . . so loud . . . hurting. Hurting. And under the pain was anger for the hurt. Red anger that bubbled and churned.

He wanted to stop the bells from ringing, stop the hurt. But the ancient region of his brain, the part buried deep under the origins of true thought, warned him to wait. There were too many of them still around. He must wait, must tolerate the pain until later, when he could move through the streets unseen. Then the anger could pour out. He could make the bells stop ringing. And when they stopped, the pain would be gone. But it was hard to wait. Hard. There was so much pain now, and the anger was pushing . . .

A pigeon on the ledge below the window lifted into the air and headed for the dormer roof. As it passed, his hand shot out and caught it in mid-flight. It was not a large bell and its death would not silence the others, but it was something.

Melanie Conroy was awakened a few hours later by a dream in which her material had somehow gotten out of order and she had sounded like a blubbering ass trying to apologize for it. Unable to get to sleep again, she finally threw back the sheet and put on her running shoes and spandex jogging outfit. She should have known that skipping her run would only make her more antsy.

Having arrived late in the day, she had not seen the *Times Picayune* warning for people to travel in groups in the Quarter or avoid it altogether. Had the night clerk not been in the toilet and therefore away from his post when she passed, he would have warned her not to go out.

Running in the rain was nothing new to Melanie. It was all a matter of discipline. If you could be deterred by a little rain, how could you expect to handle true adversity?

From her hotel on St. Louis, she went south to Decatur, then turned left and jogged past Jackson Square to St. Ann Street, where she again bore left and continued on past the old Pontalba apartments, stoically running in the light rain rather than using the balcony-protected sidewalk that ran the length of the street. At the end of the apartments, she continued to circle Jackson Square by going left on Chartres, a course that took her past the Presbytere. Impulsively, she turned into the well-lit alley between the Presbytere and St. Louis cathedral, skirting the scaffolding against the Presbytere's west face.

Unaccustomed to the humidity, she slowed to a walk as she came onto Royal and looked at the sky in pain as her lungs cried for air. The street was not as well lit as the others had been and she soon saw why: two burned-out streetlamps in a row. Nervous at being alone in such a dark place, she began to walk toward the lights a block away.

Over the squeak of her shoes against the wet pavement, she thought she heard a noise behind her. She stopped and looked back down the street, searching the darkness. But nothing stirred. There was no sound except her own labored breathing and the music of water trickling down drainpipes. About to turn and begin walking again, she saw something a dozen doors behind her . . . movement in the deep shadows.

Her eyes strained to see. It was there and it wasn't . . . a shape close to the ground or not there at all. She couldn't be sure. Still needing air, she turned and began to run as fast as she could. Giving in to the fear was like opening a sluice gate, and dread quickly consumed her. She could feel the thing behind her moving faster, so bold now that it had left the shadows, getting closer; she imagined it barely a reach away. She wanted to look back but was afraid of what she would see. A scream bulled its way into her mouth and pushed at her lips. The light ahead seemed to be getting no closer.

Then with an unearthly growl, it was upon her, grunting . . . slashing. . . . Her clear screams soon became muffled as though she was drowning, as indeed she was . . . in her own blood.

Chapter 8

When Kit heard that the third victim was a visitor to the city, it became obvious that the killer was choosing his victims at random and was not engaged in a moral cleanup campaign of the French Quarter. This fact galvanized her thoughts on the case. Bubba's reference to the killer as an animal was closer to the truth than he knew. After an hour poring over some of her own books, a trip to the psychiatry section of the LSU library, and a visit to the public library, where she spent an hour reviewing the previous week's newspapers, she was ready to tell Broussard and Gatlin what they were dealing with.

Finding Broussard's office empty, she asked his secretary where he was and was told he was in the morgue. Not a great fan of the morgue, she ordinarily would have waited for him to finish and come back upstairs. Today, that was impossible. She was simply too anxious to talk.

Like an aging woman who has had many face-lifts, most floors of the old hospital didn't look too bad if you were willing to overlook minor details such as suspended ceilings that cut across the middle of the glass transoms above the doors and the willingness of the maintenance crew to replace blocks of buckled floor tiles with whatever color they happened to have on hand.

The basement, though, was a distinct step down, in more

than direction. The elevator opened onto a vending area with a bare cement floor and grim cement-block walls that had been painted a dingy ivory color in an attempt to brighten the place up without buying a real light fixture to replace the naked bulb in a wire cage overhead. Even the vending machines looked tired. Kit thought she heard one sigh as she pushed through gurney-scarred double doors that sternly warned away all but authorized personnel.

The hall to the morgue was a dim tunnel served by more caged bulbs. At the end of it, behind a pale green door, she found Broussard, dressed in a plastic apron and looking at the face of a corpse through a camera viewfinder. There was a flash and a whir as the camera delivered an undeveloped picture.

"Is that the latest one?" Kit said, hanging back.

"Latest one to come in, but not the one you mean," Broussard said, lowering the camera. "When I first got started at all this, I thought there'd be busy times and slack times. But all we've had so far is busy. I'm still lookin' forward to slack." He took the picture from the camera and glanced at it. "Come here; you should see this."

He motioned her over to the body, which she approached slowly and carefully, trying to decide how well prepared she should be. As it turned out, there wasn't much to see. The body was that of a slim, unshaven male with no visible wounds but with a series of raised welts on his forehead.

"What do you figure was the murder weapon?" Broussard asked.

Kit shrugged, wondering how she would be expected to know.

"I'll give you a hint. It was a blunt instrument. About as blunt as they come."

She was about to suggest that the welts might be bee stings, but his hint took away even that glimmer of a thought. "I have no idea."

"Maybe this'll help." He went to the sink and took down a small framed mirror hanging above it. He gave her the picture he had just taken. "Hold the picture up toward me."

She did as he asked and he held up the mirror.

"Now, what was the murder weapon?"

She studied the corpse's face in the mirror. Suddenly, she saw what he was after. In the mirror, it became clear what the welts spelled out. "Holy Bible," she said aloud.

"Exactly. He was killed with one of those Bibles with raised letters. Probably died of a brain hemorrhage." He put the mirror back on the wall and put out his hand for the picture. "And there is no joy in Mudville, for mighty Casey has struck out." He shook his head. "Hard to believe that the guy who wrote those lines and the one who did that"—he jerked his head toward the body—"are members of the same species. Well, what brings you down here? Must be somethin' important."

"I know what's loose in the French Quarter. It's going to take a little explaining, so I'd rather tell you and Gatlin at the same time."

"We'd better get hold of him then."

They had to wait a few minutes for the dispatcher to relay a message to Gatlin and for him to get to a phone. Broussard took his call.

"Phillip, Kit says she has something on our killer and wants to talk."

Broussard covered the mouthpiece. "Where?"

"My office," Kit said.

"Her office, in . . . thirty minutes? Right. See you then."

Kit had only one extra chair, so she borrowed another from Charlie Franks, the deputy medical examiner, then spent the next thirty minutes rearranging the chairs and pacing the room. How would they take what she was going to tell them? More specifically, how would Broussard take it? Would he give her that compassionate paternal look that said he didn't believe a word she was saying but was willing to keep quiet and let her make a fool of herself? God, how she hated that look. Then she toughened. Well, if that's what he thought, he'd be wrong. He'd simply be *wrong*.

The two men came in together, as intimidating a mass of male protoplasm as she had ever seen in one place.

"Hullo, Doc," Gatlin said. "Andy's call gave me a real lift. I saw myself coming out of the property room this morning and I didn't look at all well. The pencil pushers weren't losing much sleep when the victims were 'strippers and panhandlers,' as the chief called them, but the one this morning got their attention. Not only was she 'one of us' but she was from out of town. When street people get killed, we are 'concerned.' But kill a tourist . . . Hey, now we're talking outrage." He looked at Broussard. "You know that footprint we found? It's from an Elan athletic shoe . . . made in England . . . *ten* years ago. Looks like our boy doesn't do much walking."

"Or he had a good supply laid away," Broussard said.

"Or that."

"If you'll both have a seat, we can begin," Kit said.

Gatlin sat down, took a small spiral notebook and a pen from his shirt pocket, and crossed his legs. Broussard sat with both feet on the floor, arms crossed over his belly. From the bulge in each of his cheeks, he had helped himself to a couple of lemon balls just before leaving his office.

Kit had considered standing while she spoke—for the psychological edge that would give her over her seated colleagues—but decided that simply being behind a desk was enough.

"In 1781, the mangled body of a small boy was found on a wooded lane near Caude, France. A short while later, the retarded son of the local silversmith was caught in a nearby forest, his hands covered in blood, shreds of human flesh in his clawlike nails. In court, he confessed not only to the murder of the boy but to several others. The lawyer retained by his father explained that the defendant had committed these acts under the influence of certain spells he had been having in which the odor of the victims had made him so angry that he couldn't stop himself from savaging them.

"In autumn of 1848, someone entered a cemetery near Paris and tore several corpses to pieces. At first, authorities thought that it was done by animals, but footprints in the fresh dirt clearly showed that it had been a man. That same winter, it happened again. In March 1849, a spring gun set up in a cemetery that had been the site of several corpse mutilations went off during the night. Those who had set the gun rushed to the scene and saw a man in military dress leap a wall and disappear. From blood that they found on the wall the next morning, they concluded that the man had been wounded. A search of the military installations near the cemetery turned up a young officer named Bertrand, who was suffering from a fresh gunshot wound. At his court-martial, he confessed and recounted the first time he had done such a thing.

"It was a few years earlier, in February, as he was walking in the country with a friend. It had begun to rain and he and his friend had sought shelter under a tree in a nearby cemetery. While waiting for the rain to let up, Bertrand noticed a fresh grave that had been only partially filled in. A pick and shovel in the dirt beside the grave suggested that the rain had driven off the men who had been working on it. When the rain slackened, Bertrand made some excuse to get rid of his companion and he returned to the cemetery, dug up the corpse, and in his own words"—Kit looked down at the white card on which she had copied the quote—"'tore it in pieces without well knowing what I was about. I then went away in a cold sweat to a small copse of trees, where I lay completely exhausted for several hours, taking no precaution to shield myself from the cold rain that was falling. This condition of complete prostration followed every attack.'" She looked up. "Bertrand returned to the same grave two days later, dug the body up with his hands, ripped it into even smaller pieces, and rolled among the fragments. He said that if he hadn't been caught, he thought that eventually he would have moved on to living victims.

"In the spring of 1912, the slashed bodies of a widow and her twelve-year-old son were found on a poorly traveled road near Selkirk, Manitoba. The victims had been clawed so severely that their faces were not recognizable. The marks on the bodies were those of a bear. A few days later, a canoe washed ashore at a nearby lake. In it were the similarly disfigured bodies of a young couple. A search of the woods in the area turned up Samuel Dresden—a peat digger who had disappeared from Selkirk two months earlier—living in a limestone cave. When they found him, he was in a deep sleep. In his hand was the amputated paw of a large grizzly, its claws covered with blood that contained hair subsequently shown to match samples from the latest female victim.

"At his trial, Dresden said that he left Selkirk and moved to the woods because he had begun to feel that the town was closing in on him. A week before he was caught, he shot a large bear and skinned it. As a trophy, he also took one paw. A few days later, he got a terrific headache and passed out. When he awoke, he found the paw with fresh blood on it in his hand. Since he had cut himself off from all contact with civilization, he did not know about the widow and her son. Nor did he have any memory of what had happened. He likewise had no recollection of killing the young couple. He was convicted by a scar in the heel of one of his boots that matched an impression left in the ground around the first murders."

Kit paused. So far, so good. "Collectively these cases represent several varieties of the same mental disease, an illness in which the victims suffer episodic delusions in which they behave like a predatory animal, seeking out humans, either living or dead, as their prey. And when they strike, they do so like an animal, biting, clawing, or tearing. This is what we're looking for, a victim of the disease that for want of a better word has been called lycanthropy."

Gatlin uncrossed his legs and stood up. "Wait a minute, Doc. What's the common name for it?"

"The common name is . . . misleading."

"Werewolfism, isn't that it? You're telling me I'm looking for a werewolf. Oh, the press is gonna *love* this."

Kit's presentation and Gatlin's comment about werewolves turned up the volume on the phrase that had been crying for attention in Broussard's brain since the old pathologist first had seen the body of Paula Lyons. *Never go boo-lie during a full moon.* Having heard the phrase, he turned the volume back down. A warning from his childhood. A bit of Cajun nostalgia. Interesting in a historical perspective, but of no significance for their present dilemma.

"First of all, there's nothing supernatural about this," Kit said to Phillip. "We're simply dealing with someone who has organic brain disease, a biologic abnormality like victims of epilepsy. And like epilepsy, where seizures can be brought on by certain stimuli such as repetitive flashing lights in a disco or bicycling on a street where the sunlight is coming through the trees in a dappling pattern, I think we'll find that our murderer is set off by some environmental cue."

Gatlin looked at Broussard. "Andy, what do you think?"

"I think you should listen to the expert." Gatlin sucked his teeth and considered what had been said.

"When you find him, he'll be someone who grew up in a rural background," Kit added. "For some reason, lycanthropes never come from cities. It's as if the organic basis of the disease is potentiated by early and frequent contact with animals in a natural environment. As you can see from the examples I've cited, some lycanthropes attack bare-handed. Others utilize weapons of some sort. Our killer's gardening claw is like Samuel Dresden's bear paw—an object that causes the kind of damage an animal might inflict. I suspect, though, that if our killer did not have his gardening claw, he'd find something else, something that might not relate as well to animal behavior—a knife, a club fashioned from anything handy, never a firearm. But whatever the weapon, when his victim is dead or dying, he must deliver the classical lupine coup de grace—his teeth at their throat."

"You said something about our murderer being set off by environmental cues," Gatlin said. "Like what? Not the full moon, I hope."

Kit shook her head. "The moon's in the first quarter."

"You checked?"

"Yes."

"Jesus . . . Rain then . . . what about rain? It's been raining a lot, and that one guy you told us about, that army officer, had his first attack on a rainy day."

"It's not going to be that simple," Kit said. "The first murder took place six days ago. I checked the weather section of the paper for each day since this all began. And while it's true that it *did* rain on each night there was a murder, it also rained on nights when nothing happened."

"Yeah, but two of those nights, half the department was down there in plainclothes," Gatlin said. "Maybe we scared him off."

"That's possible, but night before last, you weren't down there and nothing happened then, either. There was three-tenths of an inch of rain night before last, the exact amount we had the night the musician was killed."

Gatlin looked at Broussard. "Who knows what's going on in this nut's mind?"

Broussard had been listening carefully to the conversation. Kit knew that because he had refrained from stroking the bristly hairs on the end of his nose, a habit that always accompanied his mental departure from a room. He unfolded his arms and wiggled his index finger in Kit's direction, sighting along it like a rifle. "She knows," he said.

"Well, whatever the cue is, we're gonna be down there again tonight."

"If conditions are wrong, you'll be wasting your time," Kit said.

"But we don't know what the right conditions are, do we?"

"Not yet, but I'm working on it."

"Then we've got to be there just in case."

Gatlin went out the door first. As Broussard followed, Kit called him back. "Dr. B?" Her form of addressing him was a compromise between his wish that she call him Andy and her own feeling that he deserved more. "Thanks for backing me up."

A look of surprise appeared on Broussard's face. "Wouldn't you do the same for me?"

"Sure, but that's different. You're *always* right."

He chuckled deeply and patted her shoulder. "Then my confidence in you can't be misplaced, can it?"

Chapter 9

Left alone in her office, Kit pulled out the phone book and roamed through the state and federal listings, finally finding the number she was looking for under NATIONAL WEATHER SERVICE. The phone was promptly answered by a woman.

"May I speak with one of your weathermen, please."

"Weathermen are what you see on television," the woman said frigidly. "Here, we have meteorologists."

Kit was tempted to ask what she would call people who study meteors, but she let it go. "A meteorologist, then," Kit said.

"If you want the local forecast, you can get that by calling seven-six-seven-eight thousand."

"That's not what I want."

"I'll see if someone is available."

Mel Tormé began to sing "Stormy Weather" in the ear Kit had pressed to the phone. After a few bars of that, there was a clicking sound and a nasal voice said, "Floyd Dill, may I help you?"

"Mr. Dill, this is Kit Franklyn. I'm with the medical examiner's office. We need some weather information to help with a case we're working on and I wondered if I could come out and talk with you."

"When?"

"As soon as possible."

"I'm here until five."

"I see you're at the airport. Where exactly?"

Thirty minutes later, Kit was standing in front of the weather-service receptionist's empty desk, waiting for "The World's Greatest Secretary" to appear—if the little plastic sign in the sickly potted palm on the edge of the desk was to be believed. On the wall behind the desk, in a thin black frame, was a poem:

> Big whirls have little whirls
> That feed on their velocity.
> And little whirls have lesser whirls
> And so on to viscosity.

"Gotta remember *that* one," Kit muttered.

Reluctant to begin wandering about on her own, Kit chose to wait for the desk's occupant to return, which she did a few minutes later. She looked to be in her mid-twenties, a big-boned girl who could have drawn less attention to her mule-like face had she chosen to wear her hair up instead of long and curly.

"I'm here to see Mr. Dill," Kit said.

The girl's eyes made a quick trip from the tortoiseshell comb in Kit's hair to her new Aigner pumps, and she shifted subtly into a defensive posture, lifting her chin slightly, raising the papers in her hand into a shield that she held to her chest with folded arms. "I'll tell him you're here."

She returned with a thin man whose legs seemed to start at his sternum. "Mr. Dill, I'm Kit Franklyn. We spoke on the phone."

"Of course, come on back."

Kit followed Dill into a huge room filled with computer screens and blinking electronics. In the center of the room, there was a large circular table with several tiers of shelves rising from the center like a wedding cake. Arranged into a large semicircle around the wedding cake were several work-stations containing banks of computers, printers, and radar screens in color-coordinated shades of blue. At the worktable, a nicely dressed fellow with a skullcap of skin showing through the hair on the top of his head was drawing curving lines on a map. He didn't look up.

To her right, against the wall, was a bulletin board with a series of complex-looking maps hanging in neat rows. In fact, *neat* was the operative word here; all the equipment was laid out for maximum efficiency, no piles of loose papers, everything under control—just the way Kit liked things, just the way she kept her own office. Her penchant for neatness was probably why she hated to cook. There was simply no way to prepare a meal without making a mess of the kitchen. The complexity of the equipment made Kit understand why the secretary had taken offense when earlier she had asked to speak to a weatherman.

Dill pulled a deeply cushioned rolling chair over to the nearest workstation, motioned her into it, and turned his own chair toward her. When Dill held his head just right, his thick glasses made the tiny skin tags under his eyes look as big as grapes.

"As I mentioned on the phone, I'm with the medical examiner's office," Kit began. "And I'm working on a series of murders we've had in the French Quarter. We have reason to believe that the perpetrator of these crimes is being set off by a weather-related stimulus, and I was hoping you could give me a list of possible stimuli."

"I can tell you the various parameters we keep track of."

"That's what I mean." Kit slid her pen off the cover of the spiral steno pad she had brought and flipped to a fresh page. Dill raised one hand and began to run through a well-memorized list, ticking off each item by touching his thumb to a different finger. "Sky cover, surface visibility, barometric pressure, temperature, humidity, wind speed and direction, precipitation, evaporation and ground temperature at two different depths."

When he finished, Kit was still writing.

"Evaporation and ground temperature?"

He nodded.

Kit looked over the list. "This first one . . . sky cover. How is that expressed?"

"By a series of numbers from one to ten. One is clear; ten is overcast."

"How do you measure it?"

Dill shrugged. "We just go outside every hour and look up."

"Even at night?"

"Sure, you can usually see okay, if not by the moon, by the reflection of lights from the city."

"Do you take hourly readings on all these parameters?"

"Most of them."

"Would it be possible for me to get the hourly observations for each parameter over the last six days?"

"You can get them from the climate data center in Asheville, North Carolina."

"How long would that take?"

"If you wait for the regular report . . . about two months."

"That won't do me any good. We're trying to figure out what sets him off so we can prevent any more murders."

"Come to think of it, the Climate Center reports wouldn't help, anyway. They only show three-hour observations."

"So what can I do?"

"Well . . . what you want is all stored in our computers. I suppose *I* could retrieve it for you."

Kit touched Dill's arm lightly. "Would you? I'd really appreciate it." In the reflection of a glassed office behind Dill's workstation, Kit saw the secretary watching them, one hand poised on a jutting hip. "How long would it take?"

"Two or three days. I've got a lot of other work to keep up with."

"I wish it could be quicker, but I'll take what I can get. Would it be possible to include values for the days between now and when the data is ready?"

"I think so."

Kit wrote her name and office phone number on the edge of a page in her notepad, folded it, and tore it off. "Please . . . call me as soon as you have it."

The secretary reluctantly stepped aside to let Kit pass, then followed her into the reception area. As Kit was on her way out the door, she said, "In case you didn't know, Dill is mine."

Kit paused and looked back. "Your plant could use some water."

Hurrying to her car, Kit had to admit that Dill had one thing going for him. Neat as he kept his workplace, he probably didn't leave his dirty socks on the floor for someone else to pick up like David did.

David.

She still hadn't made that phone call giving him her decision. On the way back to town, Kit's mind played a David Andropoulas retrospective for her, juxtaposing the good and the bad: the safe warm feeling when she was in his arms, his thinly veiled lack of respect for psychologists, his remarkable ability in the kitchen, his Paleolithic outlook on the role of women in a relationship, the sex, the constant arguments about getting a family started before it was too late, the sex.

Then there was Teddy LaBiche . . . or was there? What did *that* really amount to? One night of dancing and a message left on her answering machine. *There's* a torrid romance for you. He had probably taken Maria St. What's Her Name aside and said, "Kit Franklyn? Oh, she isn't a girlfriend or anything, just a regular friend." And what if he *was* seriously interested? Was *she*?

Sure, David had faults. But who doesn't? Maybe she was being unrealistic to think that anybody had a better relationship than she and David had. People lie about things like that. David was like a . . . a car . . . an old car whose idiosyncrasies you've learned to handle, a known commodity. Why trade that for one that might have worse problems? Still, Teddy did smell *terrific*.

But he lived too far away and . . . There was another reason for resisting the attraction she felt for Teddy, one that made her feel so ashamed and so small that she tried to keep it off the table. Yet there it was, naked and ugly. He was not a professional man and, therefore, had limited financial prospects. But gosh, he smelled good.

Since it was nearly five, Kit went home rather than back to

the office. When she got there, there were two cars in the drive. The one in front belonged to Virginia Lance, the realtor David had hired. Apparently, she was showing the place.

Kit pulled in beside the two cars and went up the walk just as Virginia and her clients came out the front door. Virginia was a woman of excess: flamboyant flowered dresses with lots of material she could flip and drape over her arm, too much hair, lipstick that was too red—and could anybody really be that happy?

The couple with Virginia looked like walking mug shots. Both were dressed in purple shorts and tank tops and rubber sandals. Though trim, they both had dry skin and and stiff, lifeless hair.

"Kit dear!" Virginia crooned. "How lovely to see you. These are the Gleasons, Adras and Ozell."

Unsure which was which, Kit refrained from using any names as they shook hands.

"Dr. Franklyn works for the coroner," Virginia said. "Something I could never do . . . all those bodies. How do you manage it?"

Kit shrugged. "You sort of—"

"I think the Gleasons like what they saw inside," Virginia said in a teasing tone. She shook her finger at them as if they were naughty children. "They're trying to be noncommittal, but I can tell."

"I couldn't help noticing that you eat a lot of convenience foods," the female Gleason said to Kit. "You really should eat more fiber. Trust me; I'm a dietitian. I know about these things."

Then could I have hair like yours? Kit thought. She found herself wondering whether the whole group also had looked in her underwear drawer.

"We'd all love to talk more, but time and tide," Virginia said, herding the Gleasons down the sidewalk. "Have a nice evening," Virginia sang to the back of her clients' heads.

Later, after Kit had fed Lucky, she turned on the TV to catch the local news, which led off with an interview in which the chief of police assured the citizens of the city that every

effort was being expended to ensure that the French Quarter
would soon be as safe as their own homes and that an arrest
was imminent. But if you knew anything about body language,
you could see that even *he* didn't believe what he was saying.
The rest of the news was the usual; drug-related crime was up,
rainfall was up, there was a hurricane brewing somewhere out
in the Caribbean, and the Tulane Greenies had split a double-
header with somebody. Another half hour of the national news
and Kit was ready for dinner.

In the kitchen, as she looked over her collection of micro-
wavables, she thought about what the Gleason woman had
said about her diet. Probably true. She *didn't* eat very
sensibly. She looked on the back of the lasagna container in her
hand and stopped reading halfway through. Better not to
know, she thought, putting it in the microwave.

While the lasagna heated, Kit searched the refrigerator for
something with a little fiber in it and found a few leaves of
iceberg lettuce and half a cucumber, which, together with
some vinegar and oil, made a fair salad. Topping things off
with a cream soda, it was, all in all, not a bad meal. Maybe in
the future, though, she *would* keep more fresh fruit and
vegetables in the house.

While she was cleaning up the few kitchen utensils she had
dirtied, the phone rang. Even before answering it, she knew
who it was.

"Hi, stranger."

"David! I've been meaning to call you. But I've just been *so*
busy."

"I saw Fred Danson yesterday and he was getting anxious
to hear from you. Says he can't hold that job open much longer.
And he'd really like for you to have it."

"I know, but things have been so hectic, I haven't been able
to give it much thought. I guess you've heard about the
murders here."

"Are you involved in that?"

"Sure, as a consultant."

"You're not putting yourself at risk, I hope."

"Of course not. What risk would there be for me?" She was

glad he couldn't see her mental image of Bubba with his gun on that bum's nose.

"Probably none if you just tend to your job and don't overdo it."

"Oh, you mean I should have limits on my involvement?"

"Don't try to coax me into saying something that'll get me into trouble. You do that all the time. It makes me feel like every conversation with you is a walk across a tightrope."

"If your heart was pure, you wouldn't have to worry."

"The *Pope* would have to worry talking to you."

"I saw Virginia. She thinks the couple that looked at the house today is going to make an offer."

"Which if it's good enough would make it even more important that you come to a decision. Kit, I miss you. I miss holding you—"

"I miss that, too."

"Then join me."

"I don't know . . . In any event, I can't make a decision until this killer is caught. It's occupying so much of my mind that there's no room for anything else."

"Well, there's more to life than work. We've invested a lot of time in this relationship and I'd hate to see you throw it away."

There's more to life than work? Kit thought. This from a man she hadn't seen for days at a time if he had a big case pending. "I'll keep that in mind," she said evenly.

"What? What did I say? I know that tone. You nailed me again for something and I don't even know what it was. It's in the Bill of Rights, Kit. The accused must be informed of the charges against him."

"It's nothing . . . really," Kit said, consciously putting a convincing warmth in her voice. "I'm simply a little tired."

"I understand. By the way, I saw an article the other day that said a woman has about four hundred thousand eggs in her ovaries when she's born but every year about ten thousand die. That means you've already lost about three hundred thousand of them. It's something to think about."

"David, you'd have made a great salesman for driveway coatings."

"What's that supposed to mean?"

"Nothing. I'll think about everything you've said."

"Well, I hope so. Meanwhile, take care of yourself."

"I'll call you soon."

Later, Kit went to Radio Shack and bought a police scanner, well aware that she stood little chance of picking up any communication between the undercover cops and their command post, but *would* likely be able to intercept messages from the command post to dispatch. She spent the evening beside the scanner, working on her book, which would eventually be called either *Suicide: The Ultimate Act of a Troubled Mind* or, more simply, *Self Inflicted*, with maybe an additional phrase of some sort tacked on the end. While her work was often interrupted by the crackle of the radio as it picked up verbal police traffic, there was nothing that sounded like the trouble for which she was listening. At midnight, she took the radio into her bedroom and listened for as long as she could stay awake. By 1:30, it was playing only to Lucky, whose ears lifted whenever it emitted one of its throaty messages.

In the morning, she telephoned homicide to see whether anything had happened. It hadn't.

The next night was a replay of the previous one except it rained. Again, nothing happened.

Floyd Dill came through at two o'clock the following day and provided her with all the data she had asked for, including the current day's readings up to twelve noon. Eager to begin her analysis, she took them directly to her desk.

The simplest approach seemed to be to extract for each of the last eight days the highs and lows for each climatological parameter and then determine whether there was any correlation between these values and the murders.

Turning a yellow legal tablet sideways, she listed the days across the top and put asterisks by those when the killer struck. She then began to work her way down the list of numbers, making no attempt at analysis as she went but simply recording values, being careful to note the time each high and low had occurred. This took about forty-five minutes. Then she began to look for correlations.

All three murders took place a few hours after midnight. In no case did the hours between midnight and the murder show notable values. Her comparisons, therefore, involved highs and lows for the day before each killing.

On each of the days leading up to a murder, sky cover was a ten all day: that is, completely overcast. But this also occurred on several days when nothing happened. Maximum visibility at some point during the day before two of the murders was twenty miles, the highest value possible. Kit scratched her head. How could you have maximum visibility on days that were completely overcast? Something to ask Dill. The day before the other murder, maximum visibility was fifteen miles. These maximal values occurred on other days, as well. Nor was there any correlation with minimum visibility. These results were not terribly disappointing, since she hadn't believed sky cover and visibility were likely candidates, anyway.

But as she continued to find nothing in the more likely parameters of barometric pressure, temperature, and humidity, her hopes waned. Wind direction and speed, rainfall—which she had already checked in the papers— evaporation rate, and ground temperature were equally unrewarding.

She tossed her pencil onto the papers in front of her, leaned back in her chair, and spoke to the ceiling. "Nuts." The office suddenly seemed cramped and hot. She needed a walk.

While Kit waited for the old elevator to arrive, Broussard came out of his office with a pile of file folders on his hip and joined her.

"Havin' a bad day?" he asked.

"Does it show?"

"Guess it's too late to say no. What's up?"

"I've just spent an hour going over climatologic data for the last eight days that I got from the weather service, trying to find something that would explain why our killer strikes when he does."

"No luck, huh?"

Kit shook her head and idly worked the elevator DOWN button like a telegraph key.

Broussard shifted the file folders higher on his hip and said, "When I was a kid, an old fellow that knew the swamps better than anybody around told me that the best way to judge distance over water was to bend down and look at whatever object you were interested in, from between your legs. That sounded plausible to me, so I gave it a try. He was real tickled that I had bought this load of hay and he got quite a laugh at seein' me all bent over, but I got somethin', too. I got to see a familiar place in a way that I had never seen before. And that seemed like somethin' worth rememberin'."

They heard the old elevator jerk to a stop and its doors clattered open. Broussard motioned for Kit to precede him, but she stepped back.

"You go on. I've got work to do."

Buoyed by Broussard's story, Kit returned to her office and sat down at her desk, where she asked herself how she could look at the data in a new way. Maybe minimum and maximum values were not as important . . . as . . . as what? Not as important as . . . She scanned the numbers for relative humidity, which were not static but fluctuated from hour to hour, going down at some points, up at others.

She made a list of the amount and direction in which the humidity changed from one hour to the next for each day of the sample period. Finishing with that, she did the same with all the other parameters. When each of them had been converted to this new set of numbers, she took a deep breath and began to look for correlations.

A few minutes later, she found something. Between 2:00 and 3:00 P.M. the afternoon before the first murder, the barometric pressure had dropped 6.2 millibars. Murder number two had taken place following a 5.8-millibar drop between 8:00 and 9:00 A.M. the previous morning. The afternoon before the third murder, there had been a 6.4-millibar drop between

5:00 and 6:00 P.M. The largest decrease on any of the other days was four millibars.

Kit quickly scanned the other parameters but discovered nothing of significance. She had found the trigger. Their killer was set off by a decrease in barometric pressure.

Chapter 10

Kit anxiously looked at her watch: quarter to five. Good. Dill should still be there.

The weather service had changed the tune they played for callers who had to wait. This time it was "You Ain't Woman Enough to Take My Man." Kit couldn't help but believe that Dill's sweetie had set it up just for her call.

The music stopped and Dill came on the line.

"Floyd, this is Kit . . . Kit Franklyn." She had decided to call Dill by his first name to put their relationship on a personal level. That way, he might be more inclined to do what she was about to ask of him.

"Was that data I gave you any help?" he asked.

"Immensely. But now I need another favor."

"What's that?"

"Do you have a fax machine?"

"Yes."

"Would it be possible for you to send me the hourly barometric pressure readings every day at five o'clock?"

"For how long?"

"A week, maybe two." Actually, Kit had no idea how long it would be needed. Better to keep his initial commitment relatively short. Otherwise, he might balk.

Dill hesitated, and Kit wished she had gone out there. While she usually felt a little ashamed afterward, she wasn't above using her large brown eyes to get men to do things. In this case, it wasn't necessary.

"Since it's only pressure you want, I could do that," Dill said.

Now the other shoe, Kit thought. "I'd also like to keep up with the readings through the evening. Would there be any way that someone could call my answering machine at midnight each night and leave the hourly values that come in after five P.M.?"

Dill hesitated again. "Well . . . there *is* a night man. . . ."

"Would he do it for me? It's extremely important."

"Sure, why not. It's a little slow at night, anyway."

Kit gushed her thanks and gave Dill the number of the office fax machine and her home phone number. Before hanging up, she had Dill give her the most current pressure readings unaccounted for in the material he had given her earlier, which even as she wrote them down were obviously of no interest.

The plan she had devised contained two flaws. If the pressure strayed into dangerous territory shortly after midnight, she wouldn't be aware of it until it was too late. In addition, she couldn't be exactly sure what represented dangerous territory. All she knew was that a 4-millibar drop appeared safe, but a drop of 5.8 or more was not. The effect of anything in between those values was unknown. But it was the best she could do.

For the next three days, Dill and the night man performed reliably, neither one missing his scheduled delivery time by more than a few minutes. During those three days, the barometric pressure remained clearly within safe limits. On the fourth day, Dill sent the readings through at 5:03. As usual, Kit went directly to her office with them and began calculating the hourly fluctuations.

In the early morning, the pressure had not varied more than one or two millibars from one hour to the next. Between 5:00 and 6:00 A.M., it had gone *up* one millibar, then up slightly again between 6:00 and 7:00.

Having spent three days at this already, Kit's sense of expectation had diminished to where the activity had become almost a rote exercise. That all ended with the entries for 9:00

and 10:00 A.M. When she saw those numbers, it felt as though she had suddenly been thrust into a frozen-food locker. Her hair danced on the back of her neck and her arms erupted in so much gooseflesh that they resembled the pebbled belt she always wore with her best Bleyle knit. Between 9:00 and 10:00 A.M., the barometric pressure had fallen by 6.5 millibars. Snatching up the printout from Dill and her own calculations, she dashed to Broussard's office and burst in without knocking.

He was sitting at the microscope on a low bench to the right of his desk. From the stereo on a shelf above the microscope came the relaxing sounds of *Swan Lake*, which, according to Broussard, was the ideal music for studying tissue sections.

At the sound of her entrance, he turned from the microscope and ran his hand down the thin black cord at his neck to his glasses, which dangled just under his bow tie.

"Tonight's the night," she blurted out.

Broussard put on his glasses, stood up, and turned off the stereo.

"Our killer *has* to try something tonight. Here, look."

She rushed to him with her papers, then realized that she had never shown him the earlier supporting material. She lifted a finger. "Wait. I'll be right back."

Dashing to her office, she gathered up the rest of what she needed and hurried back to Broussard, where she spread everything out on his desk. She told her story and waited for his reaction.

He continued to stroke his beard and look over the sheets of paper for a few seconds, then began to nod, a little more slowly than she would have liked.

"Keepin' in mind that the sample period is rather small, what with your whole case restin' on three murders in twelve days . . . I'll admit it looks like you're on to somethin'."

It certainly wasn't effusive and it wasn't even praise, but considering the source, it was enough. For the first time since she had met Broussard nearly a year ago, she had begun to feel like a colleague instead of a green kid.

Broussard reached for the phone and put in a call to homicide. This time, Gatlin was there to take it.

"Phillip? . . . Andy. Kit has just shown me somethin' you should know about. Here she is."

Kit took the phone from his chubby hand, grateful that he hadn't told Gatlin what she had discovered.

"Lieutenant, that environmental cue we talked about . . . the one that triggers our killer . . . it's barometric pressure. Whenever the pressure drops a certain amount in an hour, it kicks him off. But he doesn't react immediately. He waits. Each time he has killed, the pressure drop occurred long before the killing. It's like . . . setting a bear trap. Once it's set, it's dangerous until it's sprung. He waits until the time is right . . . until he can catch a victim alone . . . when his risk is minimal. And Lieutenant, the pressure readings for today say he was set off between nine and ten A.M. Tonight's the night to catch him."

Broussard helped himself to two lemon balls, slipped them into his mouth, and sat on the edge of the microscope table.

"Tonight?" Gatlin said. "You sure? Because I haven't seen my bed in so long, I wouldn't know what it was. For the last week and a half, I've spent my days asking people who don't know what planet they're on where they were on the night of each murder, trying to figure out if we're dealing with a domestic or imported fruit. Nights, I've covered more sidewalk than I ever did as a beat cop, wearing clothes that by comparison'd make the sheets in a home for the incontinent smell like cinnamon rolls. I was planning to let somebody else wear those clothes tonight while I got some sleep. But not if the party's on. I've got too much time invested to miss the fun. So you're sure?"

"I'm sure."

That night, to make certain she wouldn't fall asleep while listening to her scanner, Kit took a NoDoz at 7:00 P.M. and began on page one of *Lonesome Dove,* a paperback she had bought on the way home. Four hundred pages, two pots of tea, and three trips to the bathroom later, she had not heard a single promising squawk from the scanner.

Hoping that the communication regarding apprehension of the lycanthrope had somehow gotten by her, Kit called homicide as soon as the thin light of dawn struggled through the windows, only to hear what she already knew. There had been no arrest and no attack. The decoys had gone through the entire night without seeing anything unusual.

As she hung up the phone, Kit could feel her face stinging with humiliation. "You sure?" Gatlin had said. "I'm sure," she had replied. She should have hedged. But how would that have sounded? I'm *pretty* sure. I *think* it'll be tonight. *Maybe*. But she *had* been sure. And now she looked like a jerk.

Always having found solace in the lakefront, she went to her car and pointed it in that direction. When she arrived, she pulled into a parking bay and sat staring out over the choppy gray water that dashed against the cement steps lining the shore. Overhead, the sun was completely shut out by a leaden sky.

Eventually, she got out and walked to the steps through dew-laden grass that left her canvas shoes nearly as wet as if she had been wading in the lake. Ignoring the benches scattered along the lakefront, she sat instead on the first step leading to the water. With her elbows on her knees and her chin in her hands, her thoughts drifted to Shreveport and the job that waited there for her, a job where Broussard wouldn't be looking over her shoulder every time she screwed up. She thought about David, hundreds of miles away when she really needed him. Having Lucky around helped a lot, but sometimes you need more than a dog.

In thinking about the comfort David could have provided if he was nearby, she forgot all the times she had neglected to confide in him when he *was* available, her memory shaping him into a far more sympathetic person than he had ever been.

A middle-aged couple in matching silver and white running outfits came up quickly from her left, passed behind her, and jogged off into the distance. As Kit watched them depart, she noticed that they even ran in unison, like a little jogging drill team.

Mistakes. God how she hated making mistakes. It was

competence that separated you from all the clucks in the world who were bumbling through life doing the best they could and coming up short, people who were tied to each other as surely as if they were handcuffed. And she preferred to *pick* her colleagues, thank you, not have them thrust upon her by her failures.

She moped on the steps for another twenty minutes and then took a long stroll along the lake. Finally, figuring that she was going to have to do it *sometime*, she returned to the car and drove slowly to the office.

When she got off the elevator, she stayed to the left of the hall so that Broussard couldn't see her shadow through the frosted glass panel in his office door. She barely had slumped into the chair behind her desk and begun to doodle on a legal pad when a shadow fell on her own door. The knock was hesitant, the way you might announce your presence to a woman whose husband had just died.

"It's open," Kit said.

Of course . . . it was Broussard.

"You heard?" he said, pausing halfway in.

"That they didn't get him? Yeah, I heard."

Broussard came in, pulled the extra chair over to the desk, and sat down. "Want to talk?"

"Maybe not ever again."

"Do you know what 'inside baseball' is?" he asked.

Kit shook her head warily. "No."

"It's a philosophy in which you choke up on the bat with no intention of hittin' anything more than a single or a double. It's the way baseball was played before Babe Ruth came along."

Oh no, Kit thought. A Babe Ruth story. In their relatively short association, Kit had noticed that Broussard dispensed inspirational Babe Ruth stories only when someone had made a real doofus out of themselves.

"The Babe was the first one to consistently grip the bat at the end. No singles for him, no bunts. He thought bigger than that. Every swing had thunder in it and every pitcher knew it. When he missed a pitch, he practically screwed himself into the ground. And he missed a lot of 'em. But nobody thought anything about it because of what he might do to the next one. You see, they respected his intent. They knew that the price for big results is sometimes big misses."

Kit got up and went to the window. She separated the blinds with her fingers. "I've been thinking about moving to Shreveport."

"I know."

Kit turned. "How?"

"Couple lives together awhile, one of 'em takes a job in another city, short time later the other one goes for a visit—"

"There's a job there . . . editor of a psychology journal."

"You'd be good at it."

As Kit looked at the old pathologist, she longed for him to ask her to stay, give her some sign that he didn't want her to leave. "I need advice."

Broussard took a deep breath and let it out slowly. "Much fun as it is to meddle in other folks' affairs, I've learned it's an itch best left unscratched. But I will say that if you decide to go, you should be sure you're goin' *toward* somethin' not *avoidin'* somethin'."

Kit watched Broussard fish a lemon ball from the pocket of his lab coat and slip it into his mouth. His hand then went back for the one he usually offered her, which, of course, she never accepted, what with it sitting there naked in the palm of a hand that regularly handled the most awful things. Would it be so hard for him to say, "Kit, I realize you have to do what you think is best, but you should know that you've done a fine job here and you're going to leave some pretty big shoes to fill." Or maybe, "The place won't be the same without you." *Something*.

Broussard brought his hand out of his pocket and extended it toward her. "Want one?"

About to decline as usual, Kit saw instead of a naked lemon drop, two of them, individually wrapped in cellophane.

"Got to thinkin' that you might not be too keen on eatin' somethin' somebody had his hands all over. So I got these for you."

Kit stared into the old rascal's eyes for a few seconds and

saw there what she had been looking for. She took the lemon drops from his hand, unwrapped them, and put both of them in her mouth. "Thanks," she said, the two candies clicking together.

"If you put one in each cheek, that won't happen," Broussard said, getting up to leave. At the door, he paused and looked back. "And I've got more."

Chapter 11

Broussard's visit left Kit in a much better frame of mind, so much better that she began to think constructively about what had happened. Sure, the killer had taken the night off, but did that necessarily mean she was wrong about his trigger? Maybe he had figured out that the only people in the Quarter at night now were disguised cops. Or maybe he was ill. Kit paced her office, trying to think of other explanations. Suddenly, a name popped into her head, one that had been sitting on a remote mental siding while she pursued the weather angle.

Thirty minutes later, after a brisk walk through the streets of the Quarter, which didn't smell nearly as gamy as they usually did at this time of year, she stepped up to the old oak door guarding the entrance to Maison Toulouse and rang the bell. It brought a downy-cheeked young man in an ill-fitting tux who looked like more like a member of the cast in a high school play than the suave concierge he was trying to be.

"May I help you?" he asked, remaining firmly planted in the doorway.

Despite his youth, his diffident manner made Kit feel like an encyclopedia salesman. She identified herself and said, "I'd like to ask you a few questions about someone that stayed here a week ago."

He might have been young, but he certainly had his offended look down pat. "I'm sorry, but we are not in the habit of discussing our guests with . . ." Kit thought he was going to say something that would really get her steamed, but he merely said, ". . . third parties."

Considering his age, Kit thought she'd try the tough approach. "Listen, junior, this 'third party' happens to be here on official police business. So you'd be well advised to cooperate."

"So arrest me," he said in a taunting tone as he closed the door in her face. She pictured him on the other side with his tongue out and his thumbs in his ears.

Unwilling to give up so easily, Kit went across the street to a small café, sat at a table next to the window, and ordered hot tea and a Danish. After what had happened last night, she certainly didn't want to ask Gatlin to make the concierge talk to her. Better to just keep the whole idea to herself.

The waitress brought her a small metal pot of hot water, a cup with a tea bag in it, and a Danish that looked so calorie laden and so devoid of fiber that she was ashamed to be sitting in the window with it. As she bobbed her tea bag in the hot water, a car pulled up to the curb in front of the café and a young man in a starched white porter's jacket got out and went into the Maison Toulouse.

A few minutes later, a man in white shorts and a Hawaiian shirt came out of the hotel followed by a heavy woman in green clam-diggers and a T-shirt that read, GIMME SOME CHOCOLATE AND NO ONE'LL GET HURT. Bringing up the rear, heavily laden with suitcases and garment bags, was the porter who had brought the car around.

Wobbling under the load, the porter managed to get everything across the street, where he dumped it onto the pavement at the rear of the car. When the trunk was closed, the owner of the car slipped the porter his tip as surreptitiously as a CIA operative might pass a bit of microfilm. Kit slapped a five onto the table and hurried into the street.

From the way the porter picked at the bill he had been given, it had apparently been folded into a tight little packet. When he got it unwrapped, the expectant look on his face soured.

"He stiff you?" Kit said.

"Shoulda known he was a buck tipper," the porter said. "You never get mor'n a buck from a guy don't look at you at the big moment. An' he folded it up so he'd be sure he was gone when I found out. Guess he ain't plannin' to come back. Or else he thinks ain't nobody but him got a memory."

The porter had skin like melted chocolate and strong white teeth that didn't quite touch their neighbors. "That's what I wanted to talk to you about," Kit said, "your memory. Do you remember a guest named Guidry . . . Henry Guidry? He stayed with you a few days last week."

The porter was nodding and smiling craftily. "I didn't think you looked like a hooker. You a cop?" When he talked, his almond eyes grew wide and round.

"Not exactly."

"What does that mean? You private?"

"I'm a police consultant."

"So, police consultant, what's this information worth to you?"

Kit dug a five out of her wallet and put it in the porter's outstretched hand.

He made a face. "Lady, ain't you tried to buy nothing lately? You can't get *nothin'* for this."

She added another five and said, "Henry Guidry," in case he had forgotten the name.

The porter's eyes got round. "In case you ain't noticed, I ain't too far up the social ladder in there. Numbers is all I know the guests by. Mr. and Mrs. Six. Ms. Eight. What's he look like?"

"Big fellow. Deep-set eyes, heavy eyebrows, long face, saturnine expression."

The porter's face twisted into a scowl and he raised his hands in a pleading gesture. "Heyyyy."

"Sorry, gloomy . . . a gloomy expression."

"Yeah, I remember him. Scary-lookin' dude. Good tipper, though."

"How long did he stay with you?"

The porter rolled his eyes in thought, then counted off some days on his fingers. "Three."

"Was he alone?"

"When?"

"Did he share his room with anyone?"

"Hu uh."

"Why did you ask me when?"

"'Cause he had somebody with him when he left."

"Tell me about that."

"When somebody stays with us, we take their car and store it for them until they leave, 'less, a course, they need it, then we go and get it. 'Cause we ain't got any parkin' right here. It's actually a convenience, so nobody gripes. But this guy did. Wouldn't let me take his car. Said he'd find a place for it. Then the day he checked out, he got the car from wherever he put it and brought it around to the front door. Then when I took his bag out, I noticed somebody in the front seat, kinda slumped over like they was sleepin' or maybe drunk."

"Could you tell what this person looked like?"

"Nah. I never got around to that side."

"How were they dressed?"

"Couldn't tell. Sorta had a raincoat or somethin' draped over him."

"So it was a man?"

"Yeah."

"Thanks. You've been a real help."

As Kit walked away, the porter watched her for a few seconds, then called out, "You ever decide to start hookin', look me up."

Kit was so busy thinking about what she had learned that she barely heard what he said. There was someone in the car with Guidry when he left town. And the night she saw him around Jackson Square, he was looking for something or *somebody*. That's why nothing happened last night. The killer's gone . . . and Guidry knows where he is. Now what? How could she tell Broussard one of his best friends was involved. On the other hand, how could she *not* tell him?

Back at the hospital, Charlie Franks, the deputy medical examiner, had just come into Broussard's office. "If you see shotcup petal abrasions around an entrance wound, how far was the gun muzzle from point of entry?" he asked.

Broussard looked up from the monthly newsletter he wrote and sent around as an educational service to his counterparts in the less populated sections of the state. Franks was referring to the evenly spaced rectangular bruises produced by the plastic sleeve around the pellets in certain types of shotgun shells as the petals of the sleeve open after firing.

"Thirty to ninety centimeters," Broussard said, reciting the accepted litany on the question.

Franks grinned and waved the journal in his hand. "Guess you haven't seen the latest issue of *JFS*." He went over and laid the open journal on top of Broussard's papers. "This top picture is the pattern produced by a Baikal four-ten with full choke firing number seven and a half I.V.I. Imperials at a range of seven point five centimeters. See the petals?"

Broussard leaned down for a close look at the path the shell had made as it penetrated the white Foamcore test material. "They're not real clear, but they're definitely present."

"Here"—Franks pointed at the second picture—"the distance was twenty centimeters."

"No question about them. So what's the conclusion?"

"Most every four-ten they tested and every kind of ammo showed petals at less than thirty centimeters, except for the Koon Snake Charmer. There it did take thirty centimeters."

"Course a Snake Charmer's got a real short barrel."

"They weren't sure if it was that or its cylinder bore."

"Wonder how come you got your copy before I got mine?"

"Age before beauty," Franks said.

"I can live with that."

"Damn, I mean the other way around."

The phone rang. "You got the morgue this mornin', right?" Broussard said, his hand poised over the phone. Franks nodded and turned to go. "And leave the article, will you?"

Broussard picked up the phone and said his name into it. On the other end was Joe Epstein, owner of Epstein Imports, an antique gallery on Royal Street.

"Listen," Epstein said, "I got a real nice Severdonck in yesterday and I thought you'd want to know."

"Sheep?"

"Seven of them and a couple a ducks. But it's mostly sheep."

In addition to his long-held passions for good food, '57 T-birds, and his work, Broussard had recently added a fourth: nineteenth-century oil paintings featuring sheep. Though he was not conscious of it his attraction to this field was traceable in large part to his job, where his senses were daily assaulted with evidence of the transient nature of corporeal existence. The survival of a painting produced before he was born showed that genius, at least, lives on. As for subject, what better than a docile animal to serve as counterpoint to the brutality he saw in his own kind.

Ordinarily, he would have waited until lunch to visit the gallery, but since there was something else tugging him toward the Quarter, he decided to go now.

When Epstein saw Broussard come through the door, he began to rub his hands together like a praying mantis. "Hullo, hullo, Dr. Medical Examiner." It was the way Epstein always addressed him. As usual, he was wearing a shiny gray pinstriped suit that left a good inch between the wrinkled collar of his shirt and the collar of his jacket. As far as Broussard knew, Epstein had never been to college, so it was anybody's guess where he got the Phi Beta Kappa key he wore as a tie clasp.

"So, what I described to you on the phone sounded pretty good, huh?" He was leaning so far forward that Broussard thought he might topple over.

"Sounded worth a look," Broussard replied in a disinterested tone.

This was the way it always was with them, a ritual with definite steps and a proper rhythm, each partner knowing his part so well that they moved through it as smoothly as a professional dance team.

"Listen," Epstein said. "I heard a good one the other day."

Now the joke. Always a joke to start.

"Rabbi goes to visit a friend who's a Catholic priest. You

Catholic?" He waved his hand in the air. "Ahhh, doesn't matter, this is not bad. The priest has to hear confession, so he asks the rabbi to sit with him so they can talk between customers. Guy comes up to the window, says, 'Father forgive me for I have sinned. I have committed adultery.' Priest says, 'How many times?' Guy says, 'Once.' Priest says, 'Say a Hail Mary for penance and sin no more.' Few minutes later, another guy comes up, says, 'Forgive me father for I have sinned. I have committed adultery.' Priest says, 'How many times?' Guy says, 'Twice.' Priest says, 'Say a Hail Mary for penance and sin no more.' Now priest has to go to the bathroom. While he's gone, another guy comes up, says, 'Father forgive me for I have sinned; I have committed adultery.' Rabbi figures he'll fill in while the priest is gone. So he says, 'How many times?' Guy says, 'Once.' Rabbi says . . ." Epstein paused, his face a glassy sea, his eyes two sinking ships. "Rabbi says . . ."

As usual he had forgotten the punch line.

"He says . . . Epstein scratched his thinning hair. "Oh, what the hell, you didn't come here for jokes; you came to see a painting. It's back here," he said, unhooking the gold braid that separated the small room at the front from the large gallery in the rear.

The painting was magnificent, a jewel whose colors glowed through a soft patina that only time can produce. And there were sheep, five adults and two lambs, in a tight grouping slightly to the right of center.

Broussard leaned in and scanned the dark grasses and shrubs in the foreground. "Is it signed?"

Epstein pointed to the lower left corner. "Down here. And dated 1885. It's quality, no question."

Broussard lifted the price tag and made a face for Epstein's benefit. He *was* going to buy it. He knew that from the moment he saw it and so did Epstein, but the ritual must be played out.

Broussard forced his eyes from the painting and began to saunter down the gallery, feigning interest in other items. Halfway down was a seven-foot Renaissance-style bronze candelabrum. Broussard figured that the price of the painting would drop 20 percent by the time he reached it.

At the Louis XVI tulipwood parquetry commode just before the candelabrum, Epstein said, "Of course, I can do better on the price. Say we discount it . . . twenty percent?"

Broussard nodded vaguely and kept moving, down that side of the gallery, across the back, and up the other side, being sure to run his fingers appreciatively over a bit of turquoise inlay, a stretch of well-wrought carving, knowing that Epstein would soon sweeten the deal.

A few feet farther on, in front of a Regency-style mahogany bookcase, Epstein said, "If you were to take it today, I might be able to discount it by thirty percent."

Broussard looked at Epstein with raised eyebrows and a slight nod, then resumed the ritual. At the front of the rear gallery, Broussard unhooked the braided rope and worked his way toward the door. When he was perilously close to it, Epstein said, "For you, because you're such a good customer . . . forty percent."

"Done," Broussard replied, and walked out the door, leaving Epstein to take care of billing and delivery.

Outside, instead of turning toward Canal, Broussard went left, the direction that would take him to the area where the three murders had occurred. Around him, the sidewalks were full of people. Apparently no one was afraid of the Quarter during the day. As he walked, he scanned the buildings along the street, imagining himself in need of a place to hide, somewhere you could secrete yourself with no one noticing that you had come in the night before with blood on your clothes.

Having never looked at the Quarter in just this way, he was surprised to see that the structures lining the street presented an unbroken skin that any would-be intruder would find difficult to breach. The buildings all had strong outside doors, many of which were covered at night by metal security doors. The high walls around the courtyards between buildings were topped by sharp spikes, or in some cases, broken bottles set into cement. Courtyard doors were heavy and tall, with concertina wire or other protective devices deployed above them. And even if someone *were* able to get through these barriers, they'd be seen during the day.

A few blocks farther on, he came to the spot where the body of the third victim had been found. Though the blood had been washed away a week ago, he could still see a faint discoloration where it had been. It was like this for him in hundreds of locations. Where others saw nothing, he saw ancient blood stains, old bullet tracks, invisible skid marks, for as much as he would have liked to forget a case when it was finished, he remembered them all, and it was by these signposts that he knew the city.

He thought about the other bodies, one, a block ahead and half a block down on St. Ann; the other, two blocks straight ahead. As he stood there deep in thought, his hand strayed to his nose and began to stroke the bristly hairs on the end of it. The killings, all clustered so close to each other . . . that had to mean their man was holed up somewhere nearby.

A smartly dressed woman in heels brushed by him and walked across the dim stains that had started him on this train of thought. Ready now to move on himself, he chose a stain-free course next to the porcelain shop facing the sidewalk, fortifying himself as he went with a lemon ball from the linty cache in his pocket.

A little beyond St. Anthony's Square, his attention was drawn down Père Antoine Alley—the passageway between St. Louis Cathedral and the Presbytere—by the sound of an electric drill. At the far end of the alley, on an extensive set of scaffolding erected all across the side of the Presbytere, he saw two men affixing new copper drainpipes to the building. For want of something better to look at, he headed toward them.

Skirting the scaffolding, he went out onto the broad flagstone pedestrian mall that ran along Jackson Square to see what exactly was being done to the old building. From the white dust over the granite block covering its lower half and the small Carborundum wheels that he had seen littering the flagstones under the scaffolding, he concluded that they were repointing the block as well as replacing the guttering.

Shading his eyes, he looked more closely and saw raw wood showing through the trim around the Palladian windows. Apparently, she was getting a fresh paint job, as well. It made him feel good to know the city was keeping the old girl in such good shape.

Good shape.

The thought made him step back and look to his left, at the Cabildo, the building on the other side of the cathedral, where Napoleon signed away the rights to Louisiana. Once identical to the Presbytere, its mansard roof had burned off a few years earlier and had yet to be replaced. The symmetry of the two buildings, with the cathedral between, had always appealed to Broussard's sense of order, but the gimpy appearance of the Cabildo without its roof was like a death certificate attributing death to unknown causes, a wholly unacceptable state of affairs.

His gaze drifted back to the slate roof on the Presbytere and the four dormers that projected from it. Apparently, the painters had not yet reached the dormers or else . . . Was that . . . He moved to his left so he could get a better angle on the middle dormer. Yes . . . it *was*. One of the small panes on the dormer's casement windows was broken.

He walked quickly toward the open iron gates that kept people out of the Presbytere's portico when the building was closed. As often as he had admired it from the outside, this was the first time he had been inside. Used now as a historical museum, the front doors opened into a cavernous room with a curved wooden counter just inside where a clerk collected an admission fee. Wishing to satisfy his curiosity on an unofficial level, he paid the fee and headed directly for the wide stairs he saw in the rear, off to the left of a large glass case containing a model of a three-masted sailing ship.

On the way, he passed a wizened old security guard, who, from the way he was rocking back and forth on his heels with his eyes closed, was mentally home on his porch, which was good, because Broussard was not planning to stay in the public area.

At the top of the stairs was a long hall lined by paintings and marble busts on pedestals. To his left, running from ceiling to floor, was a heavy red drape. Slipping behind it, he found himself in the support area. To his right were the rest rooms. Straight ahead was a room in which he could see kitchen cabinets and a counter. The continuation of the stairs was on his left.

The stairs were his primary objective, but before going to them, he walked over to the room that looked like a kitchen and flicked on the light. An employee lunchroom—sink, Formica-covered table, microwave, electric can opener, coffee maker, and a sign taped to the cabinets over the sink. If you couldn't see the anger in the slashing strokes with which it had been written, it was clear from the message: CONTENTS BOUGHT AND PAID FOR BY D. HOWELL. FOR HER USE ONLY!!!

Broussard crossed the room and opened the cabinet. Inside was an assortment of canned soups and other items suitable for a quick lunch. On the way, he examined the door and found that it had no lock.

Then to the stairs, enough of them to make his pulse quicken—or was it his growing suspicions that were affecting his heart? At the top of the stairs, there was a large landing and a single door. Even from where he stood, Broussard could see the splintered wood below the doorknob, as though the throw on the lock had been rammed through the trim by a force applied from the inside. He crossed the small space, paused a moment to catch his breath, and opened the door.

Chapter 12

The door led to the Presbytere's attic, a huge dark space illuminated only by dust-laden shafts of light slicing in through the dormer windows on the front of the building.

He stepped inside and groped around for the lights. As his eyes grew accustomed to the gloom, he saw a bank of switches a little farther over from where he expected to find them, which, as it turned out, didn't make any difference, because none of them worked.

The air was musty but temperate. Apparently, even this remote area of the building was air-conditioned. As his eyes became more accustomed to the dim light, he saw why. Piled in typical attic disarray were stored displays: wooden cases with glass fronts containing old photographs whose subjects he could not make out, bits of architectural ornamentation, cards with minerals glued to them.

At the far end of the attic, he could hear the muffled sound of a drill from the men on the scaffolding, followed by the faint ring of a hammer against metal. Then there was another sound, delicate and repetitive, like a fine gold chain dangling against a hard surface—the kind of sound a crucifix might make if its owner was on his hands and knees crawling along the floor.

Broussard looked around for a weapon. Over by the nearest dormer was a two-seater bicycle with no front wheel . . . fat lot of good *that*'ll do. Against the wall near where he had come in were two Corinthian columns, way too big to be useful. *Blast.* You'd think in all this junk, there'd be *something*.

On the floor a few feet away was a motor of some kind resting on two pieces of two-by-four. The motor was not as heavy as it looked and he was able to slip one of the supports out from under it. Clutching the lumber in both hands down low where he could get the most leverage in his swing, he crept toward the sound, which was coming from the end of the attic with the broken window.

The display cases were nearly eight feet tall, and as he moved, he could see only small areas of the attic at a time from between them. After covering a significant distance, he paused at a case containing a stuffed fox holding a pheasant in its mouth, and stole a look at what lay ahead. He quickly pulled his head back, for the light from one of the dormers was casting a long shadow on the back wall: the distinct image of someone hiding behind a display case ten feet away. And he was holding a club.

Broussard turned and crept to the other end of the case with the fox. Holding his breath so as not to give his position away, he moved quickly across the space that separated him from whoever was waiting. Despite his size, Broussard was light on his feet and he managed to cover the distance without kicking anything or making a floorboard creak. This was going to have to be quick and good.

Even as he rounded the corner of the case hiding his adversary, he began his swing, a powerful roundhouse that sent the two-by-four in a curving arc of which even the Babe would have been proud. In the instant before contact, something erupted into his face with the sound of a sheet whipping in the wind, blinding him. But he had caught a glimpse of the one he was after—well-built, shirtless, and facing away from him, as he had hoped.

When the two-by-four struck home, Broussard knew that something was definitely wrong. Instead of the sound and feel of flesh, whatever he had hit cracked and crumpled. The thing that had blinded him was out of his face now and he could see again. Everything up to the waist of his adversary was still standing, but his upper half lay on the floor.

A fiberglass Indian with a hoe over his shoulder. He had just matched wits with a blasted statue. And, considering the results, had lost big.

Above him, he heard the sound that had started all this: a pigeon, its claws clacking against the top of another display case as it strutted nervously back and forth. So *that's* what had hit him in the face.

An image flashed into his head: his fireplace, with the upper half of the Indian mounted on a plaque so that it projected horizontally into the room like a moose head. Yeah, I got him with a yellow pine two-by-four with chamfered edges. I always use pine if I can get it. Fir's too splintery and cedar'll break on you.

He began to chuckle, a deep resonating sound that caused the pigeon to turn his head and inspect him with one red eye.

For the first time, he noticed that several of the cases to his right had been pulled together to form a wall that blocked his view of the dormer with the broken window. Keeping the two-by-four with him, he circled the grouped cases and looked on the other side, into a small room whose far end was closed by another wall of cases.

On the floor, some wrinkled fabric had been thrown over a pile of collapsed cardboard boxes to make a bed. Glass from one of the cases making up the far wall littered the floor between the wall and the bed. The display inside the damaged case had once suffered water damage and the title was no longer legible. The display consisted of a variety of metal objects strapped to white Foamcore: a set of iceman's tongs, a gargoyle door knocker, a half dozen square nails, a gear wheel. The presence of a hole in the Foamcore along with the location of the hole suggested that once there had been *another* object in the display, an object that had been ripped loose with such force that the strapping had been pulled through the board.

He caught an odor, sickly sweet, an old friend: decaying flesh. In the corner to his right was a pyramid of empty cans, probably from the lunchroom downstairs. Beside it was a feathery mound. He went to the mound and turned it with his foot. Hordes of maggots boiled out of the carcass in protest. He knelt to look closer. It was a pigeon with its wings pulled off. He looked around the room and saw what appeared to be a pair of wings in the corner by the window. Despite the maggots in the carcass, it looked relatively complete, indicating that the bird hadn't been killed for food.

He discarded his two-by-four and tore two pieces of cardboard from the bed, using them to scoop up the pigeon. Taking the carcass to the window, he examined the maggots in it with the tiny hand lens on his key ring. Hard to tell what species they were. Had he been back in his office, he would have let a few harden in alcohol and then examined the structure of the breathing pores in a section taken from the tail. Field guess? Since houseflies prefer manure to animal carcasses, it was probably a bluebottle.

As if irritated that he had disturbed its children, a fat bluebottle soared out of the gloom and began to buzz around his head. A swat of his hand sent it fleeing out the broken window.

The window.

He put the carcass on the floor where he wouldn't be likely to step on it and examined the latch on the window with the broken pane. It was unlocked. The live pigeon had probably not come in through the small broken pane but, rather, had slipped in when whoever had been living here had left the window open. But was it *their* man or just a harmless transient? The pigeon carcass suggested the former. Still, it could have been . . .

His eyes focused on the stone sill of the dormer window and he knew in that instant it was no ordinary transient that had been staying there. For there were scratches worn into the sill, sets of four long gouges in which the two members on the right were closer together than the others.

Broussard called Phil Gatlin from the pastry shop in the lower Pontalba building catercorner from the Presbytere, and had a

Napoleon and coffee while he waited for him to show. Gatlin had the good sense to arrive on foot and alone.

"You're certain about this?" he said.

"Judge for yourself," Broussard replied, taking no offense at Phillip's skepticism. Phillip was a good detective, probably the best in the department, and he would not let himself off lightly for failing to find what Broussard had discovered.

"Let's play this low-key and quiet for now," Phillip cautioned as they crossed the street. "We don't want to spook anybody."

To the clerk at the desk, Broussard was simply a tourist who had enjoyed the museum so much that he had returned with a friend. The security guard didn't even see them, his attention being taken by two little potential museum wreckers in tan baseball caps and polo shirts.

Broussard led the way to the red drape on the second floor and pointed out the sights behind it. "Toilets there, and over there, a lunchroom where he was able to steal food at night." At the top of the last flight of stairs, he said, "Lock broken out from the inside."

"He used the scaffolding on the side to get in?"

"Broke out a pane of glass so he could unlock the window. Come on."

When they passed the shattered Indian, Gatlin tapped Broussard on the back. "He do that?"

"Not exactly."

"Meaning?"

"I'll explain it to you later."

"Before or after you send the place a check for the damages? Was he a tough customer? I hear Indians are hell in hand-to-hand combat. But this one probably had lousy reflexes. What'd he . . . jump you from behind?"

"You here on business or pleasure?"

"Little of both, as it turns out."

"He made himself a bed over here." Gatlin followed Broussard to the open end of the arranged display cases. "Bed, empty cans from the lunchroom downstairs—"

"And fingerprints up the wazoo, I'll bet."

"Yeah, and some of 'em might even be his."

"I'd rather have lots of prints than none. What's that smell?"

Broussard pointed to the pigeon carcass. "Somethin' he did while he was warmin' up. But here's the clincher." He led Gatlin to the window and pointed at the marks on the sill.

Gatlin bent down and studied them for a few seconds. ". . . like he stood here sharpening it while he watched foot traffic through the window." He stood up, looked behind him, and gestured at the broken display case with his chin. "You figure that's where he got it?"

"I'd put money on it."

"So where is he?"

Broussard waved his arm toward the square below. "Out there somewhere."

"Wonder when he was last here?"

"I can tell you approximately when he did the pigeon. It's full of third-instar maggots, which if they're from the bluebottle as I suspect, he was here a week ago."

"Around the time of the last murder."

"That's the way I figure it."

Gatlin took a penlight out of his pocket and went to the stack of cans in the corner. He knelt to examine the contents. "Everything's pretty dried up in here."

He got to his feet and poked at his shirt where it had come out of his pants.

"I think the son of a bitch has moved." He rubbed his big hand back and forth across one eyebrow, making it look like the fur on a frightened cat. "You know what the worst part of this job is? It's doing crap that you know has practically a zero chance of accomplishing anything. But you do it because of the stakes."

"You plannin' to spend the night up here?"

Gatlin responded with the gesture trapeze artists use at the end of their act. "The thing that burns my butt is that I must have walked past that scaffolding dozens of times in the last week or so and it never registered."

"Maybe because it was at night. If it had been during the day, you probably would have noticed the broken window just like I did."

"Yeah, right." He surveyed his surroundings. "Wonder if the weapon is *stashed* up here somewhere?"

Broussard said nothing.

"Well, I can't afford to toss the place now," Gatlin said. "It'll just have to wait."

The two men went downstairs and located the security guard, who lost his bored expression the instant Gatlin flashed his badge. In hushed tones, Gatlin explained the situation, then said, "No fuss, no bother. You give me a key so I can get out if I have to, then tonight, just lock up as usual."

The old man's eyes narrowed into a squint. "How do I know this ain't a con?"

"Look, this is Dr. Broussard, the Orleans Parish Medical Examiner. Would he be involved in a con?"

The man relaxed. "No sir, it don't seem likely."

"The key?"

The old man sorted through the ring hanging from his belt and removed two keys. "This one's to the front door and this one's to the outside gates."

"I'll be back before closing," Gatlin said, pocketing the keys.

"By the way," Broussard added, "you can bill me for the broken statue in the attic."

"And they say security guards are poorly trained," Gatlin whispered as they headed for the street.

When Broussard got back to his office, he found a string of pink message slips taped to his desk lamp. The first was from the guy heading up the Pathophysiology course at LSU, wanting to remind him that his lectures were coming up next week. Seeing that the second one was from Woodsy Newsome, he first called Charlie Franks in the morgue to see how he was coming on the floater that Newsome was working, figuring that was almost certainly what the detective was calling about.

After relaying what he got from Franks, he pulled the third message off the lamp: PLEASE CALL GEORGE BURKE. URGENT.

George Burke?

He tried to place the name but couldn't. It was the area code accompanying the phone number that finally jarred the answer loose. Of course. Burke was the young fellow that had taken over old Doc McKenzie's practice in Bayou Coteau after McKenzie died. He was also the closest thing to a medical examiner they had over there. As much as he personally liked Burke, it was clear that the man was barely up to the job.

He punched in the number on the message slip and got Burke's wife, who doubled as his nurse. Her name? What the devil was her name?

Patsy.

"Hello, Patsy. This is Andy Broussard over in New Orleans. I got a message here to call George."

"Hi, Andy. George told me you'd be calling. I'll get him. How are you?"

Patsy had a deep sultry voice that didn't go at all with her petite frame and schoolgirl look. "A little older and a little smarter, I hope."

"Sound's like a good trade-off. Hold on."

A few seconds later, Burke came on the line. "Andy. Good of you to return my call. Sorry, though, that you're the one that has to pay."

For the first time, Broussard realized that George's voice would have better suited his wife and vice versa. "I think our budget can handle it. What's up?"

"Patsy and I just got back from a little vacation. While I was catching up on the papers we missed, I read about the murders you've been having. I was particularly struck by the fact that all the victims had throat wounds that had been made by human teeth."

"We would have preferred that those details not be made known, but somehow they got out."

"Might be good that they did. Shortly before we left on vacation, we had a murder over here. Not a slasher type like yours, but a beating—one so bad, you couldn't tell who the victim was by looking at the face. And there were throat wounds."

Never go boo-lie during a full moon.

Broussard sat up in his chair and hunched over the desk. "Made by human teeth?"

There was a pause. "Look, you know I don't particularly like serving as the medical examiner over here. I haven't got the training for it. But since there's no one else, I do it . . . as well as I can. What I'm trying to say is, I don't know for sure if the wounds were made by human teeth, but I think so."

"You take any photographs?"

Another pause. "No. I was planning to, but the Latiolais boy caught his hand in his combine, the Bergeron baby came early, and—"

"How about I come over there and kick the grass a bit."

"Might be a good idea. When?"

"I'll leave first thing tomorrow mornin'."

Kit was in her office wondering what her next move should be when Broussard came by. "Thought you'd like to know that we found your lycanthrope's hideway a little while ago."

Kit leaped to her feet. "And you got him?"

Broussard shook his head. "It was empty. Looked like maybe he hadn't been there since the last murder."

Just as Kit was about to tell him what she had discovered about Henry Guidry, Broussard said, "You and Charlie are goin' to have to hold the fort by yourselves tomorrow. I'm goin' over to Bayou Coteau to check on a murder they had a few days before ours started. The local ME thinks their case and ours might be related."

"I'd like to go, too," Kit said eagerly.

Broussard thought about it for a few seconds, then said, "It's all right with me. But I was plannin' on usin' the opportunity to show Bubba the knock my yellow bird develops after it's been on the road for awhile. Already set it up with him."

"That's okay. I can drive, too." This was actually *better* than riding with Broussard. This way, she would be free to pursue her own agenda, one that might even include Teddy LaBiche.

"Since I'm not sure what we'll get into over there, I can't say how long we'll be gone. To be safe, you should take your toothbrush. I'll pick up Bubba and swing by your place about eight."

"I'll be ready."

Chapter 13

The next morning, the little caravan got under way a little after eight. Bubba pointed out that if they took the southern loop of Highway 90, they'd get a chance to see some shipyards. But that plan lost two to one and they set out instead on Interstate 10, which would take them through Baton Rouge to Lafayette, where they would pick up the southern leg of 90, in all, about a two-and-a-half-hour trip.

With Broussard setting the pace, they drove a little over the speed limit and made no pit stops. A few miles after they had turned off the interstate for the final ten miles to their destination, Broussard began to signal that he was about to apply the brakes, which he did without pulling onto the shoulder. From ten yards back, Kit saw him open his door and scoop something off the pavement. A few seconds later, Bubba got out and walked down to the swamp that ran beside the road. He disappeared for a moment in the weeds, then came back to the car.

As they resumed their trip, the swamp on the left receded and the oaks opposite the spot where she had met Teddy appeared. A mile farther on, she saw a road angling gently off to the right that she had not noticed on her first trip. A few feet in front of the turnoff was a sign for the Bayou Coteau Alligator Farm. A half mile more and the swampy shoulder on the right was also displaced by a line of oaks.

In the heart of town, Broussard turned onto one of the side streets and pulled into a parking bay in front of a sprawling one-story antebellum with a pretty wraparound porch decorated with a dozen huge hanging ferns. In the well-tended lawn was a black wrought-iron sign with white letters: GEO. BURKE, M.D. Probably the ME that Broussard had mentioned.

She pulled in between Broussard's T-bird and the BMW already there, got out, and took a good stretch. Down the street, a big man in a ragged blue sweatshirt was walking behind a power mower that filled the air with the wet, sweet smell of newly cut grass. Nice town. Now, if she could just find a ladies' room. She walked over to where Broussard and Bubba were also loosening up after the long drive.

"What was all that about back there when you stopped in the middle of the street?" she asked.

"Bubba saw a turtle in the road and was afraid it might get run over." Broussard said from around a fresh lemon ball.

She looked at Bubba, who shook his head slowly and pointed his finger silently at Broussard. His left cheek looked as full as Broussard's.

"Don't worry, I didn't forget you," Broussard said. He took her hand and put two wrapped lemon balls in it. "Let's go see Burke."

"Andy, Ah'm gonna stay out here and see can Ah figure out what's causin' dat noise," Bubba said.

While Bubba looked under the T-bird's hood, Kit and Broussard went onto the porch and followed the neat sign near the front door that directed them to the office entrance around to the side.

The waiting room was done in brown rattan with peach walls. At eye level, the room was ringed with Audubon prints. At the far end, behind a pass-through, a pretty young woman with short red hair looked tickled to death to see them.

"Look who's here," she gushed genuinely. "Y'all must have left home right early."

While she came out to the waiting room, Kit considered making a dash for the rest room she saw, but she could imagine the ensuing conversation: "Where's the lady who was with you?" "Oh, she's in the toilet." And then both of them watching when she emerged. Too late now, anyway.

"Andy, you are lookin' *so* good," the woman said, coming out the door that led to the examining rooms. From somewhere in the back, Kit heard a high-pitched whine that suddenly dropped in tone and began to labor.

Noticing her interest in the back room, the woman looked at her and said, "Isn't that just awful? Makes it sound like a wood shop instead of a doctor's office. Once, I had to chase a patient all the way to Main Street to convince her that it was just the saw George uses to remove casts. Hi, I'm Patsy Burke."

Kit took Patsy's outstretched hand and introduced herself. "I love your ferns," she added.

From the look on Patsy's face, Kit could see that she had said the right thing. "Sphagnum moss," Patsy said. "That's the secret. You plant them in pure sphagnum. World ever runs out of sphagnum, I'm in big trouble. George'll be through in a few minutes. Would y'all like some lemonade?"

"That'd be wonderful," Kit said.

"Andy?"

"Never could turn down anything made with lemons," Broussard said. "Could we make it for three? We've got a friend outside."

"Three it is."

While Patsy got the refreshments and Broussard examined the Audubon prints, Kit slipped away. She emerged just as Olivia Duhon came out the door that led to the examining rooms. Behind her, without his cast, was Claude.

There were exclamations of surprise and some vigorous handshaking. Olivia gave Kit a big hug.

"How'd you find us?" Claude said. "Martin send you over here?"

"Actually, we're here on business . . . to see George," Broussard said apologetically.

"And you didn't let us know you were coming?" Olivia said. "Shame on you, Andrew."

"I didn't want you fussin' over us," Broussard said. "I know how you are. And there's three of us."

"I don't care if there's a dozen, you're coming to lunch at least," Olivia said.

"I'm not sure when we'll be—"

"We'll set it tentatively for noon. If you're going to be late, call."

"I guess that was you we heard getting his cast removed," Kit said to Claude.

"And good riddance," Claude replied. "Seems like I been hobbling around with that thing for a year."

"What happened?" Broussard asked. "Olivia find you flirtin'?"

"He'd have had more than a broken ankle if that was the case," Olivia said seriously.

"Did it trying to save my dog from a gator," Claude said.

"Did you ever get him?" Kit asked.

"No. It's like he can read minds. He won't take poisoned bait and by the time you get a gun to your shoulder, he's on the bottom and out of sight. The day he killed my dog, he wasn't even hungry. I know because I found the dog's body later."

"Claude, that's enough," Olivia cautioned, touching his arm.

"It's just that every time I think of it—"

"Claude."

"You're right." Claude's face brightened. "I guess then we'll see you around noon."

Even though his cast was gone, Claude still walked with a slight limp. As the door closed behind them, George Burke came into the room.

"Hi, Andy. Sorry to keep you waiting."

Burke had the kind of face that would make him look twenty years old forever. He had pink lips and intelligent eyes that looked out from behind glasses with thin wire frames. Dressed in sturdy olive twills and a white shirt open at the collar, he looked like someone who had spent the morning doing some serious doctoring. Kit liked him instantly.

"Bet you thought I was *never* comin' back," Patsy said, maneuvering past Burke with a trayful of slim glasses made to look as though they were covered with frost. She handed each of them a glass and a napkin and then headed outside to find Bubba.

"Why don't we talk back here," Burke said.

He led them to a room containing a huge old rolltop desk sitting against the far wall. The placement of the desk meant that Burke's back would be to the door when he sat there, an indication to Kit that he had an open, trusting personality. Above and around the desk, the wall was crowded with framed documents, including an M.D. degree from Bowman Gray and a certificate indicating that he was board-certified in family practice. Against the near wall, under another Audubon print, was a blue vinyl sofa.

"What a beauty," Broussard said, crossing the room and running his hand over the desk.

"Belonged to Doc McKenzie," Burke said. "His heirs let it go with the house. Funny how young folks have no appreciation for the past. They talked about it as if it were junk."

"Comes with youth," Broussard said. "Takes somebody who's *had* a past to appreciate one."

Burke opened one of the deep side drawers and pulled out a pile of thin ledgers held together with a rubber harness. "They didn't even want these—McKenzie's notes about all the cases he saw over the years. It's fascinating to see how little he had to work with in the way of medicines when he first started out and how his clinical skills grew over the years. I read a few pages every night to relax. But that's not why you're here." He put the ledgers away, waved Kit and Broussard to the sofa, and spun his desk chair around to face them.

Sitting next to Broussard was like sitting on a steep hill, and Kit had to brace her feet against the floor and overbalance in the opposite direction to keep from tumbling into him.

"This murder you had," Broussard said, "who was the victim?"

"Homer Benoit," Burke said, trying his lemonade. "Ran the hardware in town. Nice fellow, but small in stature. Couldn't have done much to defend himself. He and his nephew, Marc Babinaux, worked until about eleven-thirty rearranging some things in the store. When Marc left, Homer stayed behind to finish. He must have locked up around midnight, because he was killed in the parking lot behind the store at twelve-oh-five A.M."

"What makes you so sure of the time?"

"His watch. It was smashed like he had thrown up his arm to ward off a blow. I found pieces of bark in some of his wounds, so he was probably bludgeoned with a rough piece of lumber or a hefty piece of a fallen tree branch. As I told you on the phone, he also had throat wounds that could have come from human teeth."

Broussard looked at Kit. From his expression, it was clear that he remembered her earlier comment about *their* killer being capable of using a knife or a club. He turned back to Burke. "Anybody find the weapon?"

"No."

"Benoit have any enemies?"

Burke shook his head. "Small place like this, there's not much you can keep private. Patsy always says the whole town knows it every time we . . ." Burke paused. "Well, you get the idea. If he had any enemies, it'd be common knowledge."

"I hope the body wasn't cremated," Broussard said, taking a sip of his lemonade.

"It's in the cemetery you passed on the way in."

"Who's the sheriff in Bayou Coteau these days?"

"Name's Guidry, Lawless Guidry. Great name, huh?"

"Any relation to Henry Guidry?" Kit asked.

"Which Henry Guidry?"

"The cattle rancher. Friend of the Duhons."

Burke shrugged. "You go back far enough, they're probably all related. But if those two are, I've never seen any sign of it." He looked at Broussard. "You going to talk to him?"

"Thought I would."

"He's kind of a strange fellow. Owns the Texaco station where you turned off the interstate. Does all of his law-enforcement work out of a room in the back."

"What does he do when he needs to lock someone up?" Kit asked.

"Takes them to Breaux Bridge."

"Be a dull world without the strange ones," Broussard said, finishing off his lemonade. Kit did the same, and Patsy arrived to collect the glasses. After a round of departing pleasantry, Burke accompanied his guests as far as the porch, where he watched them walk to their cars. When they reached the sidewalk, he said, "By the way, watch out if Guidry offers you his hand. He's got a grip like a vise and he loves to humiliate people with it."

The air filter of the T-bird and a small tool chest were lying on the grass. A few other pieces of the engine were resting on an orange rag spread out on the fender. Bubba was hard at work under the hood with a socket wrench. In addition to his tools, he had brought along a jumpsuit, which he was now wearing.

"You plannin' on pullin' the engine right here?" Broussard joked.

Bubba looked up and grinned. "Not unless Ah get a lot more money."

"Kit and I are goin' to take a little ride in her car." He looked at his watch. "We all been invited to lunch at noon. So, we'll be back no later than quarter till to pick you up."

Bubba saluted with the wrench and went back to work.

At the Texaco station, Kit parked off to the side so she wouldn't block the entrance to the work bays. In one of them, a mechanic was using an air wrench to tighten the lugs on a car up on the lift. There was a sheriff's car with the hood up in the other.

Broussard headed toward a skinny lad wearing a Texaco cap and a baggy Texaco shirt with the tails out. Oblivious to their approach, he was leaning on a windshield-wiper display and gazing off into the distance while he worked two fingers around in a red and silver tobacco pouch.

"Scuse me," Broussard said.

The kid pulled a clump of shaggy fibers from the pouch and packed them into his mouth. "Watcha need?" he asked, his words slurred by the sludge in his cheek. Kit hoped she wouldn't have to see him spit.

"Scotty, is Sheriff Guidry here?"

Kit wondered how Broussard knew the kid's name, then saw it herself in a red stitched patch on his shirt.

"In there," the kid said, jerking his head toward the bay with the sheriff's car. His tongue licked at a brown trickle oozing from the corner of his mouth.

Kit followed Broussard inside, where they found someone leaning so far into the car's engine that his feet were off the ground.

"Sheriff?"

The man grunted and worked himself free. Kit couldn't imagine anyone looking less like a lawman. He was wearing a black Mickey Mouse T-shirt with black pants whose cuffs were stuck into the tops of badly scuffed black boots. His wiry gray hair was pulled back in a ponytail held in place by a leather thong. On one arm, he had a professional tattoo consisting of the word *courage* lettered across a pair of wings. On the opposite bicep, an inept friend had stenciled him with a dagger dripping blood.

Kit suspected that his three-day growth of beard was simple neglect and not an affectation. As derelict as his overall appearance was, his black eyes were quick and sharp. He dipped his fingers into a tin of degreaser and worked it into both hands, his narrowed eyes sizing Broussard up.

"This is Kit Franklyn and I'm Andy Broussard, medical examiner for Orleans Parish," Broussard said.

Guidry's long fingers did a slippery dance over each other, the muscles in his forearms rippling. "You're a long way from home," he said coldly, wiping away the degreaser with a clean orange rag.

Guidry offered his hand and Broussard took it without hesitation. Seeing how the old pathologist's stubby fingers were barely able to get a purchase on the other man's huge mitt, Kit understood why Guidry had such a smug look on his face. Broussard didn't have a chance.

Guidry's fingers wrapped around Broussard's hand like the petals on a Venus's-flytrap sensing dinner. His hand whitened with pressure and the veins in his arm began to bulge. Under the strength of Guidry's grip, Broussard's fingers also went white. Kit looked hopefully for the veins in Broussard's forearm but saw no sign of them. To Broussard's credit, he was maintaining a stoic demeanor, taking the pain well.

The two men stood quietly, locked in combat, for what seemed like a very long time, Guidry's sweaty forearm reflecting light off muscles that looked as though they were carved out of stone. Did Broussard even *have* any forearm muscles? There was no evidence of it. Still Broussard showed no expression. On the other hand, Guidry no longer looked so smug. He, too, had reverted to a poker face.

On the struggle went, pearls of sweat popping out on the forehead of both men. Kit felt as if she should wipe Broussard's brow. Then, hardly believing what she was seeing, a tear welled up in Guidry's eye, spilled out, and mingled with the sweat on his face. His muscles relaxed and his fingers opened. When Broussard released him, the sheriff cradled his combatant hand in the other and massaged it.

"Maybe Orleans Parish ain't so far away, after all," Guidry said. "What can I do for you?"

"What can you tell me about the murder of Homer Benoit?"

"Dunno who did it, if that's what you mean. Probably a drifter, long gone before we ever found the body."

"Why do you say that?"

"Nobody around here had any motive."

"He have a wife?"

"If he did, I'd have been all over her like grease on a ball joint."

"Was he carryin' any money?"

Guidry's face darkened. "That's the part that bothers me. He had fifty dollars and a coupla credit cards in his wallet."

"So why would a drifter kill him, especially so brutally?"

"You ever notice how much easier it is to come up with questions in a murder than answers?"

"The courthouse still in Breaux Bridge?"

"Last time I looked. Why you so interested in Homer Benoit?"

"Could be whoever killed him did three more in New Orleans."

"Before or after?"

"After."

"Then I was right, wasn't I?"

"Maybe . . . maybe not. Could be you're tryin' to put a size-eleven shoe on a size-six foot."

"Meanin'?"

"It'll go on, but so will a lot of other sizes. Trick is to find the one that fits snugly."

"Well, if you come up with a better fit, I'd like to hear about it."

"Oh, I expect your explanation is the right one. I just like to move facts around and see how many ways they can be arranged and still make sense. Kind of a hobby. Exercise for the mind. Guess we ought to let you get back to work. Not good to have the law without transportation."

On the way back to the car, Kit said, "How'd you do that?"

"Do what?" Broussard said.

"Best him in that handshake."

Broussard put on a hurt look. "You sayin' you doubted my ability goin' in?"

"Do you always answer a question with a question?"

"I don't think so. Do I?"

"Forget it."

"Forget what?"

Kit jabbed her finger at him. "*You* are cracking up."

A sound like distant thunder rolled up from some hidden grotto inside the old pathologist and he began to chuckle with his whole body. Kit tried hard to look stern, but her face wouldn't cooperate. And once the smile started, it couldn't be stopped.

Chapter 14

When they arrived at the Duhons', the butler, Martin, was down by the boat dock spreading white clouds of smoke from a wand attached to a pack on his back. From that direction, they could hear a sound like a Model T: *putt, putt, putt.*

"Schefenacker," Broussard said.

"I beg your pardon?" Kit answered.

"He's wearin' a Schefenacker. It's what folks around here use to keep the mosquitoes down."

"Martin and the Schefenacker," Kit said. "Sounds like a group that could sell a million records."

Broussard scratched his beard and shook his head. "And you think *I'm* crackin' up?" He glanced back at Bubba, who was admiring the house with his mouth open. "Bubba, you better get up here. Hungry as I am, I get in the house first, might be nothin' left for you."

When Kit saw the lunch Olivia had prepared, she understood why Broussard had been concerned about Olivia fussing over them. At the same time, she was glad to be there.

The table was set with ornate gold-plated trays and tableware, crystal with a gilded tint, and little decorated fans that matched the ivory linen tablecloth. In addition to a blood-red tomato aspic surrounded by parsley on an elevated crystal pedestal and a huge crystal bowl of oysters Rockefeller on a bed of rock salt, there were individual salads, seafood maybe, in crenelated pastry shells. At each place setting, there was a large turquoise and rose plate piled high with another kind of salad resting on a crepe and topped with a red sauce.

"Olivia, what am I goin' to do with you?" Broussard said, in awe at what she had prepared.

"You're going to sit down and have lunch," Olivia replied.

"How did you manage all this so quickly?" Kit asked.

"I've had plenty of practice, dear."

"Claude, you're a lucky man," Broussard said, patting his old friend on the back.

"Don't let this fool you," Claude said. "I get frozen dinners when we're alone."

"Mr. Oustellette, why are you standing way over there?" Olivia said to Bubba, who seemed afraid to come close to the table.

"It jus' don' seem like Ah oughtta be here," Bubba said, holding his cap in his hand. "Everything is so fine."

"Nonsense," Olivia said, going over to him and guiding him by the shoulder. "You shall sit next to me."

The food was all as good as it looked, and Bubba soon relaxed and seemed to be enjoying himself. But when the oysters were passed, he helped himself to a few pieces of rock salt along with the oysters. Kit could see what was about to happen but could do nothing to prevent it. As he popped a large piece of rock salt into his mouth, she did what she could.

"These fans are quite unusual," she said, picking one up and spreading it. "I'm sure I've seen this scene in a museum painting somewhere. Do you know who the artist was?"

With this cover, the look on Bubba's face when he tasted the salt went unnoticed by his hosts and he was able to get rid of the piece in his mouth and the ones on his plate by putting them in his pocket. Broussard, of course, saw everything.

Dessert was a scoop of chocolate ice cream surrounded by a rosette of tiny ladyfingers. Despite her fear that the Frigi-King plant in New Orleans might ship this far, Kit managed to finish it all. At Olivia's suggestion, they took their coffee into one of the parlors, where Claude finally got around to asking the question that must have been on his mind since he had seen Broussard in Burke's office.

"Andy, what exactly did you mean when you said you were here on official business?"

"Claude!" Olivia spoke his name in a shocked tone.

"Liv, everybody knows that people in small towns are busybodies. I'm just upholding an old tradition."

"Nothin' classified in what we're doin'," Broussard said. He related the whole story, then added something even Kit hadn't heard. "And now that Olivia has fed us in such grand style, we're goin' to the courthouse in Breaux Bridge to get an exhumation order for the body of Homer Benoit."

"To see if Burke was right about his throat wounds?" Claude asked.

"Exactly. And if we expect to make any progress today, we'd better get a move on."

"Are you expecting to get all that done before dark?" Kit said. "I mean, including the exhumation?"

"Kit's right," Claude said. "Wheels don't move any faster here than they do in New Orleans, maybe slower. Why don't you plan to stay the night. We've got rooms enough for all of you."

"On one condition," Broussard replied. "I take you out tonight for dinner and you keep breakfast simple." He looked hard at Olivia.

"Agreed," she said.

After Broussard called his office and told them where he could be reached, they all thanked Claude and Olivia one last time and left. As Broussard was getting into the T-bird, which Bubba believed had been successfully repaired, Kit said, "If you don't mind, there's something I'd like to do while you're in Breaux Bridge."

"Feel free," Broussard said. "You goin' with us tonight?"

"I'm not sure. Probably."

"Let me know if we should wait for you. I expect we'll be goin' around seven."

Kit followed the T-bird out of town, but at the sign pointing to the Bayou Coteau Alligator Farm, they parted company.

Two miles from where she left the town road, the pavement
ran under a large cypress sign attached to poles on each
shoulder: BAYOU COTEAU ALLIGATOR FARM. T. LABICHE, PROP. Below
Teddy's name was the same logo she had seen on the door of
Teddy's truck: a cartoon alligator with big round eyes, emerging from an egg.

Beyond the entrance, on the left, a series of long cement-
block buildings with corrugated metal roofs were arranged
perpendicular to the road. On the right was a parking lot
paved with oyster shells, beside it, a much larger version of
the small buildings. Beyond that was a trailer up on concrete
blocks, and then another row of the long buildings. Though
clean and neat, the operation could hardly be described as
attractive.

She parked in the lot, which already contained two impec-
cably clean cars heavily decorated with pinstriping. There was
also a muddy pickup with tires mounted inside out and bearing
a vanity plate that read FITCH.

Fitch.

Wasn't that the guy she had seen beside the road with Teddy
on her first trip here? Seeing no one around and hearing noises
from the first building, she went inside.

From behind a green canvas that blocked her view of what
lay beyond came a variety of sounds: the intermittent chug of
a motor, staccato bursts of rushing air, and a loud *pop* like a
balloon bursting. She parted the canvas and saw Fitch in a
rubber apron, leaning over an alligator carcass on a stainless-
steel table. He briefly worked a knife at the carcass's throat,
then, without looking up, reached for the rubber hose hanging
in front of his workstation. He placed the hose where the point
of the knife had been. There was a rush of air followed by a
loud *pop* as the scaly hide of the alligator came loose from the
underlying tissues. He let go of the hose and began to remove
the hide over the belly with his knife.

Behind Fitch and stretching across the room to disappear
behind sheets of canvas on each side was a long track fitted
with metal rollers. Scattered along the track were several blue

plastic bins that, judging from the scaly tails sticking out of them, each contained an alligator carcass.

To her left and behind the track, two other men were working with their backs to her. The first was using another suspended hose to produce the bursts of rushing air she had heard. He held up his work to inspect it and Kit could see that he was tacking each hide to a wooden frame. Apparently satisfied with his efforts, he filed the frame in a long wooden box on wheels sitting beside him. Farther to her left, another man was cutting off slabs of tail meat and tossing them into a bin in front of his table.

When Fitch finished cutting the hide free, he grabbed the carcass by the legs and was swinging around to drop it in a bin on the rolling track when he saw Kit. He flicked a switch on his table and the chugging motor that supplied the compressed air stopped.

"This area ain't open to the public," he said, scowling.

"I'm looking for Mr. LaBiche," Kit said.

"He ain't here. Went to New Orleans to get some feed."

One of the other men looked as though he wanted to say something, but a glance from Fitch silenced him.

"When will he be back?"

"Didn't say."

"Suppose I wanted to buy all the alligator hides you could supply?"

"Then you'd have to get in line. Findin' buyers ain't our problem. Keepin' nosy tourists where they belong *is*."

"No, Mr. Fitch, I believe your problem goes far deeper than that." Before he could reply, Kit turned and stalked out. Fitch *could* have been telling the truth about Teddy being in New Orleans, but she doubted it, especially when she looked down the road and saw Teddy's truck at the far end of the cluster of buildings beyond the trailer.

A few minutes later, when she opened the aluminum and glass door to the building closest to Teddy's truck, she was nearly floored by the heat and the stench. Inside was a small room containing clouds of flies and an industrial water heater that looked like a spaceship. Behind the next door was a long, gloomy chamber even hotter and smellier than the first room. And there was music—"I Get Around" by the Beach Boys—coming from a portable radio wired to a roof support. On each side of the central walkway that ran from front to back, the room was divided into a series of cement-block enclosures.

Peeking into the nearest enclosure, she saw that it was a concrete-floored pit, filled with small black and yellow bodies: little alligators about ten inches long. In one of the pits at the far end of the walkway, she caught a brief glimpse of Teddy's head and shoulders. Then he disappeared.

Each pit had a low central area in the middle flanked by raised areas front and back. Running from side to side in the low area was a grate set into the floor. She found Teddy working on one of these grates with a screwdriver. All the little alligators in that pit were clustered in a tight mass in the far corner, as far away from Teddy as they could get. Kit was surprised to see that they were so shy.

As she was about to speak, one of the alligators left his frightened companions and set out in a direct line for Teddy, who was down on one knee. When the little fellow was no more than a foot away, it opened its mouth and hissed at him. Then it turned and scuttled away.

"Looks like a born leader to me," Kit said.

Teddy looked up. "Kit!" He got to his feet, slipped the screwdriver into his back pocket, and joined her at the pit's wooden gate, where he took hold of her hand and sandwiched it between his own. Despite the oppressive heat, his flesh was refreshingly cool. Oddly, she no longer felt repulsed by the place.

"You never struck me as a Beach Boy fan," Kit said.

Teddy's brow wrinkled in confusion, then he got it. "Oh, the radio. It's not for me; it's for them." He motioned to the huddled alligators, leaving her hand disappointed at the loss of his touch. "If it's too quiet in here, they get nervous when we go in and out. We tried classical music, but that makes it worse. Hard rock kills their appetite, mine, too, for that matter. Golden oldies are the best."

"Good promo for the station," Kit said. "More alligators listen to WHBQ than any other station. Join the crowd."

Teddy smiled and the dim lighting in the building seemed to brighten. He let himself out of the pit. The little alligator that had hissed at him had not rejoined the others but had curled up a short distance away.

"That one is still watching you," Kit said, pointing at him.

"An important lesson for someone who works around gators to keep in mind," Teddy said. "Not every gator is going to obey the rules for gator behavior. There's always that one out there . . . waiting for you. One holding a grudge or that just enjoys the kill."

"Like the one at the Duhons'?"

"This one might even have that one's genes. How about I give you a little tour?"

"Do you have the time?"

"That's the nice thing about being the boss."

Outside, Teddy pointed back toward the parking lot. "That's where we do our processing."

"I know. I stopped in there first."

"Sort of wish you hadn't."

"Fitch felt the same way."

"He wasn't glad to see you?"

"Does anything make him happy?"

"He was probably just concerned that you had seen our skinning secret."

"Which is?"

"Air pressure. It takes an experienced skinner forty-five minutes per carcass using a knife, because you have to dissect away each scale separately. And if you slip, you ruin the skin. With air pressure, it can be done in a few seconds. The savings in labor costs are enormous. I don't mind sharing the secret, but that's just one more thing Carl and I don't agree on."

"So why are *you* sorry I started there?"

"Because it's the one part of the business I don't much like myself . . . the killing of such beautiful animals. They *are* you know . . . beautiful and resilient, unchanged for thousands of years. It's not often you see such perfection in nature.

It's certainly rare enough in our own species, with certain notable exceptions."

From the way he was looking at her, Kit was sure she was the exception he had in mind. But since the killing also bothered her, she did not allow this to divert the conversation.

"If you love alligators so much, why do you stay in the business?"

"I'd be lying if I didn't include money in my answer. But it's more than that. By law, seventeen percent of the gators we collect from the wild as eggs have to be released when they reach four feet in length. By then, they're old enough to fend for themselves. Nowhere near that percentage survives in nature. Everything eats young gators, even bullfrogs. By staying in business, I help the species survive." He held up a silencing hand. "Please no debate. I'm shaky enough on this as it is.

"The buildings in this area all contain little ones. When they reach eighteen inches or so, we move them over there where the pits are larger." He pointed to a cluster of buildings across the marshy pond enclosed by the curving road through the property. "When they reach two feet, we move them again, to those buildings opposite the processing operation. They stay there until they get to be four or five feet long. Then . . . well you've seen the rest."

"How long for the full cycle?"

"From eggs to harvest, about eighteen months. Come over here and I'll show you our plumbing."

Kit followed him to a shallow cement well between two of the buildings. It was filled with a small amount of water surrounding a large plastic pipe with a screen over it. "All the pits in these buildings can be drained by pulling out this pipe. The grates in the pits keep the large gators from blocking the drains and the small ones from being flushed away. When we want to fill the pits, we put the pipe back and turn on the water right here."

"Your idea?"

"Actually, no. I copied it from the sanitation system used in Egypt during the time of the pharaohs."

Kit raised her eyebrows in surprise. "The pharaohs. I'm impressed."

"Why? Because you thought I only read *Gator Quarterly*?"

Now he was toying with her. "Perhaps," she said coquettishly. If she had brought one of those fans from the Duhon lunch, she even might have hidden behind it. Teddy began to walk toward an area where the road ran along a vast swamp that stretched away from the farm in an endless vista of boggy islands and tall saw grass. Where the swamp bordered the road, it was enclosed by a chain-link fence that encompassed many acres. A long cement pad had been laid between the fence and the water.

"This is where we keep our breeders," Teddy said. "We let them breed naturally in here, then collect the eggs. It covers us in case we have a shortfall from the field. We feed them here on this cement pad."

"I don't see any."

"You aren't looking carefully." He pointed into the water. "There's one."

After staring hard for a few seconds, Kit saw its eyes: two bumps barely above the surface. She shuddered.

"Good response," Teddy said. "They *should* scare you. It's something that Carl seems to have forgotten. Lately, he's taken to offering them food and pulling it back when they go for it. Thinks it's funny when their jaws snap shut and there's nothing there. Of all the crazy thing he does, that's the one most likely to get him in trouble."

"You said you were going to fire him."

"I will, soon as I can find someone willing to help move them from one set of buildings to the next. See, we do it by hand."

Kit shuddered again.

"You do that very well," Teddy teased.

They continued walking until they came to a cypress dock that ran along the edge of the chain link that stretched into the swamp. On the opposite side of the dock was an airboat.

"Want to go for a ride?" Teddy asked, motioning to the boat. "It'll be fun, but your hair will never be the same."

"Attractive offer, but I'm going to have to ask for a rain check."

"How come?"

"I want to talk to you about something."

A look of chagrin appeared on Teddy's face. "I need to wear a button that says SLAP ME WHEN YOU'VE HEARD ENOUGH ABOUT ALLIGATORS. I should have let you talk long before this."

"Forget it. It was all fascinating and I'd like to hear more, but I'm kind of pressed for time."

"Let's go to the office, where we can be more comfortable."

The office was in the trailer. It was every bit as neat as Dill's operation at the weather service.

"Afraid I don't have much to offer you," Teddy said, looking over the contents of a small refrigerator behind his desk. "Sprite and Coke, that's about it."

"I had a big lunch at the Duhons', so I'm fine."

On the wall beside Teddy's desk was a series of pictures showing various stages of construction of the alligator farm: one of the site with no development, one showing Teddy with his foot on a shovel, the first blocks being laid on the first building. . . . But there was nothing personal around, no pictures of Teddy sailing or holding up a big fish, no books, no plants, no knickknacks on his desk that might tell her more about who he was. Of course, the absence of things could be as telling as their presence. Apparently, he kept his business distinctly separate from his personal life. She found herself wondering whether there were any pictures at home of Maria, Teddy's friend from the dance.

Teddy sat at his desk and folded his hands. "Now it's your turn."

"What can you tell me about Henry Guidry, the friend of the Duhons?"

"Not a whole lot. Runs a big herd of cattle on his spread a few miles out of town. Apart from Claude and Olivia, doesn't have many friends, keeps to himself pretty much, maybe because of his brother, Eddy."

"His brother?"

"Sad case. Retarded from birth."

Retarded. Kit's pulse quickened. One of the lycanthropes that her research had turned up was retarded.

"Since their parents died, Henry's been looking after him. Have to give him a lot of credit there. Takes the responsibility very seriously. Could be that's why he's not married. Hard to find a woman willing to take care of them both."

"What's his brother look like?"

"Big fellow. Obviously not normal. Has kind of a hollow spot in his forehead. They say there's a metal plate under there. You might have seen him around town. He cuts everybody's grass."

Kit remembered the big man mowing the lawn next to Burke's office. "He usually wear a sweatshirt with the arms cut out?"

"That's him. Why all the interest in Henry and his brother?"

Kit related everything that had happened, then said, "I'd like to meet Eddy, but I don't want to do it alone. Will you go with me?"

"Considering what you've said, you couldn't stop me."

Chapter 15

If the courthouse in Breaux Bridge had been a person, it would have been on life-support. Redbrick with a tall white cupola, it showed many settling cracks that radiated from the window-sills like crow's-feet. Inside, the old floorboards cringed with every step Broussard took. With its heavy oak moldings, rows of square columns, wide boxy staircase, and beaded wainscoting halfway up each wall, its construction must have consumed a small forest.

"Lotta decisions been made here," Broussard said.

"More likely *bought*," Bubba replied.

"Why do you say that?"

The little Cajun shook his head. "Ah jus' don' trust anything has to do with gov'ment. Mah family lived in Plaquemines for nearly twenty years. In dat whole time, Daddy never voted in a single election. Wasn't dat he didn' want to. Jus' could never find out where to do it. Dey'd moved a pollin' place to a different spot every election an' never tell anybody where it was. Didn' seem to hurt da total turnout, though. Once, we elected somebody who got a couple thousand votes more dan da number of registered voters. Not that registerin' was so easy. Registrar used to keep his office in his car. You could register if you could catch him."

"I know what you mean. I heard that an investigation of the records down there showed that in one election, all the registered voters showed up at the polls in alphabetical order."

"Even Daddy was listed in dat one."

The building directory sent them to the second floor, where they found the secretary of Judge Albert Touchet on the telephone.

"Yeah, Ah'm tellin' you dat recipe for kush kush was somethin' awful. Mah momma tried some Ah made, an Ah practically had to give her da Heimlich maneuver it was so dry. Oh, oh, gotta go."

The girl had short blond hair that she wore like the thatch on the roof of an English cottage. She had friendly bovine features and a smooth complexion. "May I help you gentlemen?" Her Cajun accent had suddenly disappeared.

"We'd like to see Judge Touchet," Broussard said. "I'm Dr. Broussard, medical examiner for Orleans Parish, and this is my associate, Mr. Oustellette."

This being the second time in one day that he had been called *Mr.* Oustellette, Bubba's posture had improved as much as the secretary's diction.

"And what is this regarding?"

"It's a bit involved and I'd prefer to explain it to the judge."

"I'll tell him you're here."

She disappeared into an office behind her desk and shut the door. She returned in a very few seconds. "You can go in."

Touchet was standing by a tall bookcase, his attention riveted on a heavy tome in his hand. He was wearing a white shirt with no tie and gray trousers held up by green suspenders with red stripes. He let his visitors stand unacknowledged for a few seconds, then closed the book and leisurely put it back on the shelf.

He didn't seem to have any problem telling which of them was the medical examiner. "Dr. Broussard, good to see you." His handshake was firm and moist. After letting Bubba see that for himself, he waved at the chairs by his desk and said, "Nothin' of importance ever got settled between men who were standin' up. So why don't we get in our negotiatin' positions."

Where Broussard was heavy all over, Touchet's weight was all in his torso, which took full advantage of the elasticity in his suspenders. Most of his clean-shaven face had a bright red hue, as though it had just come from under a hot towel. His cheeks, though, were alarmingly blue. Broussard hoped that Touchet's impending coronary would not occur in his presence.

The judge sat down behind his desk and picked up a lit cigarette that had been waiting for him in a glass ashtray with a fishing fly embedded in it. On the bookshelves behind him, between rainbow trout bookends, were well-worn copies of *Kingfish* and *Judge*, the biographies of Huey Long and Leander Perez, two of Louisiana's most famous rascals. Draped on poles in the corner were the United States and Louisiana flags, with the latter standing about a foot above the former.

"You ever run into Judge Isaaks over in big town?" Touchet asked Broussard.

"Occasionally."

Touchet took a long pull on his cigarette and pushed the smoke through his nostrils. "Next time you see him, tell him I'd like to know how his ear is. See if he blushes. Last year when we went trout fishin' in Colorado, he was so interested in a big brown workin' a pool on the other side of the stream that he forgot the willow branches over his head."

Touchet began to chuckle and wheeze like a bellows with a hole in it. "When he tried to cast"—the judge coughed a few times into his hand—"his rod tip hit the branches . . ."

Broussard had not thought it possible that Touchet's face could get any redder, but it did. Bubba was cringing in his seat like someone behind the wheel of a skidding car.

". . . An' he hooked himself in the ear with his fly." Tears of laughter rolled down Touchet's face. Shaking his head at the memory of the trip and wiping at his eyes with the back of his hand, Touchet's enjoyment of his own story gradually wound down. After a final pull on his cigarette, he stubbed it out and leaned back in his chair. "Now, let's get to negotiatin'. What kind of business do we have together?"

"Are you familiar with the Benoit murder?"

"The beatin' death over in Bayou Coteau a few weeks ago? Of course."

"I have reason to believe that the Benoit body may contain

physical evidence linkin' that murder to three that we've recently had in New Orleans and I'd like permission to exhume the body to determine if the cases *are* related."

"What sort of physical evidence?"

"The victims in New Orleans all had extensive throat wounds made by human teeth. There were also throat wounds on the Benoit body, wounds that George Burke, the ME in Bayou Coteau, thinks may have been caused by human teeth."

"*May* have been caused," Touchet said. "You don't actually know that for sure."

"No, that's why I want to exhume the body."

"Would you say that Burke is a good medical examiner?"

"For someone not specifically trained in the discipline, he does a pretty good job."

"'Not specifically trained' . . . 'a pretty good job.' Those are not what you would call glowin' compliments. I know the Benoit family. They all took his death hard and are only now beginnin' to get their lives back in order. The exhumation of his body would most certainly delay their recovery. And for what? Suspicions of a medical examiner who, in your own words, is 'not specifically trained in the discipline.' No sir, I'm sorry, but I can't give you what you want. It wouldn't be in the best interests of all concerned."

"We wouldn't even have to remove the casket from the grave. I could examine the body on the spot."

"Doesn't matter. It's the *thought* of the act that'll create the hardship for the family. We have to think of the innocent as well as the guilty here."

In the hall outside Touchet's chamber, Broussard stood quietly and stroked the bristly hairs on the end of his nose while Bubba waited patiently for the results.

"C'mon," Broussard said abruptly, heading for the stairs. On the ground floor, he went directly for the pay telephone. He fed it a quarter and ran his finger around the dial. While waiting for his party to answer, he looked at Bubba and said, "When in Rome . . ."

As Bubba wondered who was in Rome and what that had to do with them, Broussard turned back to the phone. "Claude? This is

Andy. The judge over here won't give us our exhumation order. Are you still as well connected as you used to be? . . . Glad to hear it. Can you do us some good with this? . . . Touchet. Albert Touchet. All right, we'll do that. Thanks."

"What now?" Bubba asked.

"Back upstairs."

In the hall outside Touchet's chambers, Bubba followed Broussard's lead and took a seat on the wooden bench against the wall. "Who's in Rome?" he asked.

"In a way, we are," Broussard replied. "It's an old sayin'—When in Rome, do as the Romans do."

"An' Claude Duhon is our Roman?"

"We'll see."

A few minutes later, the door beside them opened and Touchet's secretary came out with a folded document.

"Oh, there you are," she said. "I was afraid I might have missed you. The judge asked me to give you this."

When Broussard opened the document, he saw that it was the exhumation order he sought. Stuck to the face of it was a yellow Post-it bearing a handwritten message from the judge: "Antoine's . . . on you, next time I'm in town."

Kit and Teddy found Eddy Guidry a few houses down from where Kit had first seen him next to Burke's office. He was standing behind a blue lawn mower and was touching his fingers to his forehead, a glum look on his face. Teddy parked his truck by the curb and they both walked over to him.

"What's the matter, Eddy?" Teddy asked.

Eddy removed his fingers from his head and Kit saw a small bleeding cut above his eyebrow. "Somethin' hit me." Eddy whimpered. "Somethin' hard."

Anyone could see at a glance that Eddy wasn't normal. Everything about him seemed off. From the tense, awkward way he held himself, as if he were a puppet being held up by invisible strings, to the obvious scooped-out hollow on his forehead and the odd fold of skin on the bridge of his nose that made it look as though the top half of his head overlapped the bottom, he was clearly different. And he was huge—massive arms and shoulders, hands that looked as big as tennis rackets, as though his size was some sort of crazy compensation for his lack of intelligence. A man who could do unspeakable damage swinging a gardening claw, Kit thought.

She took a tissue from the pocket of her slacks. "Eddy, my name is Kit. If you bend down, I'll make it feel better."

Eddy cocked his head to one side and looked at Kit like her dog, Lucky, did sometimes. Then he bent down but quickly stood up again. "It hurts more when I do that," he moaned.

"Then kneel," Kit said.

He did what she asked and Kit dabbed at the blood with her tissue. Then, carefully folding it so the blood was inside, she put it back in her pocket. "It's only a small cut," she said. "It'll heal soon and you'll be good as new."

"It still hurts," he said.

"I know, but you have to pretend that it doesn't so people can see how brave you are."

"I can pretend," Eddy said, "if you'll kiss it for me."

Kit looked at Teddy for help, but all he did was shrug and indicate with his hands that it was her show. In the interest of getting on with things, Kit bent and placed a quick kiss on Eddy's forehead.

"Better now?" she said.

Eddy got up and gave her a lopsided grin. "Better," he agreed. He looked at her for a few seconds and she saw his pupils dilate. "You're pretty," he said. Before she knew what was happening, he put his hand on her breast. "And soft."

Teddy moved toward him, but Kit waved him back. Gently, she took hold of Eddy's arm and lifted his hand off her. "Eddy, that's not a nice thing to do. You musn't touch a lady unless she says you can."

"Will you let me?"

"No, Eddy. We would have to know each other much better and like each other in a special way."

"What kind of way?"

Not wanting to explain sex to a two-hundred-and-sixty-pound man in the middle of someone's yard, Kit tried to shift the conversation. "You're doing a very nice job on this lawn."

Eddy beamed. "I go over it two times. First, I go back and forth and then up and down. That's what makes it look so good. But so far on this one, I've only gone back and forth on this part here."

The untouched part of the lawn seemed quite overgrown to Kit. "Are you the only one who mows this lawn?"

"Only me. They like me here. Like my work. I know because they told me."

"How often do you mow it?"

"Every week."

"Did you mow it last week? It looks like maybe you forgot last week."

Eddy's eyes flashed. "Didn't forget. Didn't."

A blood vessel began to pulse ominously at his temple. His fingers curled into fists. Teddy put a hand on Kit's arm and pulled her back a step.

"Henry says if you forget things, people won't trust you," Eddy said. "I like to be trusted. It makes me feel grown-up."

"I'm sorry, Eddy," Kit said. "I was wrong to say that. I was only trying to find out why the grass is so long, if you mow it every week."

"Don't push him so hard," Teddy whispered.

The bulging vessel disappeared and Eddy's hands relaxed.

"Did you mow this lawn last week?"

Eddy put his hands in his pockets and looked at his feet. "Couldn't," he muttered.

"Why not?"

"I was sick."

"I'm sorry to hear that. Were you ill for very long?"

He looked at her blankly.

"How many days were you sick?"

As he worked on the answer, she could almost hear his brain making sounds like a garbage disposal with a spoon in it. Finally, he held up six fingers and said, "Seven days. I was sick for seven days. But I'm better now. And pretty soon I'll have all my work caught up."

"Did you see a doctor?" Kit asked.

Eddy shook his head. "Henry said a doctor couldn't help. That I'd get better all by myself."

"Eddy, where were you when you were sick?"

He looked at her with a furrowed brow.

"Were you in a different town?"

He shook his head. "Home."

"The whole time?"

"Home . . . in bed."

Teddy and Kit turned at the sound of an approaching car and saw Henry Guidry pull in behind Teddy's truck. From the look on his face as he walked toward them, he was not happy.

"Hi, Henry," Eddy said. "I've got a new friend. Her name is Kit. See, Kit, I don't forget things."

"Eddy, wait for me over on the steps."

"Okay, Henry."

When Eddy was out of earshot, Guidry said, "I know why you're here. What I don't know is why you're talking to Eddy."

"We thought that since he spends so much time in town, he might have heard or seen something that would help us figure out who killed Homer Benoit," Kit lied.

"He doesn't mow lawns at night. And isn't that when Benoit was killed?" He didn't wait for an answer. "So how could he possibly know anything about it? Maybe you've already noticed that Eddy is easily upset by things if you don't know how to talk to him . . . and you *don't*. So I'd appreciate it if you'd keep away from him." Guidry turned and walked quickly toward the front steps, where Eddy was playing with something in his hand.

"That sounds like our cue to move on," Teddy said.

While he was making a U-turn to head back toward the town square, Kit said, "Where's the nearest Federal Express pickup?"

"For what destination?"

"New Orleans."

"There's a local outfit that'll guarantee same-day delivery in New Orleans if your package is at the pickup no later than three o'clock."

Kit looked at her watch. "That only gives us twenty minutes. Where's the pickup?"

"Drugstore in town. What is it, package or letter?"

Kit took out the tissue she had used on Eddy and showed him the bloodstains. "I'm going to send this to our serology lab and have it typed."

Chapter 16

On the way back from Breaux Bridge, Broussard stopped at the Texaco station to inform Sheriff Guidry of his plans to exhume Homer Benoit. Though not enthused at the prospect, Guidry called the local funeral home to set things up. It was decided that, weather permitting, the exhumation could take place the next day at nine o'clock.

That night, Broussard took everyone, including Teddy, to Mulate's, a combination restaurant, dance hall, and bar in Breaux Bridge, where Kit finally got the hang of the Cajun two-step by watching Bubba and Olivia do it. From Mulate's, they all went back to the Duhons' for a nightcap. After an hour or so of good conversation in which alligators were not mentioned once, Teddy expressed his thanks all around and said good night. Olivia had the presence of mind to let Kit see him out.

The night air was humid and hot. In the bayou next to the house and the swamp beyond, frog armadas waged vocal warfare. Teddy paused at the steps and turned, the porch light reflecting in his eyes.

"You haven't told me how long you'll be here," he said.

"I don't really know," Kit replied. "Depends on how things develop."

Teddy stepped closer. Despite the warm night, she could feel the heat from his skin on her bare arms. "And how *are* things developing," he whispered.

His cologne drew her in and his arms slipped around her waist. "I sense a certain momentum building," Kit said breathlessly.

"I understand that momentum is difficult to stop," Teddy said against her ear.

"It's not anything you'd want to step in front of." Kit sighed.

He kissed her gently, then pulled away. "Will I see you tomorrow?"

"I'll give you a call when I see how the day is shaping up. You'll be at work?"

"After ten-thirty or so. I've got some errands to do."

He started down the steps.

"Teddy?"

"Yes?"

"I was wondering . . . do you have any idea how many eggs a woman has in her ovaries when she's born?"

"I surely don't," Teddy said, perplexed.

"Good."

As she watched his truck go down the drive, Kit leaned against one of the huge porch columns and breathed. "Oh you better *not* let them get behind you, Teddy LaBiche."

Early the next morning, Phil Gatlin went down the stairs from the Presbytere attic with a sore butt and in a bad humor. His mumbled remarks echoed in the empty building. "Damned nonsense. Sit up all night in a dusty hellhole, and for what? Nothing. Absolutely nothing." He crossed the ground-floor hall and slipped one of the keys the guard had given him into the lock in the front door.

Considering how lousy everything else was going, the gray day that greeted him was just what he expected. And wouldn't you know it, there was a bum asleep against the outside gate. He turned the key in that lock and then noticed that the bum wasn't asleep but had his face in a plastic bag. In his lap was an aerosol can of hair spray.

Gatlin jiggled the gate against the man's back. "Hey, fella, gimme a break here, will ya."

No response.

He whistled through his teeth and jiggled the gate again. "Hey, Mr. Ed, take it about three feet to your right, what do you say?"

The bum took his face out of the bag and looked up with the same expression that Joe Gunderson had had on his face the night Gatlin tagged him with a solid right in the police boxing league.

"You're blocking the gate," Gatlin said.

The bum smiled and waved.

Convinced that he would never get a useful response, Gatlin inched the gate open until he could slip out without having the bum fall backward into the portico. While squeezing through, he scraped a button off his shirt. After closing the gate and locking it, Gatlin picked up the bum's aerosol can and tossed two bucks into the bum's lap, hoping he was so addled that he might actually spend it on food. "Screws up the ozone," he said, pointing at the can. "Someday you're gonna thank me for this." Then, as he turned away, added, "Just don't call collect."

Having decided that any backup on the ground might spook his quarry, Gatlin had done this alone. His plan had been to try it two nights and give up if nothing happened. He saw now that there was no point in going on. He had simply missed him. The killer wasn't ever coming back. Might as well call in the lab now and see how *they* do.

With dust from the attic still in his nose, he stepped across to the French pastry shop in the Pontalba building and ordered coffee and a croissant. Almost from the first swallow of the hot liquid, he began to feel better. Through the shop window, he saw the two-man crew working the Presbytere arrive in a white pickup fitted out with metal racks filled with guttering. After unloading a couple of gallons of paint and sticking some brushes in the back pocket of their coveralls, they disappeared into Père Antoine Alley.

The hot buttery croissant went well with the coffee and soon all that remained of it was a carpet of crumbs on the plate and the table. How *do* you eat one of those things without spraying it everywhere? he wondered. As he left, he tossed the bum's hair spray in the shop's trash can. Instead of heading for his car, he walked down to Père Antoine Alley and looked up, first at the painters, then at the broken windowpane Broussard had discovered—sitting right out in the open where anyone could have seen it, where *he* should have seen it.

He imagined how it was the nights the killer had struck . . . how he had gone out the window, climbed down the scaffolding, gone hunting, and then returned, possibly leaving blood on everything he touched. But, of course, it had rained each of those nights and the scaffolding would have been wet. . . . His eyes traveled over the metal gridwork, tracing the likely route the killer had used.

Overhead, one of the painters left the safety of his scaffold board and climbed up on the scaffolding itself to reach a corner of the window closest to the front of the building. When he stepped back onto the board, the vibrations of his movement caused something to glitter at the intersection of the second tier of scaffolding with its cross brace. Curious about this, Gatlin stepped to the scaffolding, pulled his pants up so he wouldn't tear out the crotch, and started climbing.

A few seconds later, he saw what it was: a gold bracelet draped over the metal peg that held the cross brace in place. With one of the keys to the Presbytere, he teased the bracelet free and let it fall to the ground. After climbing down, he teased the bracelet into his handkerchief and examined it more closely.

The links were large, and although *he* wouldn't be caught dead wearing jewelry, it seemed more like something a man would wear than a woman. On a small plate attached to the clasp was an inscription: To T.L. with love, from M. St.J. He stepped away from the scaffolding and whistled through his teeth at the painters.

"I'm Lieutenant Gatlin, NOPD," he shouted. "Could you please come down here for a minute?"

When the workmen reached the ground, Gatlin held up the bracelet in his handkerchief-covered palm. "Either of you two recognize this?"

Both men had long hair that hung limply from under their caps. One had a smudge of paint under his nose where he had probably tried to scratch an itch with the handle of his brush. The other had small flecks of paint dotting his face. And this only a few minutes into their day. The one with the smudge under his nose reached for the bracelet, but Gatlin pulled it away.

"No touching," he said.

The one with the paint-flecked face shook his head. "I ain't never seen it before."

The other one agreed. "Me, neither."

"Anyone else working this job?"

A look of pride crossed paint smudge's face. "Nahh. Just us. We do it all." He groped in the pocket of his coveralls and brought out a bent business card. "Your house ever needs gutters or paint, let us know."

Suddenly Gatlin was feeling a *lot* better. The initials—T.L. Last night hadn't been such a waste, after all.

That same morning when Kit opened her bedroom door in Bayou Coteau, she found a pot of coffee and a pot of tea on a hot plate atop a small table in the hall. Next to the hot plate were several china cups and saucers, some spoons, real sugar, artificial sweetener, and cream. Though unaccustomed to such elegance, she adapted by pouring herself a cup of tea and taking it to one of the upholstered settees that faced each other in the middle of the hall. As she sat there imagining herself the mistress of the house, she listened for sounds of anyone else moving about. But all was quiet and she had to finish her tea without benefit of conversation. After returning her cup to the little table, she went downstairs and wandered through the great house until she found Olivia in the kitchen working a batch of biscuit dough.

"Anything I can do to help?" Kit said.

Olivia looked up and smiled. "No thank you, dear. You've heard the saying about too many cooks? Well, it started in my kitchen. I think you'll find Andrew outside somewhere. Mr. Oustellette is still asleep."

"The coffee and tea upstairs was very thoughtful."

"If you're like me, you need a cup of something hot just to get moving in the morning. Now go on with you."

Kit's hopes for a bright day were dashed when she opened the door. Not only was it gloomy and overcast but there was a strange expectant stillness in the air. From off in the distance, the eerie cry of a crow completed the scene. Broussard was down by the boat dock staring across the bayou.

"Nice day for an exhumation," he said as she came up behind him.

"Weird if you ask me," she replied, moving to his side. "What are you doing?"

"Soakin' up the atmosphere. Somethin' to be said for livin' out here."

"For the house and grounds, sure. But you can have the bayou and the swamps."

"Why?"

"Too many dangerous things in them."

"When I was a boy, we thought that woods over there"—he pointed across the bayou—"was the most dangerous place around. It's called Leper's Woods. They say that before the leprosarium was built in Carville, a colony of lepers lived there and contaminated everything in it. That was one place *everybody* avoided, man and boy alike. Course it was all foolishness. Even if lepers *had* once lived there, which I doubt, they took the disease with 'em when they moved on. Nobody's gonna get leprosy from goin' in there. In fact, most folks couldn't get it even if they *lived* with a leper."

"Think they're still afraid of it?"

"I'm sure they are. Old legends die hard in bayou country."

"With good reason," Kit said. "You couldn't find spookier surroundings . . . the night sounds, the brooding old trees, the black water in the bayou. Why *is* the water black, anyway?"

"Tupelo gum. Put a handful of tupelo leaves in a bucket of water, in a few minutes it'll be black as ink."

As they talked, the way their voices dominated the stillness around them began to make Kit feel uneasy, as though they were violating the sanctity of a great library. She scanned the trees across the bayou. "Where are all the mockingbirds?" she said, speaking more softly. "I thought the South was famous for them."

"Maybe they know somethin' we don't."

"Like what?"

"Hard to say, not bein' one."

"Nice obtuse answer."

"Comes from havin' a head full of ideas and no facts."

This rather odd turn to the conversation was brought to a halt by the approach of the butler, Martin. "Dr. Broussard, you have a telephone call. Dr. Franklyn, Mrs. Duhon said that breakfast will be served in five minutes."

Broussard took the call on the phone in Claude's study, an opulent room with a huge fireplace whose mantel was supported by life-size figures of heavily muscled men carved from gleaming mahogany.

"This is Broussard."

"You learning anything over there?" the voice of Phil Gatlin asked.

"Maybe yes, maybe no. We'll be takin' a look at the body of the victim this mornin', if it doesn't rain . . . and it looks like it might."

"Yeah, here, too. I hope while you were asleep in a nice soft bed, you were thinking of me up in that attic."

"Couldn't get it out of my mind. Anything turn up?"

"Not in the attic, but I did find something outside, hanging on that scaffolding." He paused.

"Make me ask, is that it, Phillip?"

"Just wanted you to appreciate what I'm about to say."

"Better be good after this buildup."

"Somebody other than the guys working on the building lost a bracelet, which caught on the scaffolding. The inscription gave the owner's initials as T.L."

"I dunno, Phillip. It wouldn't necessarily have to belong to the killer. Could have been *anybody* climbin' around there."

"Yeah, and maybe the trees won't be full of cheap beads after Mardi Gras this year. It was dropped by the killer, all right."

"Well, I'm glad to see you're earnin' your keep. I wonder if you'd do me a favor?"

"If I can."

They spoke for several minutes more, until Martin came in and announced breakfast.

Homer Benoit had been buried in Evangeline Gardens, the cemetery halfway between the interstate and the town and which they had all passed several times during their stay. As usual, Broussard and Bubba rode together in the T-bird, while Kit brought up the rear in her Nissan.

When they arrived at the cemetery, Sheriff Guidry was waiting at the entrance in a wrecker. Motioning for them to follow, he proceeded along a belt of black asphalt that wound between more moss-laden live oaks and a small city of above-ground crypts that, except for their simpler lines, resembled those in the Saint Louis graveyards in New Orleans.

Deep into the property, the crypts gave way to a grassy expanse that bore only headstones. The wrecker stopped behind a parked black Cadillac and Guidry got out and signaled for them to do the same. At their approach, a stringy old man with a complexion the color of Olivia's biscuit dough got out of the Cadillac and joined Guidry.

"Folks, this is Buster Doucet," Guidry said. "He was the one put Homer under. Buster, this is Dr. Broussard, Dr. Franklyn, and . . ."

Never having met Bubba, Guidry paused. "Bubba Oustellette," Bubba said, touching the bill of his cap.

Apparently, Guidry never wore a sheriff's uniform. He was dressed in black, much as the day before, except that today his T-shirt bore a picture of a cartoon burglar wearing a black eye mask and carrying a bag of coins. Around the picture was a red circle with a line through it. He still hadn't shaved.

By contrast, no Fortune 500 CEO was ever more elegantly attired than Buster Doucet—blue suit, pale blue shirt, crisp tie with a perfect knot, and black shoes so well polished that they were obviously about to see their first grass of the day.

All this finery on such an unhealthy-looking old man reminded Kit of the lacquer and brass on a cheap casket.

"What are we up against?" Broussard asked.

"Like most things, there's good news and bad," Doucet replied over his clasped hands. His voice was raspy, as Kit's father's had been for a month after his thyroid operation. "The good news is that it's not a Gibson Coronado, thirty-six hundred pounds of steel-reinforced concrete with an epoxy seal that would require complete excavation of the vault, removal with a crane, and several hours labor with a jackhammer and a torch to get inside."

Doucet paused and cleared his sinuses, making a sound that would have caused the others to change seats had they been in a restaurant. "The bad news is that we used a nonsealable grave liner; an unreinforced concrete box with holes in it and a two-piece lid that simply sits on the lip of the box. I tried to explain to the family that the most appropriate casket to go with a grave liner in this part of the country is a Tyler Uniseal." Doucet shook his head in admiration. "Now *there*'s a first-class casket. I once visited the factory in Illinois, where they have a pond with caskets that have been floating since 1972. Yessir, that's—"

"You're sayin' we're gonna find water in the grave *and* the casket?" Broussard asked.

"The liner already had water in it when we lowered him. And I could hear it bubbling into the casket even while the handling straps were being removed." Doucet held up a cautioning finger. "But the good news is that it's summer. We always use more embalming fluid in the summer. You understand . . . the heat. Not good for business if the corpse turns before the funeral."

"When can we get started?" Broussard asked.

Doucet cleared his sinuses again and looked down the narrow road in the direction of the entrance. "I told those boys to be here at nine sharp. That's the one thing about this business that's going to put me in one of my own holes."

"I got a coupla shovels in the wrecker," the sheriff said. "And I don't mind usin' one of 'em."

"Ah always been pretty good with a shovel," Bubba said.

"There won't actually be all *that* much digging to do," Doucet said. "The lid of the liner is only down a couple of feet."

Guidry got the shovels from the wrecker and handed one to Bubba. They all followed Doucet to Benoit's headstone.

"Here he is," Doucet said. "We cut the sod in one piece, so you should be able just to roll it up and set it aside."

Guidry and Bubba got down on their knees at the end of the grave opposite the headstone and worked their fingers under the sod to get it started. Then they rolled it up like a rug. Even with this little bit of work, both had begun to sweat through their shirts.

"I wish we had a piece of canvas or something to keep the dirt out of the grass," Doucet said. "But I guess we'll have to make do. Try, though, to keep the dirt in as small a pile as possible, will you?"

As Bubba and the sheriff worked with their shovels, Kit turned to say something to Broussard but found he was no longer beside her. Surveying the grounds, she saw him standing beside one of the crypts that bordered the area of headstones. Curious as to what he was doing, she went to find out.

"Anything over here I should—" The name on the gable of the crypt stopped her in midsentence. BROUSSARD. His parents.

"Nice view of the grass from here, don't you think?" Broussard said, looking back over Kit's shoulder. "My father was a perfectionist when it came to the lawn. Mother would always say he paid more attention to the grass than he did to her. He'd look at me, wink, and say, 'Well, next time I get out the hose I'd be glad to water you down, too.' Then she'd pinch his ear until he howled.

". . . Mother's," he said, running his hand along the crypt's polished marble surface. "Did you know that the placenta produces a hormone that gives the fetus first claim on the mother's blood glucose? Kind of sets the tone for the rest of the relationship, doesn't it? Show me the mother of a Nobel winner and I'll show you a woman that wasn't surprised at the news."

His eyes took on that distant look that usually meant he was about to stroke his nose. "First to see the good and last to see the bad," he said to himself. Then as quickly as he had turned inward, he was himself again. "And I'll bet you haven't talked to yours in weeks," he said, shaking his finger at her.

"Conservative estimate," she replied, feeling appropriately guilty.

"We'd better get back," he said.

When they rejoined the others, they saw that the digging had exposed the paired metal handling rings on each section of the grave's cement lid. A few minutes later, the sheriff brushed away the remaining dirt with the flat of his hand and pointed at the slab farthest from the headstone. "Let's do this one first."

Bubba nodded and both men took up a position with their backs to the headstone. Guidry looked at Doucet. "How much this thing weigh?"

"Forty . . . fifty pounds maybe."

"When we get her up, we'll just take her a coupla steps straight ahead and drop her. Ready?"

Kit didn't know whether she wanted to look or not as the lid came off. Finally, she did, and what she saw looked like a shipwreck: pieces of wood and twisted loops of fabric floating on a sea of muddy water. Nothing she saw looked like a corpse, though. Apparently, they were going to have to fish for it.

Doucet looked at the remains of the coffin and clucked his tongue. "Never pays to buy bottom of the line."

When Bubba and Guidry lifted off the second section of the lid, they found two empty beer cans bobbing amid the other flotsam.

"Disgraceful," Doucet clucked. "That's what I'm up against with my help. I should have watched while the lid was put on."

"Might not be from your men," Broussard said.

"Who then?" Doucet asked.

"Maybe whoever it was that stole the body."

Chapter 17

"How do you know the body's not under the water?" Kit asked.

"We'll have to look, but I'm sure it's not," Broussard said. He looked at Doucet. "How deep's this thing?"

"Twenty-eight inches."

"I'll check," Bubba said, grabbing a shovel. He put the blade of the shovel into the muddy water and slid it across the bottom of the liner. Then he raised everything it had caught: wood and fabric but no corpse. He repeated the procedure twice from different spots but still did not find Homer Benoit.

"How did you know he wasn't there?" Kit asked again.

"I suspected it as soon as we walked up to the grave," Broussard said. He pointed at the grass around them. "See how the grass is all bent one way by the ground keeper's lawn mower? Over Benoit's grave, it was bent in the opposite direction because someone had removed the sod and put it back wrong. Also, off to the side here, the grass is flattened. That's where they put the dirt on a piece of canvas."

"Why would someone steal a body?" Doucet asked. Even Kit knew the answer to that one.

"Not *a* body," Broussard said. "It was Homer Benoit they wanted. So we couldn't tie this murder to the ones in New Orleans. Actually, not a good move. With all the water in the grave, there was a chance I couldn't have learned much of anything from the body. This convinces me that we're on the right track. Sheriff, you might want to send those beer cans to the lab for prints."

Broussard turned at the sound of an approaching car: a BMW carrying Claude Duhon. He parked behind Kit's car and joined them at the grave site.

"You folks learned anything?" he asked. His eyes strayed to the grave and his face puckered. "That's pretty nasty-looking."

"Somebody beat us to it," Broussard said. "The body's gone, probably taken last night."

"Bizarre."

"What brings you out here?" Broussard asked.

"George Burke called a few minutes ago and said he needs to see you about something important. Wouldn't tell me what. Since I was coming this way, thought I'd stop and deliver the message. And now that I've done that, I'm going to leave you all to sort this out. I'll be here soon enough as one of Buster's clients. No point hanging around now. Olivia's expecting you for lunch at noon. And we'll both want to know all about this. So be prepared. Sheriff, good to see you. You, too, Buster."

As Claude walked to his car, Broussard turned to Guidry. "Sheriff, I'm goin' into town to see what Burke wants." Then to Doucet, he said, "What do we need to do here?"

"Don't worry about it. I'll take care of things. I'll have my people put it all back like it was. No sense letting the relatives of any of our other clients see this."

Broussard looked at Kit. "You comin' to Burke's?"

"I have to do something first. But it'll only take a few minutes. I'll meet you there."

Back in town, Kit pulled into a parking place on the square and got two dollars in change from the drugstore. She took the coins to a pay phone outside and called Broussard's office.

"Hi, Margaret? This is Kit . . . I'm fine. . . . Not sure. Things are still up in the air. Well, I'm sure you're handling it all just right. Could you transfer me to serology? Thanks."

While Kit waited, she noticed a darling skirt and blouse combination in the little dress shop beside the drugstore. And it looked like an eight. Maybe when all this was over she'd . . . "Hello, serology? This is Kit Franklyn. I sent you a bloodstain yesterday for typing. Has that been done yet . . . No, I'd rather hold if it won't take too long. See, I'm at a pay phone. . . . Thanks."

Serology had no music for those waiting. In fact, the phone sounded dead, no voices in the background, no chairs scraping the floor. Before witnessing the Benoit exhumation, she would have likened it to being buried in a coffin, but now she knew that even there you could hear dripping water and perhaps subterranean animals swimming. She shuddered, then quickened to a voice: "Your three minutes are up. Please deposit an additional dollar."

Kit fed the coin slot her last four quarters and resumed her wait. A young woman appeared in the dress-shop window carrying a folded screen that she put in front of the mannequin wearing the skirt and blouse Kit had admired. A few seconds later, the blouse lay draped on top of the screen. The skirt quickly followed. Kit's pulse quickened. All her shopping instincts said the same thing: *price reduction.*

Then from the phone: "Dr. Franklyn?"

"Yes?"

"The sample you sent tested out as type A."

Kit's head whirled. "Type A? Are you sure?"

"Quite sure." The voice in serology had taken on a slight edge at her suggestion that it might have been mistaken.

"Thank you." Moving in slow motion, Kit replaced the receiver. Type A. Eddy Guidry's blood was type A. But the killer's blood was type B. She wandered back to her car, all thoughts of the skirt and blouse gone. There had to be a mistake somewhere. Either the original typing was wrong or this one was. It all meshed too well: Guidry in New Orleans that night, somebody with him when he left town, Eddy being "sick." It all fit.

There were two people in Burke's waiting room—a girl about sixteen and a man in a business suit. From her nervous manner and the way she tried to hide behind her magazine, Broussard thought it likely the girl was there for birth-control counseling, probably without her parent's knowledge. His suit

and the large sample case at the man's feet pegged him as a
drug rep. Patsy Burke appeared behind the pass-through
counter at the end of the room.

"Andy. George had to go out on an emergency but he left
somethin' for you in case you showed up. Come on back."

Patsy led him to Burke's office and pointed at the old rolltop.
"He found somethin' in one of those smelly old books he's been
readin' that he thought you ought to know about. Didn't say
what it was and I haven't had time to read it myself. But there
it is." She then went to answer the telephone.

Lying open on the desk was one of the old ledgers that
Burke had shown him when they first got into town. Broussard made himself comfortable in Burke's chair, slipped a
lemon ball into his cheek, and picked up the ledger, whose
entries were printed in a thin, wavering scrawl.

The date at the top of the page indicated that this particular
passage had been written fourteen years ago.

A sad day. Two deaths, both of unusual circumstances.
After having nearly drowned a year ago in Buck's Bayou,
the oldest Arceneaux boy drowned today in a truckload
of soybeans, confirming my belief that few occupations
are more dangerous than farming. Then Bob Lague was
found in the swamp near his home, beaten to death and
with his throat ripped open. From the look of it, he had
been hunting frogs by searchlight when he was attacked.
The sheriff is looking for a vagrant with a dog, despite
my belief that the throat wound was not made by canine
teeth.

Frogs by searchlight. The phrase leapt off the page at him.
By searchlight . . . going boo-lie, as the locals called it.
Never go boo-lie during a full moon. The memory associated
with this warning came back to him. When he had been ten
years old, another man had been found in one of the local
swamps, murdered in the same fashion as Bob Lague. His
grandmother had told him that the man had been killed by a

loup-garou, a werewolf that had been roaming the area for a hundred years.

As a child, he had believed her. But as he grew up, he realized that much of what the old ones said was simply not the truth, and he had ceased to believe in the loup-garou. But now what was he to think? Nearly fifty years had passed since that murder in his childhood. Fourteen years ago, there had been another. And just a few weeks earlier, there had in all probability been a third. Three similar cases, the first and last separated by nearly half a century. Of course, he hadn't personally seen any of those bodies, so it could be that they weren't related at all. But if they *were*, there was something in this town that had been here since he was a boy and possibly long before. Which was ridiculous . . . unless . . .

He stood up, eager to head back to the cemetery. On the way out, he was surprised to find Henry Guidry sitting in the waiting room.

"Henry! How you doin', you old scoundrel?" Through Guidry's naturally morose expression, Broussard saw a flicker of pain. But mostly he saw anger.

"I'm not doing well at all. Hurt my back this morning pulling a bale of hay off a tailgate." He raised himself gingerly in his seat and shifted positions. "Andrew, I have to tell you that I'm disappointed in the way you're handling things over here . . . sending Franklyn to talk to Eddy behind my back. If there was anything you wanted to know, you should have come to me. I would have thought that after all the years we've known each other, that would have been the obvious thing to do."

The girl and the drug rep pretended not to be listening. Broussard, of course, had no idea what Guidry was talking about. "Henry I don't—"

Guidry looked away. "If you don't mind, I'd rather not get into it right now. I'm so upset with you that I might say something I'll be sorry for later."

As Broussard walked to his car, Kit pulled in beside it and got out to meet him. "What did Burke want?" she asked.

Bubba leaned out the window of the T-bird so he could hear, too.

"To show me somethin' he found in Doc McKenzie's ledger. Fourteen years ago, there was another killin' just like Homer Benoit." Not wanting to get into a protracted discussion on such flimsy grounds as he had, he did not mention the much older case and what it might mean.

"Then the killer *does* live here," Kit said. "But why was there such a long gap in the killings?"

"Could be there wasn't a gap. Might have been others we don't know about. Or maybe he was kept in check somehow."

"Like with medication?"

"That'd be one way." Broussard scratched his beard. "I just had a strange conversation with Henry Guidry in which he said somethin' about you talkin' to his brother, Eddy. What'd he mean?"

Since he already knew about Eddy, Kit decided it was time to tell him everything. When she got to the part about going down to the French Quarter with Bubba, the little Cajun pulled his head out of the T-bird's window and tried to become as small as possible in his seat. ". . . so when Teddy told me that Henry had a retarded brother, I just had to check him out. And believe me, nothing I saw put my mind to rest. He's impulsive, emotional, and *huge*. And he was out of sight around the time the murders in the Quarter were committed . . . said he was sick. When I talked to him, his lawn mower had thrown up a stick or a stone that cut him on the forehead, and I managed to get a blood sample, which I sent to the serology lab for typing. I would have bet anything that he was type B, the same as the killer. But I just found out he's type A. Now I don't know *what* to think. I would have told you about all this earlier, but seeing you and Henry are such close friends, I wanted to be sure of things before implicating him."

Broussard withdrew into his mental study and his finger strayed to the end of his nose. Kit waited nervously for the dressing-down she expected for withholding information. Under other circumstances, she might well have received it, but since Broussard was also withholding information from her, he could hardly complain.

About the time she thought he had rubbed all the hairs off his nose, his eyes shifted gears and he was back. "So what do you think?" she asked.

"I think we should go back to that house across from the cemetery and talk to the little boy that lives there."

"What little boy?"

"The one that watched from behind a tree while we got flimflammed at Homer Benoit's grave."

Chapter 18

To get to the house where the little boy lived, they had to cross a rickety footbridge over a stretch of black water that ran beside the road for miles. On the other side of the bridge, the path to the house wandered between boggy pools with a green scum on the surface. The house itself was a flimsy pile of weathered boards that would make good frames for watercolors. Resting on cypress stilts, the house was no impediment to the free flow of chickens that pecked and clucked over the property. Rather than facing the road, the porch to the house looked out on a small vegetable garden that was half underwater from all the rain. Hanging on the wall fronting the street were three drying animal skins and a large galvanized tub.

In the yard beside the house, a woman was cleaning fish on a crude wooden table with a hole in it. She was wearing a Mick Jagger T-shirt bearing a picture of a large tongue, faded by many washings. The six inches of long straight hair nearest her skull was the color of the boards on the house, the rest matched the dun color of the chicken pecking around her bare toes. Though she looked to be a late-stage anorectic, it didn't affect her ability to clean fish, for she was the epicenter of a storm of fish scales that neither Kit nor her two colleagues wished to enter.

Behind her, legs hanging over the porch, was a boy about

ten years old dressed in coveralls and with no shirt. He was shucking oysters and throwing the shells on a large pile from previous shuckings. Each time a shell hit the pile, a blue carpet of flies rose angrily into the air.

"Mornin'," Broussard said.

The woman looked up and brushed the hair from her sunken eyes with her elbow. "You want somethin'?" Her lips paid more attention to the cigarette between them than to her words. With a break in the scale storm, her three visitors stepped closer.

Broussard introduced everybody and said, "Somethin' kind of unusual happened last night over at the cemetery and we were wonderin' if you folks saw anything."

The woman shook her head. "Ah got too much work to do without worryin' what goes on ain't none of mah business."

"Maybe the boy saw somethin'."

"So ask him."

As they walked over to the boy, the woman resumed work on her fish.

"Findin' any pearls?" Broussard said.

The boy shook his head and made a face like he wasn't expecting to find any. "What's your name, son?"

"Ain't got one. Lost it over in dat swamp one day when mah pirogue sank."

Broussard chuckled and dug around in his pocket, bringing out two of the wrapped lemon balls he had brought for Kit. He held them out to the boy, who casually inspected them, then wrinkled his nose and looked away. "Do you know who we are?" Broussard asked. Behind him, he heard a slap as Kit flattened a mosquito attempting to feed on her arm.

"Heard you tell ma your names but don' remember 'em."

"We're the folks you were watchin' a little while ago in the cemetery."

The boy threw an oyster shell at one of the chickens, which squawked and high-stepped to safety. "Didn' say Ah was in da cemetery," the boy said, sticking the point of his knife into the porch floor.

"Don't have to; I saw you there," Broussard said. "What I'm

wonderin' is, did you see anybody else there last night . . . diggin'?"

The boy pulled the knife out of the floor and stuck it in again. "Maybe Ah did an' maybe Ah didn'."

Kit was growing impatient at Broussard's inept handling of the boy. "Let me try," she said, stepping forward. "Son, we're not being nosy. This is a police matter. Some people . . . innocent people in New Orleans and some of your neighbors have been murdered and we're trying to find out who did it. This person is very dangerous and until we catch him, anyone around here, even you or your mother, could be his next victim. So for your own safety, you should tell us what you saw." From the look on the boy's face, Kit could see she was getting to him. "Besides protecting your mother, you'd be acting as sort of a deputy sheriff."

The boy stared at Kit for several seconds without speaking, his mouth slightly open. Then he said with more sarcasm than a ten-year-old should be able to muster, "Deputy sheriff? Wow am *Ah* impressed."

Bubba had been hanging a few steps back while his two colleagues worked on the boy. Now he stepped up and whispered into the boy's ear. When he was finished, the boy looked at Broussard with wide eyes. "It was dat guy with da fat gut, works at da gator farm."

"Carl Fitch," Kit said.

"He dug up somethin' an' took it away in his truck," the boy said.

"Appreciate you tellin' us that," Broussard said.

"You welcome."

Broussard turned to go, then hesitated and asked the boy, "You ever go into Leper's Woods?"

The boy seemed astonished at the question. "Jus' cause Ah'm a kid don' mean Ah'm stupid," he said.

Broussard gave Kit a look that said "Didn't I tell you?"

As they passed the boy's mother, she scraped a fish head and a pile of guts into a hole in the table. Some of it missed the bucket on the ground. "Never knew da boy to back down before," she said, the cigarette bobbing between her lips. She pointed her knife at Bubba. "Mister, you got a way with young'uns. There a woman shares your bed?"

Blushing, Bubba shook his head.

"You ever get in a marryin' mood, you know where to find me."

When they were out of hearing range, Kit said, "What did you say to him, Bubba?"

"Ah tol' him that if he didn' tell us what he saw, Ah was gonna catch him alone and put his bare butt in a hill of fire ants."

"Bubba, you're terrible."

"Dat's what Gramma O keeps tellin' me."

"What now?" Kit said to Broussard.

"Go over to the gator farm and talk to Fitch."

Suddenly from the grass at Kit's feet, there was a squawk and a flap of feathers—a nesting hen that barely escaped being stepped on. Surprised by the ruckus, Kit shied into a boggy puddle that claimed one leg almost to the knee. Bubba rushed to help.

"Gimme your hand."

The puddle gave up her leg reluctantly, succumbing finally with an obscene sucking sound. Back on solid ground, Kit looked at the mud and algae on her slacks. "I don't think it's a look that'll catch on," she said. There was no way she was going to let Teddy see her in such a state. "Much as I hate to miss the action, I've got to change clothes. You two go on. I'll meet you there."

Broussard and Bubba followed Kit back into town, where Broussard used the pay phone in front of the drugstore to call Sheriff Guidry.

"What'd he say?" Bubba asked when Broussard came back to the car.

"Wasn't there. Supposed to be back any minute. I left a message for him to meet us at the gator farm."

"You think we oughtta be goin' over dere alone? Might be we're gonna stir up some trouble."

"We'll be careful not to push anybody into a corner. There

are ways to get information without accusin' folks of anything."

At the turnoff to the alligator farm, they met Teddy LaBiche coming from the direction of the interstate in his pickup. He waved and stopped in the middle of the road. Broussard pulled up alongside.

"How did everything go this morning?" Teddy asked.

"Not good. Somebody took the body for a ride. Got information that Carl Fitch might know somethin' about it." Broussard watched Teddy's face closely. The surprise he saw there seemed genuine enough. Broussard let his eyes wander to the back of Teddy's truck, where the bed was covered by a black tarp held in place by snap-top fasteners. He had first noticed it last night. At the time, the observation had meant nothing. Now though . . .

"Why don't we go talk to Fitch," Teddy suggested.

"He at work?"

"Supposed to be, but with Carl, you can never be sure. I haven't been in yet myself. So I guess we'll find out together."

Broussard followed Teddy to the farm and they both parked in the lot beside the processing building.

"There's Carl's truck down there," Teddy said, pointing at the road where it bordered the breeding pen. "But I don't see Carl. Come on, we'll find him."

Teddy looked first in the office and then they searched the processing center without luck. "Nothing to do now but work our way through the holding buildings," Teddy said. "Which makes me even more convinced that we need an intercom system connected to the office."

At Teddy's request, Broussard and Bubba let Teddy search each building by himself so that the alligators inside would be disturbed as little as possible, an arrangement that seemed reasonable. After ten minutes of this, they still had not found Fitch. To get to the last set of buildings on the property, they had to pass Fitch's truck.

"Been here awhile," Broussard said, checking the temperature of the hood with his hand. He looked in the cab and then the bed, which was clean except for one muddy smear near the tailgate.

"*Mon Dieu . . . ?*"

Turning to see what had caused Teddy's outburst, Broussard found him staring into the breeding pen, where about twenty yards out, several large gray-white objects bulged from the black water. "What is it?"

"Looks like dead gators," Teddy said. "At least three of them."

"Can we get one up on the bank for a look?"

"You don't want to keep looking for Fitch?"

"Right now, I'd rather see one of those gators."

"Me, too," Teddy replied. "We can use our egg-collecting boat there." He pointed behind them to a metal boat upside down on three sawhorses beside the road. "But first we'll need some rope." He jogged to a nearby supply shed and returned wearing a pair of knee-high rubber boots and carrying a large coil of heavy rope. "I'll need a hand with the boat."

"That'd be me," Bubba said.

The two men turned the boat over and carried it to the gate in the chain link that surrounded the breeding pen. "Okay, Bubba put her down for a minute." Teddy threw the rope in the boat and opened the gate. "Let's change ends; I've got the boots, so I should have the bow." As Bubba bent to pick up his end, Teddy added, "Just be careful not to rattle the fence. That's what we do to call them in for feeding."

Bubba stood up, confused. "Ah thought dey were dead?"

"Looks like only three of them. There're about a hundred in here."

Bubba's mouth dropped open.

"Don't worry, they're shy of boat sounds."

"Den we oughtta make a lotta boat sounds," Bubba said.

"And I've always got this." Teddy showed Bubba his little pistol.

Bubba nodded and smiled anemically.

With Bubba's eye's searching for alligators, Teddy carried the bow into the water. When Bubba's feet reached the end of the cement apron that bordered the water, they put the boat down and Bubba pounded on the side with his hand. "Boat noises," he explained, looking at Broussard.

Teddy came around to the side and climbed in. He released one of the oars from its fastenings and laid it across the seat, making, Bubba noticed, a gratifying amount of boat sounds. "Bubba, you pole us out to that one over there and I'll work the rope."

Teddy took the rope to the bow, where his weight allowed Bubba to push the boat into the water while getting only the tip of one shoe wet. Accustomed to poling his pirogue down Goose Bayou—the body of water that ran past his log house outside New Orleans—Bubba smoothly propelled the boat forward until Teddy held his hand up in a signal to slow down. Bubba let the oar drag against the bottom.

Teddy leaned over and lifted a very large scaly tail out of the water. Pinning it against the boat, he worked a noose down it as far as he could, then tightened the slip knot with a flourish. "That's it. Take us in my friend."

They switched ends and Bubba poled them back to shore while Teddy let out rope as they went. "We're going to have to get this carcass through the gate," Teddy said. "So take us in a little to one side so the boat isn't in the way."

Bubba nodded and wiped the sweat out of his eyes. A few minutes later, the bottom of the boat scraped against the cement apron. Broussard held the boat steady while Teddy and Bubba got out. Then they all pulled it up onto the apron.

"What happened?" a voice behind them said. It was one of the young men Kit had seen the day before in the processing building.

"Don't know yet," Teddy said. "Found a couple of our breeders dead. We got one on the end of this rope. Give us a hand, will you?"

Together, they pulled the heavy reptile toward them until the end of its tail lay on the apron. Teddy and his helper then retied the rope around both of the animal's thighs.

"Easy part's over," Teddy said, looping the rope around one hand and offering the free end to the others.

When all four had a good grip on the rope, Teddy gave the

signal to pull and the carcass slowly began to slide out of the water.

"How much dis thing weigh?" Bubba gasped from his position right behind Teddy.

"If I told you, you might quit," Teddy said.

Finally, with all of them breathing hard and their shirts wet with sweat, the huge reptile lay across the road.

"Congratulations," Teddy said, fanning himself with his straw hat. "You've gotten the best of about seven hundred pounds of dead weight."

"Any objections to opening him up?" Broussard asked.

"How do you know it's a him?" Teddy said.

"Thickness of the body, rugged look to the head."

"You know your gators," Teddy said. "Buddy, get us a skinning knife, will you?"

"Got one right here in my car."

While they waited for Buddy to get back, Teddy crouched at the animal's jaws. "Gator like this ever gets hold of you, you couldn't pry his jaws apart with a crowbar. When you're had by a gator, you're had good. Couple years ago, I saw a big one close on a piece of steel with so much force, he drove two of his teeth through the top of his head." He stood up and looked wistfully over the water. "Sure hope it's only three. You can't get insurance on gators."

"Here you go," Buddy said, handing Teddy a large knife.

"Let's get him over on his back," Teddy said.

The animal was so distended with gas that it resembled an inflatable fake more than a real alligator, unless of course you looked at its teeth. To preserve the skin, whose value would partially mitigate the loss of the animal as a breeder, Teddy made a large incision along the junction of the desirable belly scales with the worthless armor on the back, cutting through the musculature but being careful not to go so deep that the bloated stomach might be punctured. He carried the cut up and around the jawline and brought it down the other side, completing the circle with a transverse incision just in front of the hind legs. He rolled up the freed section of flesh and laid it on the ground a few feet away, planning to separate the skin from the muscle later. Maggoty white and obscenely distended with gas, the stomach dominated the peritoneal landscape.

Teddy waved his knife at his helper. "Buddy, there's a piece of Visquine in the shed over there. Get it for me, will you?"

When Buddy returned with the clear plastic, Teddy folded it double and draped it across the animal's exposed organs, letting it lap onto the road on each side. He instructed Buddy to stand on one of the flaps and stationed Bubba on the other. Then he plunged his knife through the plastic and into the stomach.

There was a muffled explosion that lifted the plastic cover so violently that it almost jerked Bubba off his feet. The force of it splattered the underside of the plastic with a foamy green scum. When Teddy pulled the cover aside, the air was filled with a stench worse than the smell of any floater that Broussard had ever encountered. The sudden release of pressure had ripped the stomach in both directions from Teddy's initial incision and a putrescent green ooze now issued slowly from the gash. Eyes watering, Teddy put his knife in the split and raked it toward the tail. His eyes were tearing so badly that the others saw the partially digested hand before he did.

Mouth full of brass, Buddy turned away, his own stomach churning at the sight. Now Teddy saw it. He wiped his eyes and looked closer. The hand was wearing a ring he recognized. "It's Carl," Teddy croaked.

Chapter 19

"This is all my fault," Teddy moaned. "I should have fired him months ago. Then this would have—"

"I have a hunch this might have happened whether you had fired him or not," Broussard said. "May I?" He held his hand out for the knife and Teddy gave it to him. With it, Broussard opened a long flap in the stomach and used its tip to prowl through the contents while the others hung back. Finally, he stood up and returned the knife. "Unless Carl Fitch had two right hands," he said, "we've also found Homer Benoit. And I'd guess the rest of him and some more of Fitch, too, is in those other two dead gators. Likely, it was the embalmin' fluid that killed 'em."

"Carl must have been teasing them with pieces of—" Teddy stopped, apparently unable to finish his gruesome thought. "But why? What did he have to gain by getting rid of Benoit's body?"

Broussard looked at Teddy through eyes that burned with the thrill of the chase. "All depends."

"On what?"

"On a phone call I need to make. Is there . . ."

"Up in the office."

While Teddy watched from the doorway with more than casual interest, Broussard jabbed at the telephone buttons and gave the operator his calling card number. A short wait, then

he said, "Lieutenant Gatlin, please." He looked at the identi-
fication sticker on the phone, recited the number of the
alligator farm, and hung up.

"He'll call back. Usually only takes a few minutes."

Teddy nodded, needing a whole lot more than *that* for an
explanation.

Not wanting the Duhons to see her so filthy, Kit parked behind
the house and looked for the entrance to the rear stairwell that
opened onto the second floor near her bedroom. She found it
off a dark passage in a primitive attached structure that
probably served as a kitchen back when the cooking had been
done by slaves. Here, the stairwell was crudely constructed
and merely painted. A dozen or so steps up, there was a heavy
door that led to the main house. The door opened onto a
finished landing with one set of steps leading up and another
down.

To keep from getting the stairwell carpeting dirty, Kit
removed her muddy shoes and started up the stairs that
almost certainly led to the second-floor gallery. Then she
paused, her attention taken by a small rectangular window
that looked down on the kitchen, where she saw Olivia
stacking finger sandwiches on a plate and the butler, Martin,
puttering around a wicker picnic basket. The purpose for such
an oddly placed window was not apparent. But since it could
be opened like a transom, Kit supposed it had been put in long
ago so that the lady of the house could communicate with the
help without going all the way downstairs. Realizing that this
was not furthering her wish to rejoin Broussard and Bubba,
Kit pulled herself away from the window and continued up the
stairs.

Even if time had not been a factor, she would have chosen
the shower rather than the elegant ivory claw-foot tub with
gold faucets that sat regally in the center of her bathroom.
After all, weren't tub rings proof that you can't get really clean
from a bath?

It wasn't until she emerged from the shower that she

realized there were no towels, none on the towel rack and none in any of the drawers in the built-in vanity. Now what?

Maybe in the bedroom.

She tiptoed across the plush carpet to the chest of drawers beside the door to the hall and checked there. No luck. Turning, she saw her unclothed reflection in the huge mirror over the marble fireplace mantel and modestly covered as much of herself as she could with her hands. She considered using her blouse as a towel, but rejected that idea when she remembered that it was pure acrylic, a fact that would make it about as useful as waxed paper.

The trunk at the foot of the bed, perhaps there were towels there. She went to the trunk and lifted the lid. Inside, she found a crocheted bedspread, under that, a sweater, a tablecloth, a couple of thin blankets, and that was all . . . except for . . . On the bottom of the trunk was a photograph . . . a picture of . . .

She picked up the snapshot and studied the face of the subject, a face that she had seen before, the same yet not the same. She turned the picture over and saw something that stirred the thick gumbo of facts simmering in her head.

She put the picture back where she had found it and patted herself as dry as she could with the bedspread from the trunk. Though still annoyingly moist, she dressed quickly and went to the window so she could see to hook the tiny clasp on the band of her wristwatch. As she finished, she saw Martin heading for the boat dock, the wicker picnic basket in one hand, a rifle in the other. While she watched, he placed the rifle and the basket in one of the pirogues tied up to the dock and got in. He began to paddle toward a gap in the trees on the opposite side of the bayou.

The simmering gumbo began to boil.

She rushed down the front stairs and ran to the boat dock, but Martin had already disappeared. Having no thought beyond the moment, she stepped into the remaining pirogue and nearly pitched into the water as it tilted crazily under her weight. With the boat jiggling ominously from side to side, she somehow managed to sit down without creating a disaster.

When she reached for the rope that tied the boat to the dock, her heart flew into her throat for the second time as the boat tipped wildly, nearly sinking it. This wasn't transportation. It was a damn carnival ride.

Careful to keep her center of gravity inside the boat, she pulled the pirogue tight against the dock and slipped the mooring rope off its cleat. Now, how do you make this thing go?

She picked up the worn gray paddle in the bottom of the boat and fiddled with it until the grip felt right. Then she took a swipe at the water with it. This also nearly sank the boat. *Don't lean out!* she reminded herself sternly. It quickly became obvious that you had to alternate strokes from side to side if you wanted to do anything but go in a circle. Soon she was heading across the bayou, not in a direct course, but tacking, like a sailboat going against the wind.

When she entered the cut, she saw two channels on the other side, one to her right and one to her left. Both channels curved sharply forty or fifty yards into them, so she couldn't see what lay ahead. Both were also choked with water hyacinths except for a narrow trail of recently disturbed plants running down the middle of the one on her left, the one that led into Leper's Woods.

She hesitated, picturing sackcloth-draped figures moving silently through the woods, their crutches guided by fingerless hands, spreading the leprosy bacillus on the trees, on the leaves. She saw them getting bitten by mosquitoes that would suck up the bacillus along with the lepers' blood and pass it to anything they bit, as well as giving it to the next generation of mosquitoes, which would give it to the next and the next, so that years after the lepers moved on, the place would still be dangerous.

Ouch. Heart leaping, Kit slapped at a biting sensation on the nape of her neck. Her fingers pulled back at what they felt; not a mosquito, something smooth and repulsive, like a beetle, but not a beetle . . . flatter . . . something flat . . . feeding.

Lips curled with loathing, she sent her nails after it, picked at the object until it came free. She brought it around to her eyes and sighed with relief. Nothing but a harmless fish scale—from the house where they had spoken to the boy. She told herself to calm down. There was no danger of leprosy. Hadn't Broussard himself said so? And wasn't he always right? As an answer, she sent the pirogue toward the faint path through the hyacinths.

Keeping the boat on a straight course required such concentration that she ceased to notice the pregnant silence in the air, which, if anything, had deepened in the hours since she and Broussard had first discussed it. The gray sky seemed to hang just above the treetops, capping the swamp like the lid on a pressure cooker, holding the heat from its decaying vegetation close to the earth.

The hyacinths made it hard to find the water with her paddle and they pressed against the side of the boat, slowing her progress, sapping her strength. Sweat bled through the knees of her slacks, making Rorschach patterns that reminded her that she had only one more change of clothes. Her blouse clung to her back and she could feel the wet grip of her panties on her thighs.

Still she kept on, unaware of the cold eyes that followed her progress, oblivious to the seven-millibar drop in barometric pressure that had occurred between 2:00 and 3:00 A.M. that morning.

After fighting the hyacinths for another thirty yards, she rounded the bend that had obscured her view. Her spirits rose. For up ahead, pulled onto the bank, was the other pirogue.

Another five minutes of hard work and she was there, her hands throbbing from the pressure of the paddle. She gave a final stroke and put the paddle in her lap while the bow of the pirogue nosed toward shore. Her fingers had become so accustomed to the paddle that they were reluctant to give it up.

The pirogue landed with a soft thud and Kit carefully worked her way to the bow and stepped onto spongy moss-covered earth. She hadn't known what to expect back here, but what she saw was a distinct surprise. Ten yards away, set into the dense foliage that ran beside the bayou, was an old cemetery surrounded by a crumbling iron fence. The only path led directly into it. So where was Martin?

Reluctant to move, she paused and listened. But there was nothing to hear. Suddenly, she felt eyes on her back. She turned quickly and scanned the marshy woods on both sides of the channel that intersected the bayou on the opposite bank. Nothing there. Your imagination, she thought, turning back to the path. Across the bayou, cold, unblinking eyes patiently watched her . . . waiting.

She did not want to go into the cemetery, but what was she to do, go back having learned nothing—after all that work? Cautiously, she moved toward the path, her ears straining for sounds that would help her judge the situation.

The hinges on the cemetery gate had rusted through and someone had lifted the gate out of the way and leaned it against the section of fence to the right of the entrance, a long time ago, judging from the thick woody vine that had wrapped around its bars. There were about a dozen crypts in the small plot, all of them covered with vines and moss. The inscriptions were largely illegible, being either covered by moss or dissolved away by many decades of rain. Even so, as Kit followed the well-worn path that wound between the crypts, she could make out an occasional name. And it was always the same: Villery.

Villery.

The name was like a small hand tugging at her clothing, but she was too preoccupied with finding the butler to pay attention.

The path led to a crypt that resembled a Greek temple, with stone columns down each side and sitting up on a four-tiered platform, so that the first three layers formed steps that surrounded the crypt on all sides. And that's where the path ended.

Puzzled, Kit waded through the tall grass and went around to the right side of the crypt, thinking she might pick up the path there. But all she saw was more grass. At the rear of the cemetery, the back fence was attached directly to the side of the crypt. On the other side of the fence, running parallel to it for as far as she could see, was a dense stand of bamboo that was taller even than the crypt roof. The butler had clearly not gone this way.

She retraced her steps and looked on the other side of the crypt: same scene. So where the devil was he? As she pondered the question, she became aware of a low humming sound . . . mechanical, like . . . an air conditioner. It seemed to be coming from behind the crypt.

She went up the crypt steps and studied the huge block of stone that sealed the entrance. Halfway down the left edge of the block was a stone lion's head with its mouth open. And in its mouth she saw . . . a keyhole. Hoping that those lepers Broussard had mentioned hadn't had *their* rotten fingers on it, Kit wrapped her hands around the lion's head and threw her weight onto her heels. The stone swung open as easily as her own front door. Now she knew where Martin had gone, for the crypt, which was empty and had no back wall, led to a path through the bamboo.

With absolutely no idea of what she would say if she should suddenly meet Martin coming the other way, she moved into the crypt, leaving the door standing open in case she might want to make a quick exit.

The bamboo was very tall and the path through it looked gloomy and dark. Too stubborn to turn back, she went down the stone steps of the crypt and stepped onto the path. Entering the bamboo was like passing into another world, a dark place where the rules that governed events in the light might not apply. She proceeded cautiously, comforted on the one hand by the fact that the bamboo was so dense that she was vulnerable from only two directions. But this also meant she could easily be trapped if someone closed and locked the crypt door. About ten feet in, the path curved to the right, then back to the left. Suddenly, she was in a clearing.

At first, she was confused by what she saw: something large and green with a dark cleft in it . . . a house, painted to blend with the foliage and covered with leafy vines. The cleft was a door and on the ground in front of the door . . .

She rushed to the butler's body and recoiled in horror, for he had no head, at least nothing that resembled one. Where his head should have been, there was only hair and bloody pulp. And his throat—it was gaping open so that he looked like some gilled creature that had been pulled from the swamp and left to die.

Kit's head spun, and she began to gasp for air, the sheer horror of the scene driving the breath from her body. She heard herself grunting like an animal but couldn't stop. She forced her eyes from the carnage and her lungs pulled at the hot swamp air, which suddenly seemed devoid of oxygen.

Gradually, she got hold of herself. Her breathing slowed and her head began to clear. The pounding in her skull faded. But she was still grunting.

Grunting.

No, *not* her. *Behind* her.

She whirled around and the sweat running down her back turned to ice. Standing in the black doorway was a hulking figure wearing a tan jumpsuit splatted with blood. He was bent over in a simian stance, a heavy table leg clutched in one hand. The face was the same as in the photograph from the trunk in her room, but changed, distorted from human to inhuman, the brow beetled, the jaw jutting, eyes sunken and burning with purpose. Spittle dribbled from the corner of its mouth, mixing with the butler's blood.

Kit ran, ran like she had never run before. She plunged into the gloomy path through the bamboo. The boat. Must get to the boat. She could hear him behind her, grunting. The fear inside her pressed against her chest, threatening to rip her apart. How close was he? She didn't dare look. It sounded as though he could reach out and grab her.

Something pulled at the neck of her shirt, but she was too frightened to scream. Then she was free of it. The second turn in the path. Now she could see the crypt. Would the door be locked?

The grunting behind her was practically in her ear. She felt a breeze blow past the back of her head and heard the club crash into the bamboo beside the path as he swung wildly at her. Her toe missed the first step to the crypt and she nearly went to her knees, but she caught herself with her hands. As she barreled through the crypt, the stone walls threw her own ragged breathing back in her face.

Out in the open. Down the steps. Moving too slowly. Too slowly. Onto the path.

Again she felt a breeze lift her hair, followed by the sound of wood striking stone. The gate . . . nearly there. The boat . . .

NO!

Her boat was floating several lengths from shore. Without hesitation, she ran to the butler's boat and, in one motion, gripped the sides and pushed with all her remaining strength. The boat slid a short distance into the water and then stopped, having reached the end of its rope, which had been looped around a metal stake driven into the ground. Unable to check her momentum, Kit's hands slid along the boat's gunnels, picking up splinters that knifed into her skin. She lost her balance and slammed onto the seat midway between the bow and the stern, knocking all the air out of her. She slid across the seat and crashed into the bottom of the boat, hitting her head on the rear seat support.

A bright light mushroomed behind her eyes and broke into a multicolored shower of sparks that glowed brightly and then died, to be replaced by a shrill voice screaming for oxygen. She rolled onto her back and sucked air through her mouth. Coming off the peak of pain and need, she plunged again into the depths of stark horror, for standing to her left was the lycanthrope, the club poised over his head.

The club began its descent. She covered her face with her hands. The boat was rocked by the blow and she heard the sound of splintering wood as a fiery finger slashed across her forehead.

Blood.

She felt it run, wet and warm, into her ear.

The force of the first blow had been largely taken by the rear seat and the side of the boat, which now had a gaping hole in it that almost reached the waterline. She had been struck by only a sharp edge of the club, but now, with most of her protection destroyed, she would be an easy target.

He swung the club over his head again and Kit tried to flatten herself against the bottom of the boat. Her hands felt something hard beside her: Martin's rifle. Somehow she got it around in front of her.

Actually, it wasn't a rifle at all, but an old Ithaca single-barrel twelve-gauge, which was one of the most fortunate events in Kit's life, for she knew nothing about guns and would have been thwarted by a safety. She pointed the wavering barrel at the leering face above her and her brain screamed, *Take this you son of a bitch*, as she pulled the trigger.

Jammed.

The gun was jammed. Or . . .

Remembering all the cowboy movies she had seen as a kid in the little theater back in Speculator, New York, her thumb went to the hammer and pulled it back. An instant later, she closed her eyes and fired.

The recoil tore the gun from her hand and it toppled onto her, the hammer digging into her belly. Her nostrils were stung by the acrid odor of gunpowder and she heard the lycanthrope roar in pain. She opened her eyes in time to see him stagger backward, a red stain spreading over the left arm of his jumpsuit. *Your* blood this time, Kit thought triumphantly.

He disappeared from view and Kit struggled to a sitting position, expecting to see him on the ground. But he was still standing. It wasn't enough.

He wasn't hurt enough.

When Broussard came out of Teddy's office after talking to Phil Gatlin, everything had fallen into place. He knew who the murderer was. But he wasn't happy. He was worried, because he had let Kit . . .

In the distance, he heard a gunshot, from the direction of Leper's Woods.

"How far are we from the Duhon place?" he asked, a cold hand closing around his heart.

"Not far," Teddy said. "From the turnoff, the road runs around behind the town, so it's just behind those trees."

"That airboat down there, is it gassed up?"

"Sure, why?"

"I think Kit may be in trouble at the Duhons'."

"Then let's go," Teddy said, breaking into a run. Fat as he was, Broussard could still move when he had to, and Teddy was only a few steps ahead of him when they reached the dead alligator.

"C'mon," Broussard said to Bubba as they sped past. "I think Kit needs us. Buddy, when the sheriff gets here, tell him we're at the Duhons'."

The three men piled aboard Teddy's boat and Bubba threw off the mooring line. Teddy reached for the ignition and turned the key. The big engine in the wire cage sputtered and caught but did not start. He cranked it again with the same results. "Damn it," he muttered, trying again.

Seeing that the engine was nothing more than the motor from an old Chevy, Bubba reached into his pocket and said, "Open dat cage."

Teddy opened it and got out of Bubba's way. With the screwdriver on his Swiss army knife, Bubba made some adjustments on the carburetor. "Try it now."

Teddy turned the ignition key and the engine coughed, sputtered, ran spasmodically for a few seconds, then died. "Again," Bubba urged, turning his finger in a small circle in the air.

The engine coughed, shuddered for a few cycles, then began to run smoothly. Bubba shut the cage and barely had time to get to his seat before Teddy opened her up. Soon the boat was flying down the bayou, the sound of the engine a deafening roar in their ears. Up ahead, an egret sitting on a partially submerged log across the bayou awkwardly lifted itself into the air and sought quieter surroundings. The boat closed on the log and greased over it with ease.

They shot through a cut into the open swamp, a myriad of small lakes and channels that crisscrossed between boggy islands of cypress and tupelo ringed with saw grass. Teddy turned the wheel sharply and the boat skidded to the left. It seemed to Broussard that it had been a very long time since they had heard the gunshot.

Teddy jabbed his finger at a cut in the trees coming up on the left and angled toward it. It was a place that he had not entered for many years, not since someone had cut down a huge cypress and allowed it to fall across the entrance.

Gradually over the years, the tree had sunk deeper into the muck at the bottom of the bayou, but it was still a foot out of the water, much too high to simply slide over as he had that other one. He brought the boat in close and cruised slowly past the obstacle. . . .Maybe . . . just maybe . . .

He poured on the gas, took the boat out for a running start, and spun it around. Throttle open all the way, he sped toward the tree. Having even helped *build* airboats, Bubba had known that the first log back by the alligator farm would be no problem. He was just as certain that there was no way they could clear *this* one. As they closed on it, his eyes widened and his hands gripped the seat like channel locks. Broussard was holding on just as tightly, thinking of all the folks in Orleans Parish who had looked forward to a day of boating and ended up in his care as a maimed corpse. It was not the way he expected to die. Poisoned by a chef who didn't know how to properly prepare fugu, maybe, but not in a boating accident.

Teddy pointed the blunt bow toward two closely spaced branches on the cypress that came off the tree about eight inches above the waterline and ran at an angle down into the water. "Hold on."

The boat hurtled up the submerged branches and shot into the air. Bubba felt his cap blow off but refused to let loose of his seat to save it. They landed with a jolt that made Bubba's teeth snap and would have caused the loss of Broussard's glasses had it not been for the tether on the earpieces.

On this side of the fallen cypress, the bayou went in two directions: to the right, where they would have eventually found Kit, and to the left. To take advantage of the two branches he had used so successfully, Teddy had come in at an angle that had led him naturally into the wrong channel.

Chapter 20

The lycanthrope stood with a bewildered look on his face, the club dangling by his side, blood trickling down the opposite leg and onto the ground. Kit prayed that he was mortally wounded and just hadn't realized it yet. But it was a prayer unanswered, for he bared his teeth and charged, a growl rattling in his throat.

She tried to get out of the boat, but her vision blurred and she fell backward. Dimly, she became aware of a splashing sound as the lycanthrope waded into the bayou.

Her vision cleared. Once again, he was standing over her, this time with a strange bubbling sound in his breathing. Below her line of sight, his blood ran into the bayou, mingling with the black water. His arms lifted, carrying the club into the air. Kit remembered the butler, his head crushed, his brains . . . She tried to move, to raise her legs to ward off the blow, but they wouldn't respond.

In this last moment of her life, she wondered what would become of Lucky when she didn't return for him. Would the vet find him a good home or would he send him to the pound? It wasn't fair that Lucky should have to suffer for her mistakes. The club began to descend and she closed her eyes for the last time.

There was a loud splash and a scream. The club crashed into her. . . .

No . . . not the club.

She opened her eyes but could see nothing. A heavy weight lay across her, then it was sliding, scraping across her face. Whatever it was, was squirming and she heard more screaming, much closer than before . . . beside her. The lycanthrope's face slid over her own, his mouth moving against hers as he screamed.

The boat tilted to the damaged side, taking on water. The lycanthrope slid into the bayou and his head went under, his scream changing abruptly to a cascade of bubbles. The water exploded. A huge tail whipped out of the hyacinths and tore more wood out of the hole the club had made in the boat. Through the enlarged hole, Kit could see the water boiling, a bloody soup of hyacinths, brown scales, and tan fabric.

Then the bayou grew quiet. A bit of tan fabric buoyed by an air pocket bobbed to the surface, pushing aside broken hyacinths. A few feet away, the back of the lycanthrope's head appeared. Drawn by an unseen force, the head began to move through the water, away from the boat. Kit let out the breath it seemed like she had been holding for hours.

It was over. She was safe. She was not going to die.

Still weak from belly flopping into the boat and hitting her head on the seat support, she threw each arm over the gunnel and pulled herself to a sitting position. The resulting pain on the top of her head felt like a cap she could reach up and touch.

She knew she was sitting in water and she planned to do something about it in a few minutes. Her eyes drifted over the flowering carpet that stretched down the bayou, so pretty, yet so deceptive, hiding scaly death beneath it.

A dozen feet out, the hyacinths began to move, something under them bumping their roots. She could judge its progress as more and more of the plants came under its influence. There was no mistaking the direction. It was heading for the hole in the boat.

Three feet away, two black eyes broke to the surface, emotionless eyes that didn't know the difference between innocence and guilt, eyes that didn't care whether you already had been to hell once that day.

The hyacinths in front of the eyes rose into the air and floated to the side, carried by the rivulets of water that ran between the valleys on an armored snout. The creature filled itself with air and its enormous length popped to the surface. Its mouth opened and a mind-numbing hiss erupted from its glottis as a powerful flick of its tail propelled it forward like a missile. Its head went up and over the gunnel. Kit was sure it had her, but its heavy jaw muscles caught on the jagged wood where the club had wrecked the boat, so that the force of its charge simply pushed the pirogue sideways. Kit flattened herself against the side wall, the gator's sharp yellow teeth barely an inch from her face.

She could see directly into the animal's glistening white mouth, could see the huge tongue lolling there, the narrow opening into its throat. It hissed again and she could feel the wind blow across her eyes and could smell the half-digested frogs in its gullet. Its jaws snapped shut and it threw its head from side to side, splintering wood, its tail lashing the water.

As Teddy guided the airboat the wrong way, Broussard looked down a cross channel and saw the commotion the big gator was causing. He also saw the two pirogues. He rushed to Teddy and yanked on his shirt. When Teddy looked at him, Broussard made a circling motion with his finger and jerked his thumb back toward the cross channel.

Teddy nodded and put the boat into a tight turn. They shot into the cross channel and flew over the meadow of hyacinths like a hydrofoil, barely disturbing them. Teddy saw the alligator and also a pair of arms looped over the gunnel on the pirogue under attack. As much as he hoped they weren't Kit's arms, he knew they were.

The boat's engine missed a beat, then another. It sputtered for a few seconds, gave a last surge, and quit. Succulent hyacinth fingers grabbed at the hull, dragging the boat to a halt. Bubba rushed to the engine, his army knife already out, but he tripped on a life jacket none of them had thought to put on and the knife flew from his hand. It went through the wire cage and lodged in an inaccessible crevice between the engine and its mount.

The alligator slid backward and sank from sight. Kit felt a momentary rush of relief. But where had it gone? Not seeing it was almost as horrible as having its head in her face.

Teddy knew where it had gone. He pictured it curling its tail against the soft bottom, preparing to launch itself into the pirogue.

Suddenly, the water exploded and the great reptile came hurtling toward her, its mouth gaping. . . .

Kit heard six puny sounds like a ruler slapping a table. The alligator writhed in midair, its convulsions altering its course so that it crashed onto the rear of the pirogue, crushing the flimsy wood and tumbling back into the water. It rolled onto its back and grew still, its legs in the air like a cat wanting its belly scratched.

Still a good forty yards away, Teddy put the empty chrome pistol back in his pocket and relaxed, for he had seen enough head-shot gators to know that this one wasn't going to be bothering anyone ever again.

Bubba retrieved his knife and got the boat's engine working. After hearing a very abbreviated version of what she had been through, they gathered Kit up and headed for the Duhons' boat dock, where they found the Duhons, the sheriff, and Henry Guidry waiting.

Teddy cut the engine and let the boat glide along the dock, so it had almost stopped on its own by the time it nudged the shore. As Broussard and Teddy helped Kit onto the dock, Claude asked the obvious question.

"What happened?"

Broussard looked sadly at his old friend. "Claude, I'm afraid Martin's dead. And so's your son."

Olivia moaned and collapsed.

Claude and Henry carried Olivia into the house and up to her bedroom. Not wanting to miss a word of the conversation that would surely soon be taking place downstairs, Kit insisted that she be taken to the chaise longue in the parlor, where they tried to plunk her down without taking any precautions to protect its flowered fabric from her dirty clothes. She called their attention to this mental lapse, and Broussard smiled, happy to see any spark of normality in someone who looked so awful. Bubba ran to the kitchen. He came back with the oilcloth from the kitchen table and draped it over the chaise.

Though the sheriff was eager to ask them all some questions, he decided to wait until a more appropriate time. Broussard cleaned the blood from Kit's face, making a purring sound when he saw that it was only a severe scratch. He shined his penlight in each of her eyes and purred again.

"Well, Dr. Franklyn, looks like you're gonna be okay."

"Thanks to all of you," Kit said, clasping his hand.

"No thanks necessary. Anything happens to you, I gotta break in a new assistant. Boys, see if you can rustle up a cup of tea for her while I find the others."

After checking on Olivia and agreeing with Claude that she be allowed to rest, the three men went downstairs and joined Kit in the parlor, where instead of tea, she was finishing the last of a small glass of sherry that Teddy had brought her.

"Feeling better?" Teddy asked.

"If I'd had some of this back in the swamp, I might not have needed help with that alligator."

Claude crossed the room and as he passed, he let his hand trail over Kit's shoulder. "Dr. Franklyn, I'm sorry for what happened to you." He went to the window and looked out, his back to the others.

"I get the impression I'm the only one doesn't know what's goin' on around here," the sheriff said. "Who's gonna bring me up to speed?"

With his back still toward them, Claude said, "It was the summer after Tommy graduated from high school." He turned to face them, his eyes sad and watery. "He was the class salutatorian, did you know that? God but he was a bright kid, interested in everything. He could divide one five-digit number into another in his head and give you the answer to three decimal places. That year, he turned a hundred-dollar paper investment in the stock market into a five-thousand-dollar portfolio in just six weeks for a school economics project."

Claude tapped his head with his finger. "Smart. Very smart. He was accepted at Princeton but decided instead on LSU. Would have started in the fall, but two weeks after graduation, he began to complain about odors no one else could smell. But we didn't pay any attention . . . just passed it off.

"Then his mind began to go. Little things at first—losing his train of thought in the middle of a conversation, misplacing his car keys, running out of gas, that sort of thing. We began to think he might be on drugs, but he denied it and there wasn't any real evidence to the contrary, so we believed him. Before long, he could barely hold his own in a conversation. It was like . . ." Claude's voice faltered and became tremulous. "Like he had become a child again."

He covered his eyes with his hand and massaged his temples. When he began again, the tremor was gone. "We felt so sorry for him, we ached inside, but . . . we were also embarrassed at what he'd become. So we kept him home and invented excuses when people asked why they hadn't been seeing him around. We took him to a neurology clinic in Houston, but they were totally baffled as to what was wrong or what to do about it. From there, we took him to Philadelphia, then to L.A. It was always the same. No one could help us. . . . No one . . ." He paused, obviously remembering the futility of their search. "Then it got worse. Sometimes just before a rain, he'd get violent." Claude's eyes filled with wonder. "And it was so strange. At the same time, his reflexes would become unbelievably quick. In one of those spells, he smashed the window out of his bedroom and somehow climbed down the side of the house. When I heard the noise, I went to his room and watched out the window as he chased and caught a rabbit. And then he"—Claude shook his head and looked at the floor—"held it by the hind legs and beat it on the ground until it was dead. Then he . . . tore at its throat with his teeth, like an animal."

Claude let out a long breath and continued to stare at the floor. In a few seconds, he looked up and resumed his tale.

"After that, we had heavy hardware cloth installed over his bedroom windows to keep him in. We began seriously to consider having him institutionalized, but Liv couldn't do it. He was her only child and she was not going to desert him, which is the way she saw it."

From the doorway to the hall, another voice said, "That was when we got the letter from the last hospital we had tried." It was Olivia, looking so frail and weak that she almost seemed transparent. Claude went to her and put his arm around her shoulder.

"Liv, you shouldn't be down here. Let me take you . . ."

Olivia patted Claude's hand. "This is where I should be now."

Claude helped her to a chair by the fireplace, then sat at her knee on a footstool, their hands entwined. "The letter was from the hospital's genetics laboratory," Olivia said. "They had found something in the blood samples we had given them, something in my sample—a genetic defect on one of my sex chromosomes?" Her voice went up with uncertainty about whether she was using the correct terms. Receiving a reassuring nod from Broussard, she went on.

"They thought that Tommy's trouble had been caused by the defect. They said it had probably been in the family for a long time. I don't know all the details, but they said that the females in my family were carriers and that only male children would show the symptoms. And it wouldn't be all the males, only the ones that got the defect. Does that make sense?"

Broussard nodded again.

"So you see"—tears welled in Olivia's eyes—"this was all my fault."

"Why do you insist on that nonsense?" Claude said sharply, shaking Olivia's hand in his own. Then more tenderly, he said, "Tommy was *our* child, not just *yours*. And we didn't know. If we *had*, we could have . . ." Apparently unwilling to suggest that they should never have had a child, Claude left the thought unfinished.

Olivia picked up the story. "While we were trying to figure out what to do, Tommy got out again and was gone nearly all night. When he came home, he was covered with blood but he wasn't hurt. We thought it was just another rabbit, but then the next day we heard that a man had been found in a nearby swamp with his throat torn out. Though we didn't want to believe it, we knew it was Tommy who had done it. But there was no way we were going to turn him in. So what were we to do? We couldn't contain him in the house. We needed a special place . . . a place like the old building out in the woods."

The cemetery in Leper's Woods. Suddenly, it all fell into place for Kit. "Villery." She breathed the name aloud. Olivia was a Villery.

"You know about the Villery trial?" Claude asked.

Kit glanced at Broussard. "Villery was the name of the man convicted of being a werewolf in Caude, France, in 1781. Remember? The retarded son of the silversmith. It's one of the examples of lycanthropy that I told you and Phillip about."

"That's when the Villerys left France and settled here," Claude said. "Probably to escape the notoriety from the trial. We learned about the timing from a genealogy search we had done."

Never go boo-lie during a full moon. The phrase ran through Broussard's brain as Kit's revelation brought the final obscuring walls of the case tumbling down. The fellow who had been killed in the swamp when Broussard was a boy had fallen victim to an earlier Villery descendant. And the other sporadic murders the Villerys undoubtedly had committed since they had come to this place collectively became the legend of the loup-garou, the association with a full moon probably arising from the occasional murder that coincidentally took place at the end of a lunar cycle. Those were the ones that would be remembered. And that's why the building was *in* the woods— because it had been needed before.

"So we had the building fixed up to hold Tommy," Claude said. "I brought the workmen in from out of town a trade at a time. Picked them up at the airport, kept them on the grounds the entire time they were here, and took them back to the airport when they were finished to make sure they didn't talk to the townspeople.

"It was a perfect place. With everyone in town believing that you could get leprosy by going in there, we didn't have to worry about someone accidentally stumbling onto our secret. I suspect that the ones who originally had the building constructed started the leprosy rumor. To keep casual boaters away, I had the big cypress dropped across the bayou.

"We covered Tommy's disappearance by saying that he felt such an obligation to his country that he had joined the army for service in Vietnam. Gave the whole story credibility by getting a small article about his enlistment run in the local paper. Then, a few months later, we said he'd been killed in a helicopter crash. Obviously, we couldn't produce his body, so we just said that the army was unable to recover it for reasons that were never made clear to us. Even had a memorial service over at St. Anthony's for him and made sure there was another article in the paper."

Claude looked at Broussard. "Your sympathy card is still around the house somewhere. When people would suggest that Tommy might have survived the crash, I'd say that eyewitnesses in another helicopter believed that no one could have survived. If Olivia was around, she'd say that she knew in her heart he hadn't made it. Then as the years went by . . ." He squeezed Olivia's hand again. "I'm afraid that Liv herself began to believe the story we had made up. Oh, she knew Tommy was out there in the woods all right, but a part of her wanted him to be that hero we were telling everybody he was."

Claude leaned out and looked fondly into Olivia's eyes. "Don't you think that's true?"

Olivia nodded. "He could have been anything he wanted to be until . . . until he became ill. And since it was my fault . . ."

"Olivia!"

She shook off Claude's censure. "It was my duty to see that his name stood for something. After all I *am* his mother. . . ."

"I could see what was happening," Claude said. "But it seemed to make it all easier for her, so I went along. Even made that little charade there last year when she asked me to." He pointed at the shadow box containing Tommy's picture and the medal he had supposedly been awarded for bravery. "In a way, Liv had two sons, the one in the box there and the one in the woods. And mostly, the one in the box made her life bearable. But sometimes when it thundered, it'd all come back to her and her nerves would go."

Claude put his finger under Olivia's chin and tilted her face up to him. "Do you mind my talking about you this way?"

She squeezed his hand and shook her head.

"But what Tommy had done was not the kind of thing you can forget and it lay on our minds, eating away at us. For Liv, thunder made it worse, because it had thundered the night Tommy had . . . had made his first . . . human kill." Claude's face looked as though his words left a bad taste in his mouth.

"Then three days before Dr. Franklyn visited us, Tommy got loose again. I don't know how, except as the years went by he didn't get any more normal but he did get more cunning, while the rest of us were getting old and careless. However it happened, he got out and killed Homer Benoit. And he didn't come back home. So we didn't know where he was or who might be next."

He looked at Kit. "So that's why Liv dropped her cup that night when it thundered. When the story of the murders in New Orleans got to us, we figured it had to be Tommy and we decided to try to find him and bring him back. Except I had broken my fool ankle and . . ." Claude paused as though uncertain about what had happened next.

"He asked *me* to find him," Henry Guidry said, "which I did."

"How were you able to handle him?" Kit asked.

"Tranquilizer pistol. We use it sometimes on our cattle. You have to understand, the night I found him he'd already killed that last woman. There wasn't anything I could do about that."

"But *why*, Henry?" Broussard asked. "Why go out on such a limb?"

A look of surprise appeared on Henry's face. "Isn't that what friendship is?"

"It's the sort of thing he's been doing for me all my life," Claude said. "It wasn't Henry that did all those crazy things in high school. It was me. He just took the blame."

"Because we were friends," Henry said. "*Best* friends."

These revelations were like a knife in Broussard's heart. He had thought they were the three musketeers, equals. But now it appeared that there had always been only two musketeers . . . and him. Though deeply hurt, he didn't allow it to show. "Henry, did Tommy have a gardening claw with him when you found him?"

"Yes. I threw it in the Mississippi."

A question formed on Claude's face. "Andy, when you landed at the dock, you said my son was dead. How did you know who that was out there? Did you see the . . . see his body?"

"I did see the body, but I knew he was there, before that. The first thing that made me suspicious was that medal." He pointed at the shadow box with Tommy's picture. "The note by it says Tommy was in the army. But that's a meritorious service medal for the merchant marine. Then later when I was outside, I noticed that some electrical lines come out of the service panel and go underground in the direction of Leper's Woods. Those two things made me curious enough to ask Phil Gatlin—the detective that called me just before breakfast this mornin'—to check with the army to see if they had any record of Tommy enlistin'. A few minutes before I heard Kit fire off that shotgun, I'd learned from Phillip that they had no such records. It was then that I knew for sure." He looked at Kit. "But what were *you* doin' out there?"

"I found a picture in the bottom of that trunk in my room. It looked like Tommy, but he was a lot older than in that photograph over there. And the date on the back said it was taken two years ago."

"Liv had Martin take Tommy's picture every year on his birthday." Claude said. "She kept them in an album in that trunk. When we knew you were all coming to spend the night, I moved the album, but I guess that one picture fell out."

"At first, I didn't get it," Kit said. "Then when I saw Martin taking a picnic basket and a gun into the swamp, it hit me."

"Claude, if you had such a secret, why on earth did you invite us to stay with you?" Broussard asked. "Surely you saw the danger in that."

"We didn't feel as though we had any choice. It was what would have been expected of us. If we hadn't volunteered, we thought *that* in itself would be suspicious. That's why I got Touchet to give you that exhumation order even though I had called him a half hour earlier and asked him not to cooperate."

"And that's where Carl Fitch came in," Broussard said.

Claude's eyebrows shot upward. "You know about that, too?"

Broussard nodded.

"I don't know why we tried to hide anything from you. We should have just put a sign in the yard—'The killer lives here.'"

"Even if I hadn't found out about Fitch, he probably would have talked to someone eventually," Broussard said.

"I'm not *that* stupid, Andy. He didn't know who hired him. I simply slipped an envelope with some cash in it under his front door along with instructions on what he was to do and how much more money there'd be if he did it before daybreak."

"What made you think he'd do it?"

"I've known him for years. He used to work for me until I fired him for the same traits that made me hire him this time. Now if you all don't mind, Liv and I would like to be alone for awhile." His eyes shifted to the sheriff. "Would that be all right? I mean could you wait until tomorrow to do whatever's to be done?"

"Don't see why not."

On their way out, the old couple paused at the door and Olivia gently moved Claude aside so she could look back into the parlor. "We didn't mean for anyone to get hurt. We just wanted to protect our son. But it all went wrong. It just all went . . . wrong."

When the Duhons had gone, the sheriff shifted his attention to Claude's accomplice. "Henry, I'm afraid that legally you're in pretty deep, as well. But I'm willin' to give you the same consideration I gave Claude and Olivia. If you'll promise not to disappear."

Head hanging, Henry nodded and stood up to leave.

Broussard followed him into the hall. "Henry, wait a minute."

Guidry spun around, a hostile look on his face. "Friendship, Andy. Think about the word, because I don't believe you have the faintest idea what it means." Without giving Broussard a chance to reply, Guidry turned his back and went out the door.

Upon returning to the parlor, Broussard heard the sheriff ask Teddy, "Where exactly are those bodies?"

"I'd be glad to show you," Teddy said.

"Would you be willin' to bring them in after I've looked things over?"

"Sure, but we'll have to bring them back to this dock. I won't be able to get my boat past that tree Claude mentioned without a chain saw."

"Maybe I should go, too," Broussard said. "Kit, you seem to be feelin' okay, but I'd like for Bubba to take you over to Doc Burke's for some X rays just to be sure. We'll meet back here in an hour and see where we stand."

Kit looked at her hands. "Maybe Burke can get these splinters out."

"Dr. Franklyn, sometime before you leave, I'd like to get your statement on tape," the sheriff said. "But we'll worry about that later."

"Something just occurred to me," Teddy said. "Suppose the boat goes on the fritz again. Bubba should be there to fix it. So how about having him go with you and I'll take Kit to the doctor? I can show Bubba in about ten seconds everything he needs to know to run the boat."

"Sounds okay," Broussard said.

Kit got carefully to her feet. "I'm not going anywhere until I get cleaned up and change clothes. And it better be the last time, because my wardrobe is exhausted."

"Can you make it up the stairs?" Teddy asked, preparing to catch her if she fell.

"Everything seems to be functioning," Kit said. "You go on and show Bubba how to work the boat. I'll be down in a few minutes, providing someone can tell me where I can find a clean towel."

"I think there's a linen closet next to the doors that open onto the upstairs porch," Broussard said.

Kit wiggled her fingers at him in thanks and went off to see whether he was right.

As the others were filing out of the parlor, Bubba said, "Dere's jus' one thing Ah don' understan'."

"What's what?" Broussard said.

"How'd Teddy keep his hat on da whole way over here in dat boat?"

Chapter 21

When Broussard and Bubba returned to the Duhons' parlor, they found Teddy and Kit already waiting.

"So what's the verdict?" Broussard said. "Your X rays didn't make Burke faint or anything, did they?"

"I'm as healthy as you are," Kit said.

"Dunno if I'd be happy about *that*. By the way, Teddy, Phil Gatlin—the detective workin' the case in New Orleans—found the bracelet you lost. It was near the place where Tommy hid durin' the day. My guess is that you were the one that took him to New Orleans, not knowin'ly of course, but as a stowaway under the tarp on your pickup, which is probably where he found the bracelet. When you parked near Jackson Square to visit the perfumer in the Pontalba building, he slipped away."

Broussard's explanation jogged Teddy's memory. "Now that you mention it, I *did* go to New Orleans the day Homer Benoit's body was found. And I also went to the perfumer on the square. But how did you know all that?"

"Your cologne, Cajun Musk. They mix it on the premises and have no other sales outlet. Add that to the bracelet . . . all makes sense."

"How long have you known about the bracelet?" Kit asked.

"Since Phillip told me about it in that phone call this mornin'."

"Didn't that make you suspect Teddy?"

Broussard shrugged. "His feet are about two sizes smaller

than that footprint we found at the first murder in New Orleans."

"Did you recover Tommy's body?" Kit asked.

"What was left of it."

"And his shoes?"

"Triangles and squares on the soles just like we expected." Broussard's gaze went to Tommy's picture. He looked at it for a few seconds, then said, "Think I'll stick around for one more night so I can speak to Claude and Olivia in the mornin'. Kit, no need for you and Bubba to stay here, so why don't you go on home. I'm sure the sheriff will let you mail him a tape of your statement."

"You're all welcome to stay the night with me," Teddy said.

"Thanks, but I'm ready to see my dog and my own bed," Kit replied. Had Broussard and Bubba not been there, she might have accepted Teddy's invitation to stay the night, because she had come to see that giving up David for Teddy wasn't like swapping one old jalopy for another. It was more like trading *up*. And as far as Teddy's financial prospects, this was biology, not estate planning.

"I'll be in New Orleans in a few days," Teddy said. "Maybe we could have dinner together."

"Whenever you like, my treat."

Broussard's eyes brightened. "Does that mean . . ."

"As much trouble as I seem to get into, you sure couldn't save me if I was in Shreveport."

Despite the sadness Broussard felt about the way the case had worked out for his friends, Kit's announcement that she would be staying on made him smile.

It took only a few minutes for Kit and Bubba to gather up their belongings and put them into the trunk of Kit's car. She then offered Bubba the keys. "Do you mind?"

"Anything Ah like better'n drivin' an airboat, it's drivin' a pretty lady home after she been chased with a club," Bubba said.

Kit turned to Teddy, rose up on her toes, and kissed him lightly on the lips. "Thanks for saving me." After she got in the car, she rolled down the window and shook her finger at him. "And don't you dare—"

"Let them get behind you," they said together. "I won't," Teddy said. "I promise."

Kit watched Teddy in the rearview mirror until Bubba turned onto the road out front, then she watched him through the side window until he was no longer visible.

When Kit and Bubba were out of sight, Teddy said, "What about you, Andy? Since you're staying on, you might as well do it at my place. I just had it fixed up and I'm dying to show off. Kit said you grew up here, so you probably know it, the old Tabor estate?"

Broussard's eyes rounded in surprise. The Tabor house was the finest in Bayou Coteau, larger even than Oakliegh. "Looks like gators have been good to you."

"I'd admit to that."

And so Broussard spent the night a short way from town in a twelve-thousand-square-foot Georgian mansion filled with antique pieces equal to the best he had ever seen at Joe Epstein's. The next morning after a pleasant stroll around the grounds and a light breakfast, he thanked Teddy for his hospitality and set out to see Claude and Olivia.

As he climbed the steps to their porch, he wondered what he would say to his old friends. Despite their attempt to deceive him and his discovery that he had never been as close to Claude as Henry had, he still cared deeply for them and wished he had not played so prominent a role in their downfall. What do you say under such circumstances?

He rang the bell and waited, fighting a childish impulse to run back to his car and drive away before they answered. Getting no response, he rang again.

How would they receive him? Surely they understood what a terrible thing they'd done. Not like Henry, who didn't seem to appreciate the gravity of it all. Maybe if Henry had seen the victims . . .

No answer. He rang again.

Hopefully, Olivia and Claude would see his side of it. He had to follow up every lead. It was his job. He couldn't look the other way, no matter who was implicated.

Still no answer.

Thinking that perhaps they had gone out, he followed the porch around to the rear of the house to see if the car was there. As he descended the back steps and proceeded along the brick walkway through the patio with its huge ferns in baskets hanging from the gnarled oaks, he noticed that the grounds were as quiet as on the previous morning when he and Kit had talked by the boat dock. He went down a final set of steps and looked through the window in the garage door.

"Oh my, no," he moaned.

He pulled the door up and stood transfixed by the sight of a vacuum-cleaner hose running from the exhaust of Claude's BMW to the trunk. Through the rear window, he could see two occupants, neither of them moving. Reluctantly, his feet as heavy as his heart, he approached the driver's side and opened the door.

Claude and Olivia had never looked better, their complexions rosy with health. He shut the door and looked at the ceiling for a long minute. Then he left the garage and began to stroll over the grounds, onto the boat dock, where he stood for awhile with his hands in his pockets, staring out at the cut in the trees on the other side.

After a time, he walked farther out onto the dock, his eyes looking into the black water for answers. A dragonfly winged into view and landed on a bit of debris among the reeds beside the dock. There was a sudden splash and the dragonfly was gone, eaten by a baby alligator on whose nose it had landed. Across the bayou, he saw a nutria come out of the trees and forage in the saw grass next to the bank, frightening a small turtle, which slid silently from a nearby log and slipped beneath the surface.

Cycles of the swamp.

Events that had gone on since he was a child and would continue whether he was there to witness them or not.

A great continuity.

It was the way of things, not only in the swamp but outside it as well. With a last glance at the gray sky, he turned and walked back to the house to call the sheriff.